The Duke and the Darkness

The Dukes of Darkness
Book 1

By Anna Harrington

ARE YOU SIGNED UP FOR DRAGONBLADE'S BLOG?

You'll get the latest news and information on exclusive giveaways, exclusive excerpts, coming releases, sales, free books, cover reveals and more.

Check out our complete list of authors, too!

No spam, no junk. That's a promise!

Sign Up Here

www.dragonbladepublishing.com

Dearest Reader;

Thank you for your support of a small press. At Dragonblade Publishing, we strive to bring you the highest quality Historical Romance from some of the best authors in the business. Without your support, there is no 'us', so we sincerely hope you adore these stories and find some new favorite authors along the way.

Happy Reading!

CEO, Dragonblade Publishing

Chapter One

London
May 1817

DEVLIN RAINES, DUKE of Dartmoor, watched the dealer turn over the last card. An ace. He bit back a curse as the dealer scooped up the coins and kept them for the club.

Luck was not on his side tonight.

With a grimace, he stood, excused himself before another hand could be dealt, and made his way through the crowded game room toward the bar.

Good Lord, he was having a terrible night at the tables. If he were a superstitious man, he'd say that fate was out to get him.

Not just tonight, either. For the past few weeks, he couldn't buy a win at cards, and the losses were starting to add up. Worse, they were damnably embarrassing, and he had a reputation as a gambler to uphold, even here at Barton's where they let in any man as long as he had enough money to back his bets and any woman as long as she was beautiful.

That was what he liked best about this particular hell. Here, no one cared about titles or family histories, or that he'd spent years working as a mercenary before becoming a duke.

Here, he could simply be himself.

He needed that. Especially tonight.

Before arriving here, he'd detoured to Seven Dials to speak to two men he knew there from the days of his father's criminal enterprise, when the old Duke of Dartmoor had been involved in all kinds of illegal businesses from smuggling to child prostitution. Devlin had put an end to all that ten years ago, but ever since, he had remained on guard in case any part of what his father had created managed to crawl its way back into the light. His contacts told him that a new criminal ring had formed in London's underworld, one that had nothing to do with his dead father.

Devlin wasn't so certain. A lingering unease ached down in his bones, the same way old sailors felt approaching storms.

He prayed he was wrong.

"Cognac," he ordered, then selected two cigars from the box on the bar. He slipped one into his breast pocket for later and lit the other on the silver brazier at his elbow.

He puffed at the cheroot and watched as the smoke curled slowly upward. His mother and sisters didn't like it when he spent all night at the clubs, preferring to have him at home with them. A chagrinned smile tugged at his lips. They would have suffered apoplexy if they knew he came here instead of going to one of the more respectable places in St James's. But he couldn't find proper escape in those clubs the way he could here, where he could lose himself in the middle of a packed, noisy room.

It was the same reason, all those years ago, that he'd studied fighting at Eton under Anthony Titus, *maître d'armes*. During the rigors of training and the bouts of fencing, he had been able to lose himself, if just for a few hours. Only later did he come to realize that what Titus was teaching him wasn't how to fight but how to remain in control.

Devlin had learned to take his solace wherever he could, including on nights like this. Especially since he'd soon have to give them up completely in favor of Lady Catherine Carlow, daughter of the Earl of Northrop. The woman he'd decided to marry.

The attendant set a glass of cognac in front of him. Devlin held the glass up to the light to check the golden color, swirled it, then lowered his nose for a long inhalation, all before taking a sip.

Notes of jasmine, vanilla, earthy black truffle… *Perfect.*

He doubted Lady Catherine would ever understand how a glass of cognac in the middle of a crowded hell could calm him the way few other things could. But she would be polite enough to pretend to.

Pretense. Duty. Eventually perhaps affection. Above all, turning a blind eye… He grimaced into his glass. The makings of every good society marriage.

Nothing had been publicly announced yet because the marriage settlement was still being hammered out by family attorneys on both sides. But he'd offered, she'd accepted, and he expected to officially announce the engagement by month's end. Well-educated and proper with an appreciation of the arts and no concerns about his military past, Catherine was charming and pretty, and they bumped along well. Oh, there was no love between them, but that didn't bother him. Theirs would be a marriage tempered by tolerance, friendship, and a sense of shared obligation.

Still, Devlin didn't think she would appreciate a husband who spent his nights at places like Barton's. She expected a good husband and father to their children, and he planned to be that.

The exact opposite of his own father in every way.

But he wasn't leg-shackled yet, so he returned to the tables. Dawn still lingered hours away, and several thousands of pounds remained to be wagered. He sat and tapped the table to be dealt the next hand.

A woman slipped gracefully onto the chair next to his, then tossed a couple of coins to the dealer with a flick of her slender wrist.

Devlin slid his gaze over her—and caught his breath. *Sweet Lucifer*, she was striking.

He thought he knew all the women at Barton's, but he certainly didn't recognize this one. Not with that chestnut hair piled on top of her head in loosely pinned curls, not with those dark blue eyes and creamy skin that looked as smooth as marble. Yet something about her struck him as familiar.

Impossible. She'd never been here before, he was certain, and he would have remembered meeting a woman like her at one of those tedious society soirees his mother forced him to attend. *You are Dartmoor,* she always told him, *and it is expected...* So he went just to please his mother, even if he hated every minute.

No, this woman didn't belong in gilded drawing rooms with their tame entertainments, at stuffy balls with their regimentation, or at boring ladies' garden clubs. One look at her proved that. With an aura of confidence surrounding her like fine perfume, she belonged right here. Barton's was one of the few places in London that welcomed women through its doors and at its tables, where uniformed attendants brought glasses of liquor to the ladies as well as the men, and where it was accepted that no one inside need fear for their reputation. The hell belonged to the underbelly of London society, an exclusive club whose name everyone in the *ton* knew but which no one would ever dare admit to having entered, where gentlemen and ladies mixed with courtesans and high-end prostitutes of both sexes.

Which was she, lady or courtesan? She was certainly dressed for an evening of pleasure. Her midnight blue velvet gown draped teasingly off both shoulders, giving the impression that a slight shrug might send the entire bodice slipping away. Oh, what a damn shame if that happened...to bare to his eyes the full breasts beneath, whose rounded tops were just teasingly visible beneath the satin-edged neckline. A small tilt of her head as she watched the dealer accentuated the length of her elegant neck, encircled by sapphires as blue as her eyes.

She wasn't simply beautiful.

She was raw temptation.

Yet unlike the courtesans, she paid no attention to the men around her in the hell who stared as if she were a delectable feast they wanted to devour as greedily as the roasted pheasant in the dining room. Instead, her attention remained fixed on the cards as the dealer placed them in front of each player.

The hand played out, bets were wagered on each card, and Devlin won. *Finally.*

He eased back in his chair. "I haven't seen you here before," he said to the woman, unable to resist engaging her in conversation. "How are you finding Barton's?"

Not looking at him, she curled her red lips as if in faint amusement at a private joke. "It's everything I was told it would be."

"And what were you told?"

"That it's home to ruffians, blackguards, libertines of all kinds…" Her gloved fingers sorted the money she had placed on the table before her. "And those are just the women."

He chuckled and turned toward her on his chair as the dealer placed down the first round of cards. She shone like a blue diamond, putting the handful of other women in the club to shame. Already, he was certain, bets were being placed over which man would be fortunate enough to leave with her.

He didn't blame them. She was stunning…and strangely familiar. He knew her, but how? "And how are you finding the men?"

"Entertaining." She doubled her bet on the next card. "Intriguing." Then doubled it again on the next. At that, two of the other players dropped out of the hand, unwilling to match her wager. "Challenging."

He suppressed a smile. She might as well have been describing herself. When she won the hand and two hundred pounds with only a pair of tens, he realized exactly how much of a challenge she posed.

Finally, the evening had become interesting.

They played on, the stakes growing steeper with each card. The winnings divided themselves fairly evenly around the table, but one of the other players left the game, claiming the play had grown too rich for his accounts.

The dealer paused the game to bring out a new deck of cards and exchanged a few words with the club manager.

An attendant appeared at the table. "Another drink, Your Grace?"

"Please."

"And for you, ma'am?"

She eyed Devlin's drink. "What are you having?"

"Cognac."

"How very Continental of you." Her eyes gleamed as she turned them on the attendant. "I'll have the same. Please bring the bottle and a second glass."

The attendant looked questioningly at Devlin, who nodded his consent. Then the man hurried away to fetch the brandy.

She tossed in a handful of coins as the dealer laid out the next hand, bringing the opening wager higher than it had been all night. "I didn't realize I needed a man's permission to drink here."

Devlin would have said that pique drove her bet, if not for the cold control in her voice. He explained, "The brandy is from my private stock." He matched her wager. So did the other three men at the table, and the next cards were laid down. "I keep a case here for my own use."

"You often spend evenings here, then?"

He noted wryly that she didn't thank him for the brandy. "A few."

"Playing games?"

His lips curled. She made gambling sound like a children's afternoon in the park. "Something like that."

"Are you any good?"

"I have my moments."

"Yes, I'm certain you do." She won the hand, and the dealer pushed her winnings toward her. "Occasionally."

That stung his pride, both the barb and the loss. Yet Devlin doubled the amount of the opening bid on the next hand.

She didn't blink in matching it. "Do you often lose?"

"No," he drawled. "Usually I win."

"What a coincidence." She smiled but didn't glance his way. Was that flirtation…or amusement at his expense? "So do I."

As if to punctuate her comment, one of the other players rose and left the game. Only three of them remained at the table now, and the stakes increased as they played on until each hand was worth over one thousand pounds.

The attendant brought the bottle of cognac and a glass on a silver tray, then set them at Devlin's right elbow. Devlin tossed him a coin and splashed a small pour of brandy into the glass. He held it out to her.

She arched a disdainful brow. "That's a rather small pour, don't you think?"

"I wouldn't want you to assume I was attempting to get you foxed." But he added a second pour to the glass.

This time, she accepted it. "And in my experience," she said as she smiled against the rim of the glass, keeping it raised to her mouth and his attention on her ripe lips, "men greatly underestimate ladies' abilities."

"In drink or cards?"

"In everything."

His gut tightened. Surely, she hadn't meant that as sexual entendre, yet her words wound through him, leaving an aching tingle in their wake. Who the *hell* was she? Why couldn't he place her?

"I don't believe we've been properly introduced." He held out his hand. "Devlin Raines."

She held out her glass for topping off. "A pleasure."

With a chuckle, he splashed more cognac into her glass.

This woman was sharp, whoever she was. He was still no closer to ascertaining if she was a lady or a courtesan. Or why she stirred shadowy memories in the back of his mind that frustratingly he couldn't quite uncover. He wasn't a eunuch, for God's sake. He should have remembered everything about an encounter with a woman like her.

"And you are...?" he prompted.

"Going to win."

Devlin grinned. Her confidence was damnably alluring. He

enjoyed witty women who were able to hold their own in any conversation. Throw in the way she looked, all warm and soft and sensual, with enough flesh revealed to make him wonder what the rest would look like when she was bare—

"You seem to be a man who appreciates a woman who knows what she's doing."

His mouth twisted at that veiled flirtation. "What gentleman doesn't?"

"Before this night is over, I'll be on top."

His cock jerked in his breeches. *Jesus.* There was no veil that time.

"Surprised you, did I?" A cat-like smile turned up the corners of her mouth. "I'm not a courtesan out for your money, if that's what you're thinking," she told him loudly enough that a man walking past the table faltered mid-step before moving on.

He chuckled. He admired her audacity, even if he found her mysterious enough to give him pause. "Good to know my fortune's safe."

"Oh no, you misunderstand. I'm definitely out for your money." She rested her elbow on the table and her chin in her palm, then gazed at him with an expression of such forthright honesty that he bit back a laugh. "But I'm not a courtesan."

"Thank you for putting my fears to rest," he drawled.

But she hadn't. It bothered him that he couldn't place her. She wasn't one of the Spanish or French women who had entertained him on the Continent, nor one of the widows who had so eagerly thrown themselves at him since he'd returned. Nor was she a mistress seeking a new protector, although that was more likely given that he hadn't seen her in society before—if she were *his* lover, he'd certainly keep her locked away from all other gentlemen.

So who the devil was she?

The last man left the table then; only the two of them remained. The dealer called for a pause and left the table to speak again to the club manager, surely to inform him that the stakes had grown even higher.

Devlin laid his arm across the back of her chair. "You're very beautiful."

"You noticed," she murmured, her eyes almost glowing as she turned them onto him. Those eyes...not just blue, but multiple shades of blue. The shadows of memory stirred faster in his mind, but nothing came into focus. "How perceptive of you."

He wasn't blind, for God's sake. "In that dress...you want to be noticed."

He moved his hand to trail his fingertips over her bare shoulder in a soft caress. He smiled when she trembled.

"Who are you?" he drawled. "And what is it you want?"

"You."

His fingers stilled against her skin. He froze, except for his cock which began to ache with longing.

"You said you weren't a courtesan," he reminded her.

"I'm not. I'm not for sale." She removed her right glove, then dipped her fingers lightly into his glass of brandy. He watched as she sucked the drops of golden liquid from her fingertips. "But I *can* be won."

He stared at her, transfixed, her brandy-wetted lips glistening in the lamplight. A small drop clung to the corner of her mouth. He reached slowly to wipe it away, then licked it off his thumb. It tasted of her. Of brandied cherries, rich and sweet with a hint of tartness, and it left him craving a deeper taste.

She leaned toward him to bring her mouth close to his ear, and the soft brush of her breast against his arm stole his breath away.

"If we're going to play together tonight," she purred, her breath tickling warmly against his cheek, "then let's make it worthwhile, shall we?"

His blood heated with anticipation. "What do you have in mind?"

"Winner takes all." Her lips slid across his cheek in a feather-light caress as she shifted away. The challenge in her sapphire eyes was undeniable.

"I'll win," he warned, his deep voice husky with desire.

She settled back in her chair, pulled on her glove, and lifted his arm away from her shoulder, returning it to his side. Her attention turned back to the dealer as he returned with a new deck of cards in hand and the club manager at his side to oversee the game.

"You won't," she whispered, but with such icy intensity Devlin would have sworn he saw her shiver.

He frowned. "If you're not comfortable with—"

"Deal," she ordered.

The dealer nodded and placed three upturned cards on the table in front of her, Devlin, and himself.

With a king in her cards, she placed a stack of banknotes onto the table. "One thousand pounds."

Devlin smiled and matched her wager for that card. And the rest. When the hand was over, he'd won five thousand pounds, only to lose it all and more on the next one. He didn't care. Either way, when the game ended, he'd escort her upstairs to one of the private rooms and into bed. As she'd implied earlier, it was simply a matter of who would be on top.

He opened the next hand with the same thousand-pound wager as before, then watched as she coolly swallowed the last of the brandy in her glass. He watched the soft undulation in her elegant throat and wanted his mouth, right there, on her so badly that his hand shook as he reached for his own glass to distract himself.

But she did say that the winner would take all, and he planned on taking all of her. Repeatedly.

She tripled the wager on the next card. That got his attention, and also that of the club manager, who nodded to accept the bid when the dealer looked at him questioningly. Ten thousand pounds rode on the last card.

When the dealer flipped it over, the manager blew out a relieved sigh. The club had won.

"We don't have to keep doing this," Devlin told her beneath his breath, to keep from being overheard by the crowd of gathering onlookers. "We both want to end the evening the same way."

For a moment, she didn't reply. Then she turned her head and boldly looked at him. "I want to win."

So do I. He glanced at her rapidly dwindling winnings, then slowly moved his gaze over her...down her delicate neck to the temptation of her full breasts beneath the soft velvet he wanted to rip from her body. "Can you afford to lose?"

She laughed, her spellbinding eyes gleaming as they found his. "Can *you?*"

Overwhelming need twisted his gut. More than anything in the world, he wanted to be inside her when she closed those shining eyes and cried out with pleasure. The damned seductress knew it, too.

She placed all her remaining money—one thousand pounds—on the first card of the next hand, surprising him. Deliciously so. Because if she had no more money to wager on the rest of the cards in the hand, then...

"When I win this hand, what will you offer me in winnings?" he murmured as he brought his mouth close to her ear. He still didn't know if she were courtesan or lady, if he'd ever met her before or not. Suddenly, he didn't give a damn either way.

"What would you like?"

He went hard as all kinds of wanton thoughts spilled through his mind. Her coming on top was the least of them, but it would be a damnably fine way to start.

"Everything," he drawled. And meant exactly that.

Her gaze held his. "Done. But at least give me the chance to win some of your money on each of the cards."

"Done."

She gestured to the manager to lean down and spoke quietly into his ear.

The man's gaze flicked to Devlin. He said something to her

with a pointed lift of his brows. When she answered, he nodded, then straightened and circled behind the table. Then the manager signaled for the dealer to step aside so he could finish the hand himself.

"The club is out," the manager informed them, rapping on the remaining deck with his knuckles. "Understand?"

"Of course," Devlin answered. She and Devlin would be on their own against each other, negotiating their own wagers. Perfectly fine terms with him.

The first cards were dealt. A queen for Devlin...and a king for her.

"And your wager for the next card?" Devlin asked, leaning toward her again. He expected her to whisper something scandalous into his ear—

"Ten thousand pounds," she announced loudly enough for the manager to hear.

"The lady stakes ten thousand," the manager called out, which circulated curious whispers and stares throughout the crowd that had gathered to watch. "And you, Your Grace?"

"Match." Devlin knew she was bamming everyone in the room, except for him and the manager who both knew she didn't have those kinds of funds. She was wagering with air on each card. But they weren't playing for money now.

The next card brought a five for him and an ace for her. He was ahead, but not by much. So he leaned over and whispered into her ear exactly what he wanted for this card's wager, sparing no details.

Her cheeks flushed at his wanton wager. "All right." But she couldn't utter the bet aloud to the manager. Instead, she cleared her throat and said breathlessly, "We've agreed on...a private wager."

Snickers and guffaws went up from the crowd pressing in around the table, which only made her blush deepen. Delectably.

Not keen on letting all of Barton's know what the two of them would be doing upstairs for the rest of the night, he reached over and carefully removed her sapphire earbob and set it onto the table. "There. Your stake, my lady."

Let them think she was too proud to admit to wagering away her jewels. He'd give them back to her when she was lying naked in bed with him.

But from the irritated look she threw his way, she didn't seem at all pleased.

Devlin won both the card and control of the hand. Without a word, only a wolfish smile that told her exactly what he wanted for his wager, he removed her remaining earbob and set it beside the first.

She won the card and edged him out of the lead. Barely. But enough that she was allowed to set the wager for the final card.

"Twenty thousand pounds," she announced.

The room instantly fell silent, the laughs choking off into startled whispers.

She smiled coyly at Devlin. "Unless you cannot afford it?"

He laughed. Not afford imaginary money? He had nothing to lose but a thousand pounds from his original bet, and hours of pleasure to be gained. "Matched."

His luck had finally changed. The hand rested on one last card he was confident he'd win.

The manager placed down the last cards. A deuce for Devlin, a four for her.

A moment's hesitation gripped the room as all the onlookers held their breaths, followed by shouts of disbelief that Dartmoor had been beaten. By a woman.

Devlin laughed good-naturedly along with them. The damage to his reputation would sting for a while, but he knew what the true wager had been and how he would ultimately emerge a winner tonight regardless of the cards.

He pushed himself away from the table, then held out his hand to help her to her feet. He squeezed her fingers as they rested in his and sketched her a shallow bow. Hours of wanton pleasure were promised in that gentlemanly gesture.

She slipped her hand away and unassumingly collected her coins and banknotes as the crowd around them dispersed back to the other tables, the spectacle now over. He was glad of it. Fewer people would notice that they were about to leave the game room at the same time, and not for the front door.

She rested her hand on his bicep, and the soft touch radiated up his arm and into his chest. "If you'll excuse me, I'm going to find the retiring room. I should refresh myself before we continue the rest of this evening's games." As she picked up her earbobs, the sultry look she gave him made his mouth water. "Don't you agree?"

He would have agreed to nearly anything as long as she kept looking at him like that. As if she wanted to hunt him like prey.

She turned to the manager. "Would you be kind enough to settle my tallies on His Grace's account?"

The manager's eyes darted curiously to Devlin, who nodded his consent. "Of course, ma'am."

Devlin chuckled at her audacity. She'd not only publicly bested him; now she expected him to pay for her food and drinks for the evening, as well.

But of course he would. And breakfast, too.

As she began to move away, he took her elbow from behind and stopped her. He lowered his head over her shoulder, close to her ear. "Who are you? Tell me now. I have to know."

She tensed beneath his fingertips. For a moment, he thought she wouldn't answer—

"Lady Payne."

He scoffed at that with a short laugh. "You're lying."

She slowly pulled her arm from his light grasp and said cryptically beneath her breath, so softly he was certain he misheard, "When you meet the devil in the darkness, he never gives you his true name."

Then she slipped away through the gaming room toward the front of the hell, smiling her appreciation as she went to those gentlemen who congratulated her on her play.

He stared after her, frowning. *The devil in the darkness...* What the hell did she mean by that?

But he wasn't concerned. After all, he had the rest of the night to wheedle her true identity out of her. And enjoy himself immensely in the process.

Devlin pulled the spare cigar from his breast pocket and lit it on the tabletop brazier. "Patton," he ordered the manager, "I'm going to need a key to one of the upstairs rooms and a fresh bottle of cognac. We'll want breakfast in the morning."

Patton hesitated. "Perhaps you should settle up first, Your Grace."

He laughed. "What's to settle?"

"Thirty-one thousand pounds."

His heart skipped. For a long moment, he only stared at the manager, the cigar clamped between his teeth as he tried to fathom... "She had no money. She wagered air."

"But she did have funds, Your Grace." Patton gaped at him. "I thought—I thought you knew—"

Cold dread seeped through him like ice water. "Knew what?"

"She took out a marker when she arrived, using a land deed as collateral. For forty thousand pounds. All her bets were backed by the club."

Christ.

By the time Devlin rushed through the front doors and outside into the night after her, she had already vanished.

Chapter Two

F ROM THE DARKNESS of her unmarked carriage, Peyton Chandler slipped a gun and knife out from beside the seat cushion. She peered through the window at Barton's.

Dartmoor.

He'd run out of the club in pursuit of her, just as she knew he would. He stood on the narrow footpath and looked up and down the street, searching for her. But there were too many people coming and going, too many carriages of all sorts in the midnight street, for him to figure out where she'd gone. He ran a hand through his sandy blond hair in aggravation with what she was certain was a harsh curse. He was angry, embarrassed, undoubtedly frustrated…and now decidedly poorer.

Good. The bastard deserved all that and more.

And she would be the one to rain it all down upon his head.

She pounded the hilt of the knife against the ceiling. The driver snapped his whip, and the team started forward slowly so as not to draw any attention. Exactly as she'd instructed earlier. She watched just long enough to be certain Dartmoor wasn't following her, then leaned back against the leather squabs.

A long sigh seeped from her lips, and she closed her eyes.

The evening had gone exactly as she'd hoped. Better, in fact, because she'd been able to add the humiliation of losing to a woman to Dartmoor's losses. It had been so easy! Armand Marchand, the former Imperial Guard member and *maître d'armes* whom she had hired to teach her to protect herself, had been right about cards and this particular game. As long as the dealer didn't shuffle the deck between hands, she could easily keep track of which cards had been played, noting them in her head as each one was laid down. Then she'd used her beauty against Dartmoor by letting him believe the game was turning into foreplay. Whenever he'd started to win, she'd simply distracted him with a well-timed innuendo or flirtation.

She laughed darkly—tasting the brandy from her fingertips had been a stroke of genius. For a moment, she'd thought he might just start panting!

He had been so caught up in the idea of tupping her tonight that he never stopped to think she might be tricking him. She had warned him outright that she planned on winning, but he'd underestimated her anyway.

Why did men always think there was never anything of substance behind a pretty face? Inexplicably, she'd expected more from Dartmoor.

She'd managed to take his money without him recognizing her—although why would he? He hadn't seen her in ten years, not since she was sixteen, fresh from the schoolroom and still in braids. Even then, he had never truly *seen* her. Not the Marquess of Truro, whom he had been before inheriting, the dashing young twenty-two-year-old who had freshly returned from the wars. He'd paid her no more mind that spring than a piece of furniture. Yet in less than a handful of meetings, when he'd said nothing more to her than empty pleasantries before turning his attention to the glamorous society women surrounding him, Peyton had fallen completely in love. She'd thought him nothing short of perfect.

In truth, he'd been nothing but a self-absorbed young man who cared so little about his country and family that he'd hired himself out as a mercenary during the wars. Then, four years later, when army life had become too difficult, he returned to London to take up where he'd left off as a rakehell in the making. He had cared only for what the Raines' family name and fortune could do for him, what doors would open to him as heir to a dukedom. Especially bedroom doors of beautiful young widows, unfaithful wives...

"Opera singers," she muttered into the darkness, remembering that night from so long ago when Truro had vanished from his parents' party with the Italian soprano his mother had hired for entertainment.

No, not *remembering* because that night never left her. It was always at the forefront of her mind, in everything she did, in every breath she took. She would never be able to forget how her parents' carriage had been attacked on their way home from the party at Dartmoor House, how Papa and Mama had been pulled from the carriage and murdered, how she had nearly been killed herself. The only reason she was still alive was that her attacker had attempted to rape her before slitting her throat, and in that moment's pause, she'd somehow managed to escape. She didn't know how, having fallen unconscious in the struggle, and she might never discover how—but she *had* survived, and being haunted every day by the memory of that night was now what kept her going.

Half an hour later, her carriage stopped in front of the townhouse she was renting at the edge of Marylebone. It was located close enough to Mayfair to keep an eye on Dartmoor, yet far enough away that she wouldn't be recognized by anyone who might have known her from before, although that wouldn't happen.

After all, she'd changed so much she barely recognized herself.

When the tiger opened the door, she hesitated before stepping outside as a silent warning slithered down her spine. It was the same feeling she'd had since the moment she'd disembarked from the ship six weeks ago: she was being watched.

"Ma'am?" Misreading her hesitation, the tiger held out his hand to help her down.

"Thank you, but I'm fine." Yet she cautiously glanced around in all directions before stepping to the ground on her own.

If the footman was surprised she'd emerged from the carriage carrying a pistol in one hand and a knife in the other, he didn't show it. But she hadn't expected him to. He was a former soldier, after all, hired specifically because he'd proven his bravery in battles on the Peninsula and wouldn't hesitate to kill if necessary.

It had taken her years after the attack to be comfortable riding in carriages again, and only then when she was armed and surrounded by men she'd personally hired. She couldn't give up carriages and night travel completely. They were both necessary evils. But she could stack the odds considerably in her favor and give second thoughts to anyone who dared to consider coming after her.

The butler, who had served as a captain beneath Wellington, opened the door as she hurried toward the townhouse. She nodded her thanks and slipped inside the dark house.

"You're back," John Wilkins called out from the first-floor landing above the stair hall. "How did it go?"

"Incredibly well." She handed her cape to the butler and walked up the stairs past Wilkins.

Her old friend fell into step behind her, as she knew he would. He'd most likely been pacing the townhouse as he waited anxiously for her return. She smiled to herself. At thirty-eight, if Wilkins hadn't already lost most of his hair, she was certain his worry over tonight's plan would have left him completely bald.

Ostensibly, John Wilkins was her estate manager. He oversaw all her finances, protected her interests, and made certain her household ran smoothly.

In reality, he was so much more. He ensured she was safe by helping her rent the townhouse, by hiring the household staff who were more soldiers than servants, and by serving as her primary bodyguard. Wilkins had been twenty-eight and in her father's employ as a footman when her family's carriage was attacked. He had been leading the carriage through the fog with a lantern, and he had never forgiven himself for not noticing the men waiting in the shadows, for not being able to stop the violent attack.

Since then, he'd guided Peyton as surely as if he were still holding up that lamp for her to see her way. He was her confidante, her dear friend, the man she trusted with her life—and one of only two people in the world who knew that she was still alive.

Wilkins followed her into her bedroom as he had done countless times in the past. Neither of them thought anything of that far-too-familiar intimacy.

She circled behind the Chippendale writing desk positioned next to the fire. As she set her pistol and knife onto the desk, she smiled at him. "Dartmoor is now thirty-one thousand pounds poorer."

His eyes gleamed with delight. "Exactly as you planned."

She pulled at the fingertips of her left glove to remove it and corrected, "As *we* planned." The long glove dropped to the desktop. Then she started on its mate. "I couldn't do any of this without you and Betty."

Betty Proctor had entered her world more than thirteen years ago as her mother's maid, but the woman had since become a second mother to her. Her own mother might have given birth to her, but Proctor had pulled her back to life.

Wilkins protested modestly, "We do it out of love for you. Betty and I consider you—*all* of us—to be family."

Her eyes stung with gratitude as she whispered, "As do I."

Turning her face away before Wilkins accidentally saw any stray emotions, she reached to remove her earbobs. She paused, tingling at the unbidden memory of how Dartmoor had so audaciously removed them tonight, as if he had the right to undress her.

Unlike Devlin, Armand Marchand *had* been given that right.

A former soldier who had been forced to flee Paris after a failed assassination attempt on Napoleon, Armand had been hired to teach her to fight with knives, guns, and even her own hands so she would never feel defenseless again. Thanks to him, she had also learned how to be vulnerable and trust in men again in a way she never thought she could. Eventually, she gave her innocence to him. But Armand had always made her feel safe.

What had happened between them hadn't been love, she knew that; theirs was simply a joining of bodies. Armand would never let it become anything more. After all, he had also been protecting her heart.

But Armand had been living on borrowed time. When he disappeared last year, with signs of a scuffle left behind in his room above the barn, she was certain Napoleon's men had finally found him, taking his life for bravely attempting to stop a tyrant.

Devlin Raines was *nothing* like Armand.

She snatched the bob from her ear. "I want you to go to Barton's tomorrow. Patton will have the money waiting for you." Then she removed the other bob and set both on the desktop next to the knife. "He knows to expect you."

"Of course."

"Add it to the other winnings from Dartmoor."

Winnings that amounted to a small fortune. For the past few weeks, she'd been setting hired men against Dartmoor at the tables, funding their stakes and paying them twenty percent of their winnings. Only one of them had disappeared with her money. The others were eagerly waiting to earn more.

That she was using one of Dartmoor's greatest pleasures against him was a delicious bonus. She'd take that pleasure away from him, too, before she was finished. Just as she planned on taking everything from him...his money, his reputation, his fiancée and family. Just as he had taken away all that had been most dear to her that night ten years ago.

"He's making you a very wealthy woman," Wilkins murmured, unaware of the dark place where her thoughts had strayed.

"I'm already a very wealthy woman," she reminded him grimly. She certainly didn't want Dartmoor's blood money mixed with hers. "As soon as it's in the bank, I want you to start donating it as planned."

He nodded, repeating her previous instructions, "No donations so large as to draw suspicion, all paid out to a dozen different charities."

"All supposedly from an anonymous yet progressively minded society matron on the verge of death who has no surviving children on whom to bestow her money."

A thin smile tugged at his lips. "And who cannot stomach the thought of giving it to the Church."

Peyton arched a sardonic brow. "Who can?"

Wilkins laughed, although a bit stiltedly. He was the one who had suggested she return to London to make Dartmoor pay for his crimes. If her revenge failed, he'd blame himself. She couldn't let that happen. Wilkins meant too much to her.

So far, though, all was going according to plan. She'd never believed that destroying a duke would prove so easy.

"You'd planned to speak with the new investigators." She reached up to unpin her hair, needing to keep her hands busy as she broached the topic she had always hated. "Did they learn anything more about the attack?"

"Raines left Dartmoor House only a few minutes after you and your parents, apparently in a flustered rush after speaking to his father."

Disappointment panged hollowly in her chest. "We knew that already." With a deep sigh, she set down a hairpin and reached to remove another. "He went to a gambling hell in Westminster."

The investigators she'd hired had discovered that the attack had not been a random act of violence but a targeted assassination, and all the evidence pointed to the late Duke of Dartmoor, Devlin's father. The timing of events was still unclear, and she had yet to uncover a motive for her parents' murder or enough evidence to prove that Devlin was at the scene of the attack.

Wilkins had been unable to see any of the attackers' faces in the foggy darkness that night, being too confused and frightened by the unfolding chaos to do anything more than run for the night guard. She, herself, had fallen unconscious without seeing her attacker's face in the darkness, able only to claw at his neck and tear loose a button from his waistcoat while she struggled against him as he pinned her to the ground from behind. Everything else was darkness.

Wilkins drawled, "But the new investigators have determined there was a two-hour time gap between when he left Dartmoor House and when anyone remembered seeing him enter the hell."

Her fingers froze. *Two hours.* More than enough time for Devlin to oversee the assault in person and then hurry to the hell to create an alibi.

Her eyes darted to Wilkins. "Are they certain?"

"They have sworn statements from witnesses."

Straightening her back to steady herself, she removed the last of the pins and shook out her hair, thankful to hide the trembling of her hands by running her fingers through her locks.

Devlin had been at the attack; all the evidence now placed him there with enough time to spare. *But why?* Why would he commit such evil? That question nagged at her more than she wanted to admit, especially after seeing him again tonight.

But everyone told her that Devlin had been part of it—the detectives, Wilkins, Betty, even the bits of evidence she'd managed to find on her own—and she had no reason to doubt them. Except...*why?* Why would Devlin take part in his father's murderous plans, and why would a rake like him, who had been invited into the beds of the most beautiful London ladies, want to rape a scrawny girl like her?

After spending time with Devlin tonight, that question demanded an answer more than ever. Yet it was an answer she simply didn't have. Nor most likely ever would.

Wilkins watched her silently. Neither of them thought any-thing of her taking her hair down in front of him, so long had they known each other and so closely had they lived together in France. Although he was a decade older than Peyton and had come from a completely different background in London's east end, he had cared for her during the dark days immediately following the attack with an attention born from deep remorse for being unable to stop it. He'd seen her at her worst then, beaten and bruised and barely clinging to life, and he was still with her now as she sought revenge.

Only the kindness and care that Wilkins and Betty Proctor had given her allowed her to survive. She owed them everything and trusted both with her life.

"And you believe the investigators?" she pressed. "You're certain Dartmoor was there that night?"

"Absolutely."

Her shoulders sagged with a disturbing mixture of relief and regret, and she nodded slowly as she accepted that last piece of missing information. Despite the whispers of lingering doubts from the corners of her mind, all the evidence pointed irrefutably to Devlin.

"Do you have new instructions for me?" Wilkins asked quiet-ly.

She shook her head faintly as she reached for the wooden keepsake box siting on the fireplace mantel and made her decision. "We stay the course." She placed the sapphires inside. Then her gaze fixed on the silver button tucked into the corner of the box. "That will be all for tonight, Wilkins. And thank you...for everything." She glanced over her shoulder at him. His face blurred beneath her unshed tears before she looked away. "Would you please ask my maid to attend me?"

"Of course." Yet he remained where he was for a long while, as if wanting to say something more, before murmuring instead, "Good night."

Then he left, closing the door behind him.

Alone in her room, Peyton sucked in a ragged breath and reached into the box for the button. She held it up to the firelight. She'd kept this button for a decade, long enough that the silver had tarnished black. It was a brutal reminder of that night.

Everyone thought she'd died shortly after the attack, including Dartmoor. Truly, Peyton Chandler *did* die, only to rise from the ashes as someone else. She had been able to keep living by taking one breath after another, one step at a time. Each breath slowly turned into uneasy hours, then entire days and months, and eventually into years, just as each step eventually turned into miles. Through it all, the only thing that had kept her going was her determination to make Dartmoor pay for what he'd done.

How had she gotten away that night? She still had no idea. The last thing she remembered was tasting the acid of panic and terror on her tongue, her hands and knees scraped raw against the cobblestones as she'd tried to crawl away, the sinking of her nails into her attacker's neck as he grabbed for her, the ripping of her skirts and bodice as her dress tore away, the weight of the man pressing down upon her from behind as his leg shoved hers apart—

She woke two days later with this button clenched in her fist in a death grip.

She'd been delivered, half-dead, by an unknown stranger to a surgeon. At some point during the night, Wilkins and Proctor had come for her. Fearing another attempt on her life, that the men who had killed her parents would come after her again if they thought she might be able to identify them, the two had secreted her away from London to a small cottage in Richmond. Then, they'd told everyone she'd died. When word spread of the vicious assault, no one questioned a third coffin joining those of her parents' in the churchyard.

As soon as she was well enough to travel, she fled to France with Wilkins and Proctor, where they started new lives.

There, in the warmth and anonymity of the southern French countryside, she was able to grieve. Proctor looked after her as if she were her own daughter, and with Wilkins's help in tracking down old business contacts, Peyton was able to regain a large portion of her father's fortune, which he had invested into accounts and business ventures across Europe. Eventually, Armand had come to join them, to train her to fight and help her heal, and they had all lived together on the small farm like a real family.

Through it all, though, she was haunted by the attack. She had hired investigators, the best money could buy, who began to piece together what had happened. Through their help, she learned who had directed the attackers, how the assault had been carried out...

All the evidence pointed to the Duke of Dartmoor and his son, Devlin Raines.

The old duke had avoided punishment by dying seven years ago, but she wouldn't let his son escape so easily. As the sixth Duke of Dartmoor, Devlin was untouchable in the criminal courts; such a high-ranking peer would never be found guilty, not even for murder. But there was more than one way to ruin him, and Peyton planned to do exactly that—ruin him but *not* kill him. After all, he deserved to suffer for his crimes, just as she'd suffered. He deserved to have everyone and everything he held most dear stripped away from him, until he was left with nothing. Just as she'd been. Until he wished he was dead.

Before she took her last breath, she would rain fire and brimstone upon Dartmoor's head, until the flames of hell consumed him and swallowed him whole.

She tossed the button onto the desk. It pinged against the wood, then rolled to a stop. From several feet away, she couldn't see the tarnished design, but she knew what it was. It was engraved on her soul as surely as it was engraved in the silver...the entwined initials D-R.

Devlin Raines.

"The Devil Reigns," she murmured.

But not for much longer.

Chapter Three

THE BELLS OF St Giles in the Fields rang three times over the city's streets and faded into the black night as Devlin made his way down the damp street. The bells were the only presence of God in this forsaken area of London, an area that made Devlin doubt if God even cared that the people who lived here existed, or if He'd simply resigned them to the damnation that was life in Seven Dials.

The thin blade of the long knife he kept shielded beneath his jacket sleeve pressed against his palm, the sensation a constant reminder to stay on guard.

Be aware of your surroundings at all times, Anthony Titus had repeated during their long hours of training, starting when Devlin had still been little more than a boy. So young, in fact, that he'd barely begun to shave.

A wild animal never goes against its instinct. It never willingly puts itself into danger. Never do the same.

He nearly laughed at that. Hadn't Devlin done the exact opposite of that, launching himself headfirst into danger after danger?

The first time was against his father, when he'd stood up to the tyrannical bastard for physically abusing his mother and his sister Margaret. Never had he taken more satisfaction in any act than when he'd backed his father against the wall with a knife and threatened to slit the bastard from balls to throat if he ever laid a hand on his mother or sister again. And *never* had he been so terrified—not of retribution from his father, but of himself and what he was truly capable of doing. He'd been barely eighteen, but five years of study under Titus, a former mercenary and Captain of the Guard at Windsor, had prepared him well for that confrontation, if only because he'd possessed enough control not to kill his own father.

The next time came when he left England for the Continent to put as much distance between himself and his father as possible. Fighting in the wars had nearly killed him, but he'd felt compelled to rush head-long into the fray. He'd been young and stupid, and so had his three friends—Lucien Grenier, Seamus Douglass, and Chase Maddox—who fought for the Prussians alongside him.

Yet he'd felt the danger most of all four years later when he returned to London at his mother's urging and learned what the Duke of Crewe, Charles Chandler, and his father had truly been doing all those times when the three men had secreted them-selves away with their port and cigars in their studies. Instead of gossiping over drinks about horses, hounds, and Parliament, the three men had been creating a web of criminal businesses. No evil had been overlooked in their pursuit of power and money, nor did they care how many lives they ruined in the process. Including those in their own families.

Devlin had put a decisive end to all that business, closing them down one by one, by scattering the pieces to the winds, and doing it all in complete secret so no one would ever know the extent of those crimes. Now, after seven years of living as Duke of Dartmoor, of burying and reburying his father's atrocities every time a new one revealed itself, he thought he had finally put all the old ghosts to rest. That the pact he and Lucien Grenier, the current Duke of Crewe, had made to keep their mutual silence of what their fathers had done was still being enforced.

He'd always believed he could trust Crewe.

Until tonight, when a beautiful siren in blue velvet had so distracted him that he was still reeling from the encounter. It was as if she knew all his weaknesses, and the only way she could have known those was if Crewe had told her.

His old friend had been playing a bad joke on him, which was just like Crewe to do, especially if the joke was to make Devlin lose at cards to a woman. Such a prank would buy him dark gossip about himself for weeks and serve as a warning to those gentlemen who wrongly thought they might wheedle their way into becoming Crewe's confidantes or cronies. After all, if Lucien was willing to play such a prank on Devlin, no one was safe.

And if it wasn't a joke, then Lucien had let slip information he shouldn't have to the prostitutes he was so fond of spending time with, who then passed it along to the woman who'd taken advantage of him tonight.

Either way, when he found Crewe, Devlin planned on hurting him. Repeatedly. Tonight's encounter, hot on the heels of dark rumors circulating through London's underworld of a new criminal enterprise rising from the ruins of what their fathers had done, wasn't at all amusing.

But it wasn't the new he feared as much as the old, and one old enemy in particular—*Horrender*.

Where Josiah Horrender had come from, no one knew, but as a child, he'd haunted the nighttime streets of the Almony as nothing more than a common pickpocket. He'd insinuated himself into London's criminal underbelly by the time he was in his teens, working for gin palaces and brothel owners and steadily raising himself to distinction as one of the most vicious men in St Giles. He had established his own businesses by his early twenties, with a hand in all kinds of crimes—smuggling, fencing stolen goods, extorting so-called protection from merchants and gin distillers. But his reach had been local, his crimes minor. Until he met the Duke of Crewe.

Lucien's father had strayed out of his usual King Street

haunts, for once making use of a brothel in Seven Dials to which Horrender had a connection. It only took a handful of conversations for the two men to realize the potential of joining forces and how the reach of their crimes could grow to encompass most of London. But with the involvement of Devlin's father and Charles Chandler, an astute London businessman, their reach could be limitless. While Horrender and his men oversaw the hands-on aspects of the crimes, Dartmoor and Crewe used their influence as peers to protect their growing enterprise, and Chandler used his business acumen to hide their money. Their crimes exploded in scope, and smuggling became the least of it...forced child labor, the slave trade, the sex trade, extortion, bribery—

"Murder," he muttered to himself as he quickened his pace.

God only knew the size of the fortune they'd made or how far the tentacles of their criminal enterprise reached. Just recently, Devlin had uncovered evidence that their fathers had illegally purchased slaves from Africa and shipped them to the sugar plantations in the Caribbean, that they'd supplied women for sex parties for East India company officials in Calcutta and child laborers for secret factories in Ireland. They'd managed to do it all beneath a cloak of secrecy.

But on one horrific evening ten years ago, their schemes all went to hell. All thanks to Horrender.

Before that night was over, three innocent people would be dead in an assault so grisly that even the two old dukes were stunned at what they'd done. Worse, one of the men involved had been captured, and to save his neck, the brute had named Horrender as being responsible. His testimony by itself wouldn't have been enough to make Horrender swing, but the additional proof that Devlin could provide would have ensured it. Horrender fled England to save his own neck and had not been heard of since. Left in his wake, their two fathers thought they'd escaped all scrutiny.

That was when Devlin coolly explained to both men that he would personally turn them over to the authorities and watch them hang if they dared to so much as even consider restarting their enterprise. The courts might not believe the word of a common criminal, but they would certainly believe Devlin. An agreement was struck—if either duke so much as even whispered a word to anyone about what they'd done, they'd both be tossed into the flames.

It was an unholy accord that Devlin and Crewe had no choice but to continue when their fathers both died three years later. It was either that or face the destruction of both dukedoms, their families, and everything they held dear. Perhaps even imprisonment for covering up their fathers' crimes. More innocents would be harmed, more lives destroyed. Knowing that didn't ease the guilt nor wipe away the blood Devlin had gotten on his hands by his silence. But he'd begun to take solace, however small, in the fact that at least the blood was no longer fresh.

Yet he couldn't get that woman out of his head. Nor could he banish that feeling from his bones that she might be a portent of something wicked rising in the night. Beyond the money he'd lost to her, beyond the frustration of being denied the carnal pleasures she'd dangled in front of him, he couldn't move past the dark suspicion that he knew her.

He'd forgotten the very first rule Titus ever taught him, the one that four years fighting with the Prussians had branded on his soul... *Know your enemy.*

The lamp at the end of the street burned like a beacon against the black night—or like a torch lit from hellfire, welcoming the demons who gathered here. The light was the only signpost of the business housed within the old structure whose plain front door it illuminated. Madame Pierre's, the most popular brothel in Seven Dials. All kinds of wickedness could be unleashed within its walls, and none of it ever saw the light of day. Including her special entertainments, attended by invitation only, which included evenings of nude dancing by twelve nubile nymphs of both sexes, all of whom went up for sale, to carry on the performance in private rooms upstairs.

He walked inside without bothering to knock.

The entry hall was crowded with men and women of all ages and manner of dress and undress, and as usual, it took a moment for him to sort through those who were for purchase and those eager to spend their coin. Madame Pierre's was one of the few houses in London that catered to men and women alike without discrimination. As long as the patron could pay in advance, that is. A few special gentlemen she serviced herself in the upstairs rooms, each space individually decorated after a European city. Devlin had never partaken here himself, but he'd heard from Lucien Grenier that the gladiator equipment in the Rome Room made for an intriguing evening.

"Dartmoor." A breathy voice greeted him as Madame Pierre glided down the hallway from the back of the house. The loose flowing satin robe she wore gave proof she'd been enjoying herself tonight, so did the red puffiness of her lips and the slight flush to her cheeks. She was well into her fourth decade, yet she still possessed the unparalleled—if slightly hard-won—beauty of any society lady in her twenties, despite the silver tint of her long hair that fell freely around her shoulders. "What brings a man like you to my humble establishment?"

"I'm looking for someone."

"Well, you've *found* someone," she corrected in a low purr as she trailed her hand down his chest. "I've been rather busy tonight being a good hostess, but I think I can accommodate you."

He was certain of it. He grabbed her wrist just as her hand reached his breeches. "Where's Crewe?"

She gave a throaty laugh. "A *ménage à trois*? Why, Dartmoor, you surprise me!"

"Where is Crewe?" he repeated sternly, setting her away. He had no patience for games tonight.

She sniffed peevishly as she tightened the belt of her satin dressing gown. Unlike the rest of the women who worked here, who made do in corsets and drawers, she wore a robe and slippers. Not because their undress was particularly alluring, but because being half-naked made it more difficult for the ladies to run away before they'd paid Madame their monthly tallies for room, board, and medical examinations against the pox, by a doctor who often took his fees in the form of a night in the Paris Room.

"You know I never reveal the identities of my guests." She gestured toward the drawing room, where two middle-aged ladies were admiring a half-naked young man and where a bald gentleman was bouncing a girl on his knee. "But come inside for a drink, and we can discuss—"

Enough. "Crewe!" he bellowed and charged up the stairs. "Crewe, where the hell are you?"

With a furious glare, she raced past him and blocked him from going any further. "If you don't calm down, I will have no choice but to call for help." She waved a hand toward the downstairs hall. "The magistrate often enjoys the entertainments here."

"And I'm a goddamned duke," he growled. "He can't touch me." Pulling rank was the only thing that blasted title was good for. He shoved past her to continue his hunt for Crewe.

"I will call the captain of the night guard!" she threatened weakly as she followed him onto the first-floor landing. "He's here right now—"

"Good." He charged down the hallway to begin his search room by room. "Then I'll introduce myself when I come across him."

He flung open the first door. The prostitute inside screamed at being startled, and angry shouts came from the man between her legs. He wasn't Crewe.

"Stop this right now!"

"Then tell me where Grenier is." Leaving the door open, he stormed across the hall. "I know he's here somewhere."

"How do you know he's—"

He shot her a contemptuous look as if she were daft as a

bedlamite, then yanked open a second door to reveal two women being watched by a man while they undressed each other. Only the gentleman seemed surprised that they now had a larger audience.

He moved on, shoving open a third door to find a fat old man being ridden like a horse around the room on his hands and knees by a prostitute perched on his back, completely naked except for a pair of spurs and the riding crop she slapped at his bare buttocks.

Devlin paused, stunned.

When the man looked up and realized Devlin was there, his eyes grew wide, but he was unable to shout around the bit in his mouth.

"Bishop." Devlin nodded apologetically and closed the door.

He bellowed for Crewe again and headed for the next room.

"Stop this!" Madame slid herself between him and the door, wedging her body into the frame. "You are ruining my business!"

He leaned down, bringing his face even with hers, so close he could feel the warmth of her breath against his lips. She trembled. *Good.* He'd learned from Titus that cold control could be just as intimidating as physical threats.

"I will keep ruining it," he said quietly so she had to listen hard to hear him, spreading more fear through her than if he'd yelled, "until you tell me where I can find Crewe." When she hesitated, he leveled his first true threat. "It won't stop tonight, either. In the morning, I will go to the borough council and have your business shut down under the Disorderly Houses Act, and you and your employees will be transported to Australia. I'm a duke, remember? They'll do whatever I ask."

Her eyes flared with defeat. She nodded toward the stairs and ground out reluctantly, "Crewe is in Venice."

"Of course, he is," Devlin muttered, heading toward the stairs and the second floor.

He didn't bother to knock before throwing open the door and striding inside.

Lucien Grenier, Duke of Crewe, rolled off the gondola-shaped bed where he'd been lying with a half-dressed prostitute on either side of him. He backed away from Devlin, who threw him against the wall and pinned him there with a loosely held hand at his throat.

Devlin growled out through clenched teeth, "What the hell have you been up to?"

"Two whores," Crewe answered, holding up his hands in a sign of peace. The same old signal they'd used when they were lads-in-training with Titus whenever the fighting bouts grew too fierce. "You should try it yourself and stop attacking me."

Devlin had no patience for Crewe's antics tonight and demanded, "Was it you?"

Crewe scowled. "Who did what?"

"Was it you who sent that woman to Barton's after me tonight?"

His old friend stared at him blankly. "What the hell are you talking about?"

"The woman," Devlin repeated irritably. "The one who beat me at cards."

Crewe blinked. "You got beaten at cards by a woman?" He laughed, despite the hand at his throat. "Wish I'd been there to see *that!*"

Devlin pressed harder against his throat. This was no time for joking around. "Did you put her up to it?"

"No! I didn't send any woman to Barton's. I've been here all night."

"All night?"

"Since this afternoon when I returned from Ealing, where I've been for the past three days." His expression sobered, taking on an uncharacteristic haggardness. "After dealing with things there, I needed a diversion. Christ!" He gripped at Devlin's wrist to loosen the hold on his throat. "Titus was supposed to have taught you control."

"He did." Devlin released him with a shove and stepped back.

Still sitting on the bed and propped up by red satin pillows meant to resemble the seat of a gondola, the two prostitutes stared at them, stunned. One of them whispered, wide-eyed, "Lucien?"

"It's all right." Crewe blew out a hard breath. "We're done for the evening." He narrowed his eyes on Devlin and rubbed his neck. "I'm no longer in the mood."

The two women hesitated. They stared at Devlin as if they didn't trust leaving him alone with Crewe. Truth be told, at that moment, Devlin didn't trust himself.

"You can each keep a book," Crewe said, bribing the two women, then gestured at the door to hurry them along.

That was when Devlin saw the short stack of books resting on the utterly ridiculous bed. He blinked. Books in a brothel? That was the most surprising sight he'd seen tonight.

Crewe cajoled, "We'll start next time with *Moll Flanders*, all right?"

The two women reluctantly slipped out of bed, picked up a novel, and moved toward the door, the books held protectively in their bare arms. As they passed by the tall lamp that was made to resemble a wrought iron lantern from Piazza San Marco, Devlin got his first good look at them, and his heart stuttered. In their bare feet beneath tightly tied corsets that pushed up their full breasts, with drawers tied by pink ribbons just below their knees and wide slits in the crotch, they weren't a day over seventeen—the same age as his youngest sister.

When the two women closed the door after themselves, Crewe turned toward the tiny table in the corner that was meant to resemble one from a canal-side café, complete with a picture of the Bridge of Sighs painted on the wall behind it. He reached for the bottle of whiskey sitting on the tray.

Devlin asked incredulously, "You're teaching prostitutes to read *Moll Flanders*?"

Crewe shot him a puzzled glance as he poured the whiskey. "Why not? She turns out all right in the end."

"Giving the girls something to shoot for, then?" Devlin asked dryly.

"Always." Crewe held out the glass as a peace offering.

Devlin accepted it and gestured at the room around them. "Must you give them lessons in this room?" Carnival masks dangled from the tall prow of the gondola bed, obviously there for bed sport. He didn't dare wonder how the long oar hanging on the wall was meant to be used. "Surely there's a better place."

"The drawing room is too noisy, and we get interrupted too often in the kitchens." Crewe lifted his glass in a toast with mock solemnity. "They take great pleasure in being educated wherever they may be." He quirked a knowing grin. "And in return, I take great pleasure in them."

Devlin didn't laugh. He knew Crewe's boast was a lie. Lucien never touched prostitutes, preferring instead to spend his time helping them, although apparently, he had no qualms about lying half-dressed in bed with them.

"One of these days, someone's going to discover that you're not actually using the women here for your own pleasures," Devlin muttered. "And then what will you do?"

"What I always do." He took a gasping swallow of the cheap whiskey and rasped out, "Lie."

Devlin had been friends with Crewe for two decades, and he was one of only a handful of men who knew the truth about him. That Crewe's entire life was a lie.

"Not that I don't appreciate this social call, mind you, but the tea here is terrible." Crewe refilled his glass and turned to Devlin, suddenly serious. "So why are you here?"

He frowned. "Because I met a mysterious woman tonight."

"*Now* the conversation's becoming interesting." He eyed Devlin over his glass as he raised it to his lips. "Tell me."

Taking a deep breath, Devlin told his old friend about the mysterious woman he'd met at Barton's, sparing few details. He, Lucien, Seamus Douglass, and Chase Maddox had become brothers-in-arms while training under Anthony Titus when they'd been at Eton together. Each had been there for different reasons, but in the end, they'd become brothers in every way but blood, never turning their backs on each other when in need and even following each other into the wars. He could trust all of them with his life—and with Crewe, he did just that every day with the secret of what their fathers had done.

He just couldn't trust Crewe not to involve him unknowingly in one of his latest jokes.

Crewe was always playing some sort of game he could brag about in the clubs to solidify his place as one of London's worst blackguards, to make everyone believe he held no feelings whatsoever in his black heart. It was only a matter of time until he involved Devlin in one of them, and tonight seemed to be it.

Crewe leaned back against the ceramic winged lion and folded his arms casually over his chest as he listened. In his shirtsleeves without a cravat, his bared neck revealed even more by his unbuttoned shirt and waistcoat, he was exactly as half-dressed as the two girls had been. After all, if anyone else had come across him tonight while he was teaching them to read, he needed to appear as if he were the rakehell everyone assumed him to be.

"I had nothing to do with any of that," Crewe promised, crossing an X over his heart the way the four friends had done since Eton.

Devlin raked his hand through his hair and blew out a hard breath, believing him. Lucien might have been able to fool the world about who he was, but Devlin knew him better than anyone. And now, Devlin didn't know whether to feel relieved or even more worried.

"She didn't give you her name?"

Devlin grimaced. "Lady Payne."

"Well, that's a damned lie."

Devlin finished off his whiskey. He didn't need a reminder of how blinded he'd been by her tonight.

"Nothing at all to identify her by?" Crewe frowned. "No idiosyncrasies about the way she played cards or spoke? Nothing about her clothes that would identify her dressmaker or indicate how long she's been in London?"

"No." He'd replayed every moment with her in his mind at least half a dozen times. Nothing stood out. He'd even questioned Patton about the name on the deed she'd used to back her marker—Elizabeth Wentworth—but that name meant nothing to him.

Yet he *knew* her, damn it. He would have bet his fortune on it.

"Be honest with me." He locked eyes with Crewe. "Have you told anyone about what our fathers did?"

"Never. Not even Shay or Chase." Crewe didn't try to conceal his bitterness at being doubted, as he added, "Our agreement still stands. I haven't betrayed your trust, Devlin." Crewe returned his glass to the café table. "Besides, it would be suicide. If one of us breaks the vow, both of us are destroyed. You know that."

"You more than me."

"Not much more." He fixed a grave stare on Devlin from across the room and asked pointedly, "How are your mother and sisters these days?"

Point made. The quiet question was a stark reminder of all they both had to lose. Even now, both men could be thrown into prison for hiding their fathers' crimes, and neither dukedom would be able to save them or their families.

"You can trust me, Devlin," Crewe assured him. His face was drawn. "I would never do anything to dredge up the past."

Devlin nodded faintly. Still, unease hung heavily over him. He slowly swirled his whiskey and frowned as he watched the golden liquid sheet down the sides of the glass. "I've been hearing rumors..." He didn't want to finish the sentence and put voice to his fears. "Do you think Horrender might have finally returned?"

Crewe stiffened instantly. "If he's back, I've not heard of it," he said quietly, as if he, too, was afraid to speak the devil's name for fear the devil would appear. "And my contacts in Seven Dials and St Giles are even better than yours."

Devlin prayed he was right. "Are you certain?"

"Horrender has not returned," Crewe insisted irritably, running his hand through his already disheveled hair.

Devlin recognized that sign of aggravation in his old friend, that old frustration at being unable to strike out at the unfairness of his world. Titus had worked with Crewe to channel physical exertion into release, to keep his hot frustrations tamped down, but they had come back once he'd stopped training. He got himself expelled from university during his first term, then headed to France to become a mercenary because his father prevented him from buying an honorable commission. Men across three countries had paid the price for Crewe's frustration during those years, and even now, Crewe only found solace by engaging in illegal bouts of fisticuffs waged in dockside warehouses where he could beat his opponents to a pulp. But all the fights in all the world would never fix what his father had done, just as they could never ease the hell Crewe had gone through during the wars. More than any of the four friends, it was Crewe who'd witnessed the worst of the fighting and suffered the most for it—was *still* suffering for it.

That was why Crewe spent his nights helping prostitutes, why he secretly gave thousands of pounds each year to send poor boys to school and to buy others places in the army and navy, why he anonymously gave away the greater share of grain from his estates to people living in the Almony and the Mint. Crewe desperately wanted to make reparations, but Devlin knew he'd never be able to. None of them had the power to change the past.

Crewe continued, "We've been keeping watch and would know if Horrender was back and picking up where he left off." This conversation was bothering him enough that he'd absently set to buttoning up his shirt and waistcoat. "Besides, he wouldn't dare return, not to London anyway, not with the two of us capable of making him swing." He crooked a gravedigger's grin that lacked all humor. "He'd make certain to kill us first, and I'm still breathing. *That's* how I know he's not back."

"Oddly enough, that doesn't make me feel better," Devlin drawled.

Crewe reached for his discarded cravat and began to knot it haphazardly around his neck. "It's been a decade without any sign of him, here or abroad. Most likely he's dead and buried in some unmarked grave in America."

Devlin wished he could be as certain of that as Crewe.

"If a new criminal ring has been established, then it's not Horrender who's running it." Crewe leveled a hard look on him. "Which makes it *none* of our concern."

Devlin knew better. It would always be their concern. He was still uncovering new evidence of the extent of their fathers' crimes, even though both men had been buried for years. God only knew the number of people their evil had touched, how many lives they had destroyed.

Were *still* destroying.

"And the woman?" Devlin pressed, unable to push her from his mind. The coincidence that he would meet a mysterious woman tonight on the heels of all the new rumors was too much to ignore.

"Demme if I know." Crewe slipped on his jacket and pulled his cuffs into place. Now fully dressed yet still mussed, he looked like any gentleman coming home from a night of debauchery. But that was Crewe. The man had always been a chameleon. "Are you certain she isn't just a mistress between protectors who planned to approach you about an arrangement but seized the moment to take your money the easy way instead?"

No. She was beautiful and refined, and any man in want of a mistress would count himself lucky to gain her for company. She wouldn't have to go hunting. Besides... "Since when does a mistress own land worth forty thousand pounds?"

Crewe tossed the copy of *Moll Flanders* onto the bed and muttered wryly, "Apparently, I've been teaching the wrong book."

And apparently, Devlin was right back where he started when he'd left Barton's, having no idea who she was or why she'd come after him. "You'll tell me if you hear anything?"

"Of course. Now get out so I can continue the lesson." Crewe snatched up the book and pointed at the door with it. "We've reached the part when Moll marries her son, and I need to explain to the ladies the basics of tobacco farming."

Crewe was lying. Devlin was one of the few people in the world who knew him well enough to know that. There would be no more lessons tonight, reading or otherwise. Crewe would be out questioning his contacts about Horrender before Devlin made it as far as Piccadilly. Crewe might have put on a good show about being certain that Horrender was already dead and either in hell or America—same thing, after all—but he was just as uneasy as Devlin over the possibility that he might have returned.

Still, experience had taught them how to pick their fights—a skill that Lucien knew better than anyone—so Devlin let him have his pretense and headed back out into the night.

Around him, the city was alive despite the darkness and shadows of the late hour, which did nothing to put him at ease and everything to stir the short hairs on his nape. He wanted to believe Crewe was right, that his fears about the new criminal ring were unfounded, but he knew the pure evil that was Josiah Horrender.

That kind of evil never remained buried for long.

As Devlin made his way through the dark streets, he cut south toward Piccadilly. There, lulled by the false security of its gas lamps along the wide avenue, he took deep breaths of frigid air, allowing himself the short-lived release brought on by the physical activity of the walk. Two miles to home. He'd be there in less than half an hour at this pace, but he didn't dare slow down. *Couldn't* slow down. Because he needed the exertion tonight to burn away the pain and anger he still carried inside him from all those years ago, and most likely always would.

Prowling the streets of London at this time of night wasn't safe, but he didn't give a damn. Let the footpads and thugs come for him. *Just let them try.* He'd been beaten before and survived, and tonight he ached for a fight. Even now as he hurried on, he clenched and unclenched his left hand into a fist, while his right clasped a knife so tightly he felt the soft indention of the blade through his glove.

What he wouldn't give to be able to let loose, to take comfort in fighting the way he had when he'd been on the Continent. In pouring himself into every punch and kick, into every slash of the sword, he had exhausted himself to the point when he could barely move or catch his breath, when every inch of him turned numb. When peace could finally settle over him, for a little while at least.

He'd been beaten then, too, although in a different way, whenever he lost command of his emotions and let the anger blind him. For years at Eton, he'd studied beneath Titus to learn control. All those years spent striving for hard-won restraint... Were they nothing but a waste of time? After all, what good was a man's control when the men he wanted to punish were already dead?

A movement in the shadows—

He spun around. The knife handle slid expertly down into his palm with a small flick of his wrist. Balancing on the balls of his feet, he held his breath and scanned the darkness at the edge of the street. His blood roared through his ears with each thundering heartbeat; every muscle was tense and ready to spring.

But nothing happened. No attack came. Not even a curse at him to be gone.

As he stared into the shadows, a small form became visible in the darkness, one huddled in a narrow doorway set back from the avenue. A soft sob of fear broke through the pocket of silent stillness, and Devlin's heart lurched.

A little girl, no more than ten or eleven based upon the size of her, crouched in the doorway. Dear God, she was thin! She was little more than a skeleton as her skinny arms hugged her knees to her chest, but her large eyes stared at him, terrified.

When he put away the knife and squatted down next to her on the dirt-covered footpath, she cowered away.

"I'm not going to hurt you," he said as gently as possible. "I was just walking past and saw you."

Those eyes—wide as the moon and filled with fear. And hatred. He easily recognized that emotion in her. God knew he'd lived with it himself for most of his childhood.

She was alone. If someone was with her, they'd have come forward by now. He knew that well from all the other children he'd come across on the nighttime streets.

"My name is Devlin. What's yours?" When she didn't answer, he added, "I have two sisters. Older than you, though. Margaret who loves to dance, and Teddy who has the same color hair as you."

Actually, he had no idea what color hair she had because of the shadows. Nor did it matter if he lied as long as he was able to draw her out. The ends always justified the means. Hadn't he learned that lesson the hard way?

"I would never hurt them," he assured her. "Just as I would never hurt you."

The brutal truth of those words was as sharp as the blade pressing against his palm. But the girl didn't believe him and so didn't move an inch.

"I want to help you," he said softly.

"Don't need no help," she whispered fiercely, like a hissing kitten cornered by dogs.

"No, you probably don't. A young miss like you can take care of herself, I bet."

"An' I can, too." When her chin raised into the air, the fear in her eyes turned to fire.

"But can you help *me*?"

She hesitated. He didn't blame her. Any other man who approached her tonight would have only done so to hurt her or force himself on her. Both of which Devlin wanted to prevent.

She tilted her head curiously, studying him. "What do you need m' help for?"

He fought back the urge to smile with satisfaction at finally drawing her into conversation. "My sister Theodora's birthday is tomorrow, and I don't know what to get her for a present. What do you think she'd like? Ribbons, a doll..."

"Shoes," she whispered. "She'd like shoes. A pair with 'em fancy buckles on the toes."

"In blue?"

"Black. 'Cause then the filth won't show on 'em."

He forced a smile. "Sounds like the perfect gift to me." He repeated, "I'm Devlin. What's your name?"

"Mary."

Mary... How many Marys and Janes and Sarahs had he rescued over the years? He'd lost count. Tonight, he planned to add another to that list. "That's a pretty name."

"Yours is *odd*."

He chuckled. "Yes, I suppose it is. Theodora says so, too, all the time. She'll probably tell me that as soon as I arrive home tonight." No, she wouldn't. His youngest sister was tucked safely into bed, dreaming sweetly through the night. She'd been the only one to escape their father's wrath. "And you, Mary? Where's your family and home?"

"Don't got none," she whispered. "Just some chums."

Chums. A gang. "It's cold tonight. Would you like someplace warm to sleep? Maybe some stew and biscuits?"

Her face softened with longing, yet only for a fleeting heart-beat before hardening again. "You said you weren't goin' harm me."

"I'm not," he said solemnly. "You've heard of Brechenhurst?"

She nodded. Of course, she had. Nearly every child in this part of London had heard of the peculiar place that took in children off the streets and gave them shelter and food for the night. It had no walls and gates to lock them in. No forced Bible lessons or memorizing moral platitudes. No questions asked.

"Have you ever been there?"

A shake of her head.

"Well, I happen to know the woman who runs it, and I know for a fact that she has room for you tonight."

"But it's all the way o'er t' Seven Dials."

"It is. Too far to walk. You'll have to take a hackney." When she hesitated, he dared her, "Grownups take hackneys. Are you grown up enough to ride in one?"

She gave a fierce nod and scowled. "I'm big enough."

"Yes, you are." This one had spirit. He hoped she could be saved before that spirit was broken. "Come on then. Let's get you a hackney."

He held out his hand and waited.

A long stretch of stillness passed before she slowly put her trembling fingers into his. He pulled her gently to her feet. Only then did he see that she was wearing little more than rags. He resisted the urge to give her his jacket, not wanting to embarrass her any more than she already was.

He stepped to the curb, raised his arm, and let out a shrill whistle into the traffic, which was busy even for four o'clock in the morning. After a few moments, an old hackney cab stopped beside him.

He opened the door and put Mary inside.

"Take her to number seven Wadley Street in Seven Dials," he instructed the driver. "Wake up the woman there who runs the place—Mrs. Martin. Tell her that Mr. Hunter sent the girl to her and that she's to take her in."

The man held out his hand for payment.

Devlin fished a coin from his pocket and held it up. "Mrs. Martin will give you a sealed note that you are to deliver to Number Ten Grosvenor Square. When the footman receives the note, you will be paid well for your trouble." He stepped up onto the cab and leaned in toward the driver as he placed the coin in the man's hand. Then he warned in a low voice that was little more than a threatening rasp, "If you harm her, I will hunt you down, and I will end you."

Despite the darkness, Devlin was certain the driver paled as he nodded.

Good. No one was going to harm an innocent tonight as long as Devlin could help it.

He jumped to the ground. The driver flicked the whip and started the old horse forward. From the side of the road, Devlin watched as the carriage disappeared into the traffic and darkness, carrying the homeless child away.

Another innocent saved.

It seemed that was all he'd done for the past ten years— attempt to save innocents and keep more of them from being harmed. He and Crewe had sworn to take their fathers' secrets to their graves. With Horrender gone, they'd thought they'd succeeded.

But the devil always collected his due, and Devlin feared it was finally time to pay.

Chapter Four

PEYTON STOOD ON the first-floor landing and watched through the large fanlight over the front door as the approaching dawn chased away the night. It felt as if the world was frozen in place, the whole city pausing to catch its breath before the sun rose and the day started.

Sleep had proven impossible last night after her encounter with Dartmoor. So she'd rolled out of bed and was making her way down to the kitchens when the view from the fanlight stopped her. The rest of the house was still asleep, including the scullery maid who would be rising soon to start the fires, so she paused on the landing and let the quiet moment have her.

A key scraped in the lock, and the front door opened.

Peyton froze, every muscle tensing instantly like a coil ready to spring. She held her breath as the door opened and watched the slant of light fall across the marble checkerboard tile of the entry hall floor, waiting for the first glimpse—

"Sweet heavens!" Betty Proctor glanced up and gave a startled cry to find Peyton standing there. The older woman's hand went straight to her chest. "You scared the daylights out of me!"

Peyton bit back the urge to tell Proctor that she'd done the same to her. Instead, she leaned against the wall in her satin dressing robe and waited for the older woman to catch back her breath.

Then she frowned to see Proctor in her coat and hat. "What were you doing out so early? It's not even dawn."

Closing the door, Proctor waved a hand in front of her face to fan air at herself and subdue her fluster at being surprised. "Oh, you know me." Another wave of her hand, although this one was half-dismissive. "I'm used to being up early. All those years as a lady's maid when I had to get up early to make certain the fires were lit, the breakfast tray ready, the mistress's clothes tended to."

Perhaps, but... "Where were you at this hour?"

"Just went for a little walk to stretch my old legs." She rubbed her hip with a smile. "Feels good to get them moving, especially on cold mornings like these."

"Please don't go out alone next time. The city is dangerous. Take one of the footmen with you." Peyton hadn't felt safe herself since they'd disembarked from the ship nearly two months ago. She added quietly, "I couldn't bear it if anything happened to you."

Another dismissive wave. "No one bothers with an old woman like me." Then she crooked her head and looked sternly up at Peyton. "But why are *you* awake? You should still be in bed after the late night you had."

"I couldn't sleep." She forced a weak smile. "You caught me on my way down to the kitchen to see if there was any hot water for coffee."

"Well, we'll do better than that!" Proctor stripped off her hat and coat and laid them across a chair in the entry hall. "We'll go down together and make breakfast ourselves."

Peyton blinked. "*We'll* make breakfast?"

Proctor paused when she realized what she'd said, then nodded fiercely. "Cook makes it every day. Can't be that difficult."

Fighting back a smile, Peyton looped her arm through Proctor's. The two women walked through the house to the servants' stairs in the rear and down into the kitchens.

As they went, Proctor related what she'd seen that morning on her walk down the street to the park and back, how the flower seller was putting out his baskets and the butcher most likely shorting orders of beef.

Peyton listened with affection. She owed this woman everything.

Ever since Peyton could remember, Proctor had been her mother's maid, and not much difference in age from Mama, which was most likely why Peyton now saw her as a second mother, one who had sacrificed her own life for an adopted child. In their years of self-exile in France, she'd taught Peyton how to be a proper woman—how to take care of her hair and skin, how to choose dresses and accessories, how to deport herself—all the things she should have learned from her own mother and from her own lady's maid when she was old enough to have one. How could she have survived all those years without Proctor, to say nothing of those first few dark days after the attack? Proctor had nursed her back from the edge of death and dragged her back into the light.

Peyton had repaid her the best she could by elevating her to the status of an aunt and giving her a separate set of rooms within her home, her own maid to attend her, and a generous allowance. She'd given the same kind of luxuries to Wilkins. The two had become her family.

"And then the butcher said, 'My! That's the finest rump I e'er seen!'" Proctor stopped just as they reached the kitchen, placed her hand on her hips, and shook her finger, re-enacting the moment. "So I said, 'Mr. Butcher, you'd best be talking about a roast!'"

Peyton laughed, her hand flying up to her lips to keep back her laughter. Only Betty Proctor could be that audacious on her morning walk.

Useless in the kitchen, Peyton sat on a little stool pulled up to the long worktable and let Proctor scurry about the space, looking into all the cabinets and pantries, to make them breakfast.

Learning to cook was most definitely not a skill Peyton's schooling had prepared her for. But then, her girlhood hadn't prepared her for a lot of skills that she later found necessary, such as shooting pistols and wielding knives. Her chest tightened. How much different would her life be if she'd remained that same girl who needed to know nothing more dangerous than how to watercolor, play the pianoforte, and dance without stepping on her partner's feet? It was impossible to even contemplate that now.

"We'll have ourselves a right fine breakfast." Proctor fetched a bowl of strawberries from the cold pantry and set them on the table in front of Peyton, along with a hunk of cheese and a knife. "And prove to Cook we're capable of taking care of ourselves! How about some eggs?"

She reached for the metal basket of eggs on the wall shelf with a smile. Then she halted and frowned at the eggs, realizing she would have to cook them.

"Maybe not eggs," she mumbled as she put them back.

Peyton stifled another laugh.

Proctor set a plate of croissants from the breadbox on the table and then plopped onto a stool across from Peyton just as the young kitchen maid came back inside from the service yard in the rear. Surprised to see them, she nodded her good morning greetings, then busied herself with putting a pot of milk over the fire to heat to make chocolate.

"Now then." Proctor reached for the knife to cut off some cheese. "What's so wrong that you can't sleep?"

Peyton lowered her eyes to the croissant as she broke it in two with her fingers. "I met Dartmoor last night, face-to-face…and he wasn't the monster I thought he would be."

For a long moment, Proctor didn't move, didn't speak. Then she gestured at the kitchen maid and ordered, "Go down to the butcher and tell him that I've changed my mind. I want that roast after all."

The girl frowned. "But Cook's planning to—

"Go on! Be away with you then—shoo!"

With an irritated twist of her lips, the maid grabbed her coat and hat from the hooks beside the door, then slipped out the rear door.

"What happened?" Proctor pressed quietly once they were alone. "Did he recognize you?"

Peyton shook her head with a frown. "Not at all."

Proctor set down the knife, and her fingers pulled idly at a piece of cheese, crumbling it without realizing it. "Then your plan didn't go well?"

Her frown deepened. "The evening went exactly as planned."

"Then why aren't you happy about it?"

"Because it doesn't feel at all the way I thought it would. I thought I would hate him, that I would recoil and be sick from being near him. But I wasn't." No. The exact opposite, in fact. There had been times during the evening when the years had seemed to disappear, and she'd forgotten the events of that night, if only momentarily. And *that* bothered her more than she wanted to admit, as did the swirling doubts about him that gnawed at her belly.

"Tell me," Proctor insisted.

As she slowly ate the croissant, one nibbling bite at a time despite not having an appetite, Peyton related what happened last night, about meeting Devlin at Barton's and besting him at cards. Exactly as planned.

Proctor listened intently, nodding her head and urging her to continue with each new detail she shared…except the part about the attempted seduction, at which Proctor said nothing because Peyton conveniently excluded it. After all, Proctor was too much like her own mother to discuss subjects like that.

"That's wonderful," Proctor said when Peyton finished the story with a description of making a clean exit. She slipped off the stool and removed the milk from the fire, then set about making an urn of chocolate for Peyton exactly as she liked it, including a pinch of cinnamon in the layer of butter cream on top. "It's what you wanted—to make him pay for what he did."

"Not as much as I'd thought," she admitted. "It felt…wrong, somehow, taking his money like that."

Measuring out the cocoa powder, Proctor paused to send Peyton a pointed glance. "That man murdered your parents."

"He wasn't one of the men who pulled us from the carriage." She knew that with certainty. She clearly remembered those men, having seen their faces. They were too physically different from how Dartmoor had been then, when he'd still been the young Marquess of Truro. He'd been taller than those men, not so broad, not so stocky. His muscles had been sinuous, not bulky hard—he'd possessed the muscles of a young man who spent lots of time riding and fencing. The men who killed her parents had been older and rounder, possessing more brute strength than Devlin's finesse. After all, in the weeks leading up to the attack, she'd spent hours watching him dance at balls when he hadn't been aware that she was even present, and he possessed a natural-born athletic grace those men lacked.

"You're splitting hairs now." Proctor shot her a chastising glance as she stirred in the dark powder. "He might not have pulled your parents and you from the carriage, but he was *there*. He was part of it."

Peyton frowned at the piece of croissant as she slowly shred-ded it with her fingers. Devlin *had* been there, and she'd fought against him; the button she'd ripped from his waistcoat proved that. She'd torn it from his waistcoat during the struggle when she'd nearly been raped, and the tailor on Bond Street confirmed that it was exactly like all the others he'd sewn onto Dartmoor's evening clothes. She'd remembered seeing those buttons herself earlier that same evening before everything changed, when he'd been staring at the opera singer and she'd been staring at him, so closely that she'd noticed every detail about him, right down to the shine of the silver buttons on his chest.

"Why was he there then," Proctor pressed as she poured the chocolate into a long-handled chocolate pot, almost as if reading

Peyton's mind, "if not to hurt you and your parents?"

Peyton couldn't answer that. It was that same question that always stopped her in her tracks whenever she tried to sort through the events of that night. *Why? Why Devlin?* Even after all these years, even after all the evidence she'd gathered that pointed at Devlin and his father, she still had no motive. But it hadn't been a coincidence that he had been there that night. He knew their carriage was going to be attacked, most likely by hired porters from the docks or thugs from Seven Dials, and wanted to witness the carnage. Or worse—that he'd arranged the attack himself.

Yet even now, though, nagging doubts that had been growing inside her since her return to London rose in a chorus inside her head.

"I don't know," she whispered.

Her face dark with sympathy and grief, Proctor returned to the table and set down the now unwanted chocolate. She said quietly, "He tried to rape you."

Peyton also wasn't so certain of that any longer either, since seeing him again at Barton's. At different times during the evening, she'd felt a visceral pull toward him, a rekindling of the old attraction. How could she be attracted to the man who had tried to rape her? *Impossible.*

Yet she'd seen his face the night of the attack, clawed a bloody scratch into his neck, ripped off his button—

He had been there, had attempted to rape her...hadn't he?

Confusion swam inside her until she felt as if she might drown. Wilkins had been so adamant that Dartmoor was the one responsible for what had happened that night. Even the latest pair of investigators she'd insisted Wilkins hire to discover the last missing pieces of that night—and lay her final doubts to rest—had provided only more proof of Devlin's involvement. It had taken ten years to arrive here, but now, finally, she could claim her revenge. Ten years of fear, anger, and grief so terrible that it had nearly consumed her. Her only way forward from the darkness had been a dedication to bringing justice to the man responsible.

So why were her instincts whispering that maybe she was wrong?

Proctor took Peyton's hand in hers. "You know what kind of monster that man is. You cannot stop until he gets what's coming to him." Her eyes fixed on Peyton's. "Or do your parents' graves mean nothing to you?"

Grief struck her so fiercely she winced. "They mean everything." She slowly pulled her hand away, for once not taking any solace in Proctor's motherly gestures. Her chest burned, and she blinked hard. "Do they still—" She choked, then started again. "Are flowers still put on the graves?"

"Yes." Proctor poured two cups of chocolate, but neither wanted any now. "The woman we hired is still putting flowers there every week. I've been checking up on her since we've returned, and a new bouquet is placed there every Sunday. On all three graves."

On *her* grave. Perhaps that's why Peyton risked herself as she did. What more did she have to lose when she was already dead?

"When this is all over," Peyton promised, forcing herself to accept the cup of chocolate only because Proctor had gone to the trouble of making it, "that grave will be removed."

Not one day too soon.

Chapter Five

T HE CROWD PARTED as Peyton slowly made her way through
the crush of opening night at the Theatre Royal. All of
London society seemed to be in attendance, including the prince
regent and his latest paramour. But then, it wasn't every night
that Domenico Scarlatti's grand opera *Ambleto* was performed on
the London stage.

A secret smile tugged at her lips as she took surreptitious
glances at the crowd, not one of them realizing the private irony
she found in that. *Ambleto... Hamlet.*

Tonight was act two in her own revenge play.

She leisurely climbed the wide marble stairs that swept their
way up to the first floor, one slow step at a time. Every pair of
eyes in the house seemed glued to her as she rose above the lobby
floor, and curious whispers followed in her wake.

Good. For the past ten years, she'd hidden from the world. But
now she delighted in appearing in it, just as any smart actress
would who needed to be noticed.

She'd certainly dressed the part tonight, right down to the
glittering rubies draping around her neck and dangling from her
ears. Every one of the jewels was meant to sparkle beneath the
chandeliers and set her apart from the crowd. So was the blood-
red silk dress she wore. Exceptionally low cut in a Spanish style,

the dress flattered her figure with its tightly fitted waist, so unlike those cylindrical-shaped English gowns with their high waists and puffy cap sleeves that had become all the rage. To Peyton, those gowns looked as if ladies' maids had gotten confused and dressed their mistresses in the drawing room draperies. Not at all proper attire for a seduction.

Or in this case…a deception. After all, as Armand Marchand had taught her, a good soldier always dressed appropriately for battle. Tonight would be her second skirmish with the Duke of Dartmoor in the war she was waging against him, and she needed to be prepared.

Three nights ago, she'd begun her assault on his fortune. Tonight, she planned to go after his future.

Dartmoor was here somewhere amid the crush of bodies, which was why she moved so slowly up the stairs, each step deliberate and smooth. She wanted him to see her. Her presence tonight would make him reveal himself. He wouldn't be able to resist approaching her, demanding answers about the other night at Barton's, and then she would have him exactly where she wanted him.

Come into my parlor, said the spider to the fly…

She hadn't seen him yet, but she knew he was here. She'd heard he'd planned on escorting Lady Catherine Carlow and her parents. *Of course* she'd heard. Servants' gossip was better than newspapers for reporting the latest *on dit*. Dartmoor really needed to hire servants who were more cautious in sharing information about their employer's whereabouts. But servants employed in the household of a duke did so love to brag about what their estimable employer was up to when he was out and about. In this case, they'd shared with Proctor how Dartmoor was still attempting to formalize his engagement to Lady Catherine by continued reminders to her father that he was a duke, one powerful enough to hire the box located next to the prince regent.

She reached the top of the stairs where more whispers and

curious stares greeted her. Her heart pounded so fiercely that her chest ached, yet not a stray emotion registered on her face to show how uneasy she was venturing into society like this and putting herself at risk for being recognized. Attending Barton's had been different. Dark and smoke-filled, the club was used to patrons who wanted to keep their identities and activities secret. But here, everyone wanted to see and be seen, to be put on display for compliments or cuts. The crowd was ten times as big, the chandeliers twice as bright, and there was nowhere to hide from snooping eyes.

For the past ten years, she'd stayed away from London for fear of being recognized and having her life threatened. But she knew now her fear was unfounded. Dartmoor didn't recognize her, for heaven's sake, and she'd practically been in the man's arms at the card table. If he didn't recognize her, why would anyone else? She was a woman who was dead, after all, transformed like a butterfly from the caterpillar of a sixteen-year-old cocooned girl whom few had bothered to notice in the first place.

The crowd might have been curious about her, this stranger who so audaciously moved through them tonight in the devil's own colors, but none dared approach her. She was safe, hiding in plain sight. Yet knowing that didn't lessen her unease.

Drawing a deep breath, she walked on, just as deliberately as before. She turned toward the wide saloon that led to the private boxes and toward the one she'd rented entirely for herself for the evening.

Halfway down the saloon, she stopped.

Dartmoor.

He stood among the crowd at the end of the saloon, engaged in conversation with an older couple. Beneath the chandeliers, he looked rakishly handsome, with his blond hair just sandy-dark enough to give him a rogue's appearance even while dressed in Bond Street's finest. As if in intentional opposition to her attempt to stand out, he'd dressed in dark colors that blended into the crowd around him. Black jacket and trousers, black waistcoat—

the sapphire pin in his white neck cloth was the only splash of color in all six feet of him.

Yet if he'd meant to hide, he'd failed. Because beside him on his arm stood a young lady in dandelion yellow muslin, as bright as he was dark.

So *that* was the woman he wanted to marry. Lady Catherine Carlow. She looked so...ordinary. Not at all the kind of woman Peyton would have picked for Truro. But he wasn't the Marquess of Truro anymore, was he? He was the Duke of Dartmoor now and all that name implied. Which meant no more scandalous widows, no more adventurous wives or opera singers. He had to project a veneer of respectability, after all, even if he was wicked to the core.

Lady Catherine would certainly help with that. By all accounts, her father, the Earl of Northrop, was one of the most respectable peers in England, while she had a sterling reputation to match. Overall, the Carlow family was conservative, scandal-free, as exciting as a rainy afternoon...utterly harmless. A middling peerage with a middling fortune that would benefit exponentially by marrying into a dukedom, and a dukedom that would benefit from an unblemished family name that stretched back to the Restoration.

Lady Catherine was the perfect choice for Dartmoor. But did she have any idea of the monster he truly was?

Not at all, judging from the pleasant way she smiled at him as he stood talking to the earl. Her mother stood at her other side, her back toward Peyton. Around them gathered a half-dozen or so assorted friends. Quite the crowd, all of them enjoying the evening.

But not for long. Not if Peyton had her way.

Before the night was over, the Earl of Northrop would reconsider his plans to marry his innocent daughter to Devlin Raines, and the poor girl would have escaped by the skin of her teeth. All it would take was a private box and a few mussed pieces of clothing to convince the earl and countess that Dartmoor had engaged in scandalous intimacies tonight, right behind the back of his intended, sitting only a few yards away. Their engagement would be off before it had begun.

Dartmoor glanced up, and their eyes locked across the length of the salon. For one beat, his face registered surprise. Then it vanished, his expression once more a carefully controlled mask.

"Come into my parlor," she whispered.

Then she turned toward the private box she'd reserved, knowing his eyes were following her.

"Thank you," she told the uniformed attendant as he opened the door. She gave him a coin. "Please go somewhere else for the evening. And leave the door open."

He nodded smartly. "Yes, ma'am."

She sat in the second row of chairs in the dark box, far enough back to watch the stage yet remain in the shadows, and patiently waited.

Most of the first act passed before a prickle of awareness tingled at her nape. She didn't hear him—she *felt* him slip inside the box and close the door, felt his slow approach through the shadows. Her heartbeat increased as it always did before a fight. Every inch of her tensed, every one of her senses came alert. Yet she kept her gaze straight ahead on the stage, not turning to reveal that she knew he was there.

The air around her stirred as he came up behind her. He rested his hand on the back of the chair beside her, then lowered himself to lean over her shoulder, bringing his mouth close to her ear. "Are you enjoying the opera?"

"Not yet." She didn't dare turn her attention away from the stage, although it was firmly on the man behind her. "Although I'm certain to find it absolutely scintillating before the curtain falls. And you?"

"I hate opera."

"But you love opera singers," she purred, remembering how he had stolen away with the Italian soprano at his mother's musicale. At the time, she'd thought that to be the most terrible part of her night—that the man she'd held an affection for, who barely realized she existed, had slipped upstairs with another woman. She'd been so very wrong.

"What warm-blooded man doesn't?"

She turned her head to gaze over her shoulder at him, bringing her mouth so close to his that the warmth of his breath shivered across her lips. She paused with her mouth right there, knowing she could kiss him if she simply tilted up her chin. When his gaze fell to her lips, she knew he was considering just that, and a soft thrill of triumph sped through her.

She turned back toward the stage. "Then don't let me interrupt your evening."

He chuckled, the sound tickling her ear. Yet there was no amusement in it. "Why are you here? It isn't for the opera."

There. The invitation she'd been waiting for. "I'm here for you." Slowly, she rose from the chair and circled around it to join him in the dark shadows in the rear of the box. "To continue our game."

"But there's no card game here, so you have no way to win more of my money through duplicitous means."

"I wasn't duplicitous. I warned you outright, remember? It isn't my fault you underestimated me."

"You led me to believe you had no money but the pile of winnings in front of you."

She tsked her tongue and reached up to play with his cravat, ostensibly to straighten the knot. "You assumed that because you wanted to believe it. You, of all people, should know you cannot trust your eyes at cards, that you have to use all your senses to know what your enemy is thinking."

"Opponent, you mean," he corrected, yet he didn't put her hands away from him.

No. He was the enemy, and even more dangerous because she'd once loved him before he'd turned foe. There had been times that night at Barton's when it seemed as if they were still the same young acquaintances they'd been before. Back then, what she'd wanted most of all was to make him notice her as a woman.

Ironically, some things never changed.

"Surely you're not upset with me for being the better player," she purred. "I simply outplayed you." Or in this case, simply counted cards while successfully distracting him.

"You were attempting to seduce me."

"Not attempting." *Succeeding.* An old thrill spiraled through her, the same one that had plagued her ten years ago whenever he'd graced her with a short word or a passing smile. Oh, she'd been nothing to him then. But now… "I'd hoped the seduction was mutual."

"So did I," he murmured and punctuated his point with a caress of his knuckles across her cheek.

It wasn't a simple thrill that sparked through her then, but a deep and longing ache. She wasn't an innocent girl anymore, yet for a split second, the sensation unnerved her. And not because he was her enemy.

All these years, she'd been certain that Dartmoor had had a hand in murdering her parents, that he was the one who had attempted to rape her. But as she felt a feminine ache for him blossom inside her, the whispering doubts in the dark corners of her mind began to shout that she was wrong, and this time, they were too loud to ignore.

Confusion swirled through her. How could her body take such pleasure in his attentions if he'd attempted to force himself upon her? Surely it would remember, would be able to recognize the enemy…wouldn't it?

"And if I'd have won that hand?" He smiled, mistaking the sudden tension in her.

She forced herself to relax and pulled her concentration back to the present. Twisting her lips with chagrin, she leaned against him to whisper into his ear, "Then you would be the owner of a lovely little estate in Sussex."

He stopped her when she moved to shift back, gently taking

her arms and lightly holding her against him. Her breasts brushed against his chest and traitorously increased the throbbing ache inside her. He raked a hot gaze over her. "That wasn't what I was referring to."

"I know." As if to make her point, she pulled at his cravat, twisting loose the knot and rumpling it as she stepped away.

Knowing never to take her eyes off the enemy, she slowly retreated two steps into the shadows, until her back pressed flat against the rear wall. She placed her palms against the paneling on either side of her, arching her back and thrusting out her breasts, the same way she'd seen the opera singer do that night at the duchess's musicale to draw the attentions of the young gentlemen. To draw *his* attention most of all.

Come into my parlor...

He didn't move, his eyes fixed on her through the subdued darkness of the box. For a moment, her heart plummeted in disappointment, and she felt like the same unwanted girl he'd ignored all those years ago. No, not ignored—she couldn't be ignored if he'd never realized she was there in the first place.

Then slowly, he accepted her unspoken invitation and followed. He closed the distance between them until he stood so close she could feel the heat of his front warming the top swells of her breasts above the low neckline of her dress. So close, but not touching. *Yet.*

He lowered his head, stopping his mouth just before it found hers. "Why did you go to Barton's that night?"

"To take your money."

"And that was all?"

"Wasn't thirty-one thousand pounds enough?" Even in the shadows, she could see the glint in his eyes that told her he didn't believe her. Yet she pressed on, not caring if he trusted her to tell the truth or not. "We could return to Barton's and set up another game, should you decide to give me even more."

He chuckled softly at her audacity and leaned closer, until she could just feel the brush of his waistcoat against the red silk of her dress.

She should have been panicking that she was trapped there, between the wall and his broad body, but inexplicably, she wasn't. Her only sign of nervousness was a single hard swallow, which he took as an invitation to trace his fingertip down her throat. His touch quickened her breath, which only increased when his gaze lowered to her breasts. Instead of his fingers following after his gaze, his hand dropped to his side.

An unfathomable pang of disappointment pierced her.

"I think I prefer the opera," he confessed huskily. "Far less dangerous."

"Not at all." She'd meant that to come out as a laugh. Instead, it emerged as a throaty whisper.

"Is that why you're here tonight, alone in this box?" He lowered his head to bring his lips to her ear. "You wanted me to come after you. Why?"

His warm breath tickled against her ear, and she trembled. Her reaction earned her a smile from him, one she could feel against her cheek.

"Doesn't every woman want that?" she tossed back. "I hear Dartmoor's quite the lover."

"You had better odds with the thirty-one thousand pounds." He straightened, breaking the faint contact with her, and his frown deepened as he studied her face. "What do you want from me? And I know better now than to believe you want to be taken to my bed."

She lifted her hand to his chest, to play with the buttons of his waistcoat, and prayed that he didn't notice the trembling in her fingers.

She was no longer naïve when it came to men. Yet even with all her experience, seducing Dartmoor was proving harder than she'd imagined. She'd believed for years that he was the man who had attempted to rape her, and those feelings couldn't so easily be pushed aside. Neither could those niggling doubts that perhaps he hadn't.

The uncertainty threatened to consume her.

She forced a teasing smile. "What makes you think I don't want that?" With a soft laugh, she brushed her fingers through his thick blond hair. She'd done it to mess up his appearance, yet strangely, her fingertips itched to touch him. "Or that I'd expect a bed?"

"Because you wouldn't have fled Barton's like that." He touched her ruby earbob and slowly stroked it between his fingers. "You would have stayed to enjoy the night with me, then collected your winnings from Patton in the morning. So what do you want with me tonight?"

"Perhaps I've changed my mind about being intimate with you."

He laughed. Then he leaned in and touched his lips to hers.

Peyton inhaled sharply as a burst of electricity pulsed out to her fingers and toes, to the ends of her hair. It wasn't a kiss so much as a dare, she knew, yet a troubling part of her longed to turn it into so much more.

"No, you haven't," he murmured as he shifted away, smiling with self-satisfaction. "I can taste the hesitation in you."

Anger flared inside her—at him for being so presumptuous...at herself for not wanting to slap him.

In retaliation, she slipped free the top button of his waistcoat. Then a second. She was more determined than ever to punish him exactly as she'd planned tonight, and not spend a single second more in his presence than she had to.

When a third button came undone, his hand darted up to still hers in its downward progress.

"What do you think you're doing?" he demanded.

She gave a throaty laugh as she slipped back into her role of seductress. "Really, Dartmoor, if you don't know..." She finished that with a tsk of her tongue and a shake of her head. "It's a good thing I didn't linger at Barton's after all. I do so hate to be disappointed."

Instead of rising to that bait, he placed his forearm against the wall just above her shoulder and leaned in, searching her face. "I know you, somehow," he muttered, searching her face in the shadows. "Who are you?"

A warning pricked in her belly, yet she commented flippantly, "You know a great many women, if the stories are true."

"They're not."

"Pity." She slipped her fingers away from his and deftly undid another button.

He stopped her again, this time stunning her by lifting her hand to his lips and placing a kiss to her palm. She shivered, and her lips parted in surprise.

"You're a very beautiful woman."

Her traitorous heart skipped. *Damn him.* She could *not* be affected by him as a woman. Not *him!* Yet how many nights when she'd been a girl had she dreamt about hearing those exact same words fall from his lips? How could she thrill to hear them now, knowing what she knew about him?

Yet she did. And those doubting whispers began to shout out again, louder this time, that perhaps she was wrong...

"But your beauty won't save you if you cross me. If you're attempting to come after me or my family, if you harm one hair—"

"I would never harm them." She would *never* harm innocents. Especially family.

Yet disbelief flickered in his eyes. He'd obviously learned his lesson and wouldn't underestimate her again, which made tonight even more of a challenge. One she had every intention of winning.

His eyes turned steely black in the darkness. "Who sent you after me?"

"No one." She'd sent herself.

He lowered his face until his eyes were even with hers, until his warm breath teased at her lips. "Was it Horrender?"

She blinked. "Who?"

She had no idea who that was, nor did she care. The only

person who concerned her at that moment was Lady Catherine Carlow, to make certain the woman believed she and Dartmoor had been intimate in the box. *Which shouldn't be too hard...* The last button slipped free, and his black waistcoat fell open, revealing the white shirt beneath.

Holding her hands to stop her, he searched her face. "If not Horrender, then who? What do you want from me?"

"This." She rose up onto her tip-toes and brought her mouth hard against his.

He stiffened, stunned at her brazenness, and she seized the moment. Her wandering hands tore at his cravat and slipped it off from around his neck, then set to pulling at his shirt to leave it hanging half-untucked around his hips. With one hand reaching up to further mess his hair, her other hand grabbed at her own dress to skew her bodice and wrinkle her skirt.

All the while, her mouth was on his. She fiercely kissed him, alternating between biting at his lips and sucking, daring to dart her tongue into his mouth—doing *everything* she could to make him look thoroughly mussed when he left her box. She reached a shaking hand toward his fall—

He grabbed her wrist and stopped her. Breathing hard, with a faint expression of irritation darkening his face, he demanded, "What the hell are you doing?"

"Kissing you." Her own irritation sparked then. Why wouldn't he cooperate and let her seduce him? He was a rake, blackguard, scoundrel ...wasn't he? "Surely the infamous Dartmoor knows what do to when a woman kisses him." Then, to bait him, she challenged, "Doesn't he?"

"Yes, he does," Devlin drawled, shifting closer. "This."

Peyton tensed, readying herself for his assault, preparing to use the fighting skills Armand had drilled into her—

But there was no attack, not like that. Instead, he cupped her face in his hands and leaned in slowly to kiss her...gently, softly...so very tenderly. The surprise of that ripped her breath away.

So did the confusion he spun through her. He shouldn't be kissing her like this, not when he could be forcing himself on her. He was a monster, a man who had coldly murdered her parents and then came after her. But...he wasn't doing that. They were alone in the box, the door undoubtedly locked. For all he knew, she wouldn't be able to stop him if he forced himself on her, and the musicians and singers on stage were so loud that no one would differentiate her screams from those on the stage if she tried to cry out for help. But he wasn't even trying! *Why* wasn't he?

Instead, he coaxed each slow kiss from her, cajoling her with his sensuous lips to kiss him back just as softly, just as tenderly.

A soft whimper for mercy fell from her lips. The doubts and confusion overwhelmed her, and she began to shake beneath his unexpected embrace as each kiss remained as tantalizingly gentle as the one before.

But he gave her no quarter to sort through her confusion, and his fingers on her cheeks began to tenderly stroke her soft skin. Each featherlight touch sent her spinning back in time until she felt as she had before that horrible night, when she was still innocent of the darkness. When she still had a bright and shining life ahead of her. When he was still the most alluring man she'd ever seen... Before her world had ended.

Slowly, her lips responded to his and returned the luxurious kiss with the same decadence as he gave it. Not sweet—*nothing* about this kiss was sweet. It was sultry and sensuous with a lingering heat that only flamed hotter beneath the unhurried desire he conveyed. As if he had all the time in the world to do nothing more than stand there and kiss her, to savor her the way some men savored port...one luscious taste at a time.

"Truro," she whispered, caught up in his spell.

He froze, his fingers stilling against her face. His mouth lingered above hers, poised to take another achingly tender kiss. Instead, he demanded, *"Who?"*

Her eyes flew open. Reality slammed into her, and with a

startled gasp, she stared up into his face. The *same* face that had hovered over her the night of the attack—the same dark eyes and hair, the same deep concern...

The memories of that night flooded back in crashing waves, drowning her with their intensity and relentless confusion. Flashes of her mother's face, her father's body writhing as the life was cut from him—the pain of her own fingers digging into the wood of the carriage and forcing splinters beneath her nails as she clawed to keep from being pulled outside by the attackers and devoured by the darkness.

Panic flashed through her, and the desperate need to flee gripped her. She wanted to run away as fast as she could, to escape and *never* stop running—the same horrible desperation she'd felt that night. She'd long ago suppressed all those emotions, all those terrible memories, just to survive. But now they came rushing back in a tumultuous riot, upended by the attraction she still felt for him. Even now. Even knowing he'd played a part in that night, yet perhaps not the one she'd always assumed—

"No... *no!*" She shoved at him to force him back, to find room to breathe. "I can't—"

He was too close! She couldn't catch her breath. She shoved at him again. When he didn't move, panic seized her, and she punched at him with her fist.

He grabbed her wrists to stop her. Concern darkened his face. "What's wrong?"

He reached for her shoulder, just as he'd done the night of the attack—

"Don't!" she cried out, ripping her hands away from his. "Don't touch me!"

She shoved past him and stumbled toward the door, still facing him and instinctively keeping the enemy in sight. He'd been there that night, damn it!

Her left hand flew to her lips, which were hot and wet from his kisses. She couldn't believe she'd let him kiss her like that, that

she'd enjoyed it—

Dear God, what had she done? She stopped, her back against the door. Yet he made no move to lunge for her. He simply stood there, a damnable look of concern on his face. She scoured at her forehead with both hands. She couldn't think through the confusion and panic. Couldn't *think*!

"What's wrong?" he asked calmly.

"You're not who…" she whispered as he continued to stare at her with that dark look of worry that now filled her head and wouldn't let her go. He was a monster! He *couldn't* be concerned about her.

But his expression distorted beneath the memory of that same concerned face from ten years ago, until she couldn't tell where the memory ended and this moment began.

"Are you all right?" He reached for her arm. "Let me—"

Yanking her arm away so fiercely her sleeve ripped, she hissed out the brutal truth through clenched teeth before she could stop herself, "I'll *never* be all right!"

DEVLIN PULLED BACK as if she'd slapped him and stared at her, stunned. A sharp memory pierced him, one so dark and distant, so horrible—

Impossible.

No, she couldn't be… That girl was dead. He'd seen for himself how close to death she had been after the attack, had been told the next morning by her mother's maid that she had died during the night. He attended the funeral a few days later with Crewe, when three coffins were lowered into St Martin's churchyard.

For Christ's sake, *she was dead!*

Any icy dread pulsed through his veins as he stared at her, chilling him though to his bones. She wasn't—she simply *couldn't* be. The two women were nothing alike. There was nothing in this woman of the awkward, shy, and homely girl whose death had shocked London. And nothing of that girl he recognized in this enthralling woman.

And yet... *"Peyton?"*

Her eyes flared wide with terror. Then she threw open the door and raced from the box.

"Stop!" He charged after her. She was *not* getting away from him. Not this time.

She ran into the wide gallery that was crowded full with operagoers pouring out of their boxes for intermission—

And straight into Lady Catherine, hitting her so hard that the two women both staggered backward.

Devlin arrived a half-second behind her. He was close enough that his left hand was on her arm to stop her, his right resting on the small of her back in an attempt to stop her from spinning around and striking him but which everyone in the crowd immediately assumed was a touch of familiarity. Especially given the red and swollen state of her lips and how her hair had come loose in her struggle to flee the box, along with the ripped sleeve of her dress, her tellingly wrinkled skirts, and her bodice pulled so low that she nearly spilled out of it. Especially given his own state of undress. Every pair of eyes that saw them leaving the box together assumed they'd just had sex.

Clearly, so did Catherine and the circle of friends and family surrounding her. Bewilderment swept over her stunned expression, followed immediately by mortification. And betrayal.

A flash of red caught the corner of his eye. The woman was getting away. He started after her to stop her, to learn for certain who she was, what connection she had to the Chandlers. Because she simply couldn't—

"Dartmoor." Northrop stepped in front, blocking his path. "I demand an explanation!"

"So do I," he growled and started around him.

The earl grabbed his arm and hissed low enough not to be overheard by the gawking crowd around them, "How dare you embarrass my daughter like this?"

Clenching his jaw, Devlin stopped and dropped his arms to his sides, letting the woman get away. *Christ.* He had no choice unless he wanted to get into fisticuffs with the earl right there in the opera house. As laughter and snickers rose around him from the crowd, he blew out a frustrated and angry breath, then raked his fingers through his hair. *Control...control...control...* He internally repeated the old mantra that Titus had taught him and focused on his breathing, when what he wanted to do was toss the earl onto his arse and charge after her.

Whoever the woman was, she was gone, once more slipping away like a ghost into the fog.

Who the hell *was* she? Because that dark beauty who was working to destroy him couldn't possibly be the shy Peyton Chandler he remembered. *Impossible.* She was dead, for God's sake! He'd seen the graves with his own eyes.

But apparently, the dead were rising, and he feared this ghost had returned from hell to take his soul.

Chapter Six

"**G**OOD MORNING."

The soft female voice gently penetrated the cocoon of deep sleep engulfing him, but not enough to wake him completely.

"Devlin?"

With a grumble, he turned over. Sleep's oblivion beckoned him back, a fuzzy euphoria heightened by the warm, soft bed around him.

"Devlin!"

A hard shove to his shoulder brought both eyes wide open. Then he promptly squeezed them shut again with a groan.

"Go away, Megs," he muttered against the pillow.

But his younger sister Margaret wouldn't be deterred and gave him a good, long shake. "Wake up."

"No."

She gave an aggravated huff, and from behind his closed eyelids, Devlin could imagine her sternly crossing her arms as she'd done since she was a child whenever she didn't get her way. Which was hardly ever, considering how much he doted on her and his youngest sister Theodora.

"It's almost ten," she reported.

He groaned. Less than four hours of sleep.

Haunted by ghosts last night, he'd spent the first half of the evening being rebuked by the Earl of Northrop and apologizing profusely to Lady Catharine and the rest of it hunting down his contacts in St Giles and Seven Dials to find out anything he could about the Chandler family. But he'd learned nothing past the night of the attack. They were all dead and buried in Bayswater. He'd made a point of stopping by the graveyard himself just before dawn. Short of taking a shovel to the grave, there was no way to prove the mysterious woman who reminded him so much of Peyton Chandler wasn't her, and he hadn't had nearly enough sleep to seriously consider doing that.

He ordered in a grumble, "Go away."

"No."

The bedroom drapes flung open. Bright sunlight streamed into the room like a beacon.

He cursed and sat up so quickly that he nearly shot out of bed. With one hand covering his eyes, he gestured wildly with the other for her to close the drapes. But it was too late. A pounding ache reverberated through his skull like the strike of a hammer on iron, so painful he winced.

Margaret stood in front of the window, arms crossed and refusing to put him out of his misery by closing the curtains.

"Good God!" He squinted and turned his head away, but even half-awake and hurting, he instinctively kept his bare back from her sight. "Are you trying to kill me?"

"I am trying to wake you."

"You've succeeded." With an angry scowl, he flopped back down and threw the counterpane over his head. "Now go away and let me sleep in peace."

"No." The mattress sank as she plopped down beside him. Then she grabbed the blanket and yanked it down, exposing his eyes to the brutal sunlight. "You were out all last night."

"I was. Which is why I need rest." As soon as possible, he planned on proposing a bill in the House of Lords to make waking a man before noon a hanging offense. After all, Parliament might as well be good for something. "Go away so I can go back to sleep."

For more than a few hours, too. Because he planned on spending tonight once again tracking down that woman who reminded him so much of Peyton Chandler but who couldn't possibly be her. No, this woman was someone else. Someone who had been hired to go after him simply because she bore a passing resemblance to the dead girl whose death hung over his head.

The question was no longer who she was but who had hired her, and he would need to have his wits about him when he found her.

When he put the covers back over his head, only for her to pull them away again, he gave up, and simply squeezed his eyes shut.

"Go away," he ordered. "And close the drapes on your way out."

Silence answered that. He cracked open one eye. She was still there.

He sighed heavily. "What's the matter, Meg?"

"You were out *all* last night," she repeated for emphasis. "Again."

He shut his eye. "I plan on being out again all night tonight, too." And the next night, and the one after that...until he found out who was after him and why.

"You're on a cut, aren't you?"

"I am *not* on a drinking spree."

"Foxed to the ears."

"Not at all."

"Like a wheelbarrow."

Both eyes flew open, then narrowed suspiciously on her. "How do you know so much cant about drinking?"

She answered, deadpan, "I have Dartmoor for an older brother."

"In whose life you shouldn't be meddling."

"I should when I'm concerned about him." Her quiet words pierced him, bringing him as wide awake as the harsh sunlight. "And I'm concerned, Devlin. Mama and I both are." She paused, just long enough to bite her bottom lip in that worried way which reminded him of the little girl she'd once been instead of the twenty-four-year-old woman she'd grown up to be. "You're slipping back into your old ways."

That put an end to any more sleep. It was as good as a dunking in cold water.

He rolled out of bed and faced her. It was his turn to cross his arms and give a chastising look. "I'm not slipping back into my old ways."

She arched a disbelieving brow and raked her gaze over him, noting his wrinkled trousers. In his fatigue when he'd stumbled home at dawn, he'd been too tired to remove his clothes and had fallen into bed still half-dressed.

Her expression was damning.

"It isn't what you think," he defended himself.

"Then what is it?"

He couldn't tell her. Their father had already hurt her enough, and she still bore the scars. Just as he did. She didn't need to be punished further by dredging up dark memories.

"Just a night out," he dodged, although not technically a lie.

He snatched up the dressing robe his valet had left for him across the foot of the bed and pulled it on to cover his back. Some scars were more visible than others.

"Like all the nights you spent away from home before Father died?"

Father. Margaret was the only society daughter Devlin knew who didn't refer to her father as Papa. But then, *Papa* was an endearment, wasn't it? And their father had never been endearing to any of them.

"It wasn't like that," he assured her before he crossed the room to the wash basin, knowing she was deaf in her left ear and might not be able to hear him once he'd moved away.

"Then what exactly was it that compelled you to tup a woman in a private box the same night you'd invited your fiancée and all her family to the theatre?"

He froze. *Christ.* The story was spreading already? The London gossip mill was churning at top speed if she'd found out about that when it wasn't yet noon. Taking a deep breath, he poured the pitcher of water into the basin and reached his hands into the bowl to splash the cold water on his face, when what he wanted to do was dunk his entire head.

She followed after him and sank into the chair beside the washstand. A grim solemnity darkened her face as she waited, unmoving, for an explanation.

"I didn't tup anyone, at the opera or anywhere else." He splashed more cold water against his face in an attempt to chase away the lingering lightheadedness from lack of sleep. *Why* on earth was he having this conversation with his sister? "And Lady Catherine is not my intended."

"Not anymore."

"Not anymore," he muttered, then gave up all pretense of control and submerged his entire face into the basin. But there wasn't enough cold water in the world to shake the feeling of dread that consumed him.

When he couldn't hold his breath any longer, he flung back his head and let a spray of water fall across the floor behind him. Water dripped over his shoulders and off his chin and ran in rivulets down his chest, bare beneath the open banyan.

She held out a towel. "If you didn't tup that woman, then why does all of Mayfair think you did?"

"Because it's complicated." He took the towel and wiped it over his head, then gave her his best no-nonsense paternal glare. "And where did you learn such language?"

She arched a brow. "From my older brother."

He winced. That was most likely true.

"What happened, Devlin?" She leaned back in the chair, obviously with no plans to leave until she'd thoroughly interrogated him.

"Very bad timing." He peered at himself in the mirror. *Good God.* The sight was worse than he'd suspected. "I saw someone I'd met at Barton's." There. That was vague enough. "We had a private conversation."

"A woman?"

A ghost. "Yes."

"And when you emerged from the box, you were both half-dressed, suspiciously rumpled, and had lost track of time enough to be stunned to see that the rest of the audience had emerged for intermission."

"Something like that," he grumbled. Something *exactly* like that. So much so that his assurances to Northrop that the situation wasn't at all as it appeared wasn't enough to convince the earl. All hope of marriage to Lady Catherine was gone.

Oddly, though, except for guilt over the pain he'd inadvertently caused her, he didn't care much that it was.

"Why do I think you did more with that woman than simply converse?"

He slid a sideways glance at Meg. "You're not too old to be sent to boarding school, you know."

"Yes, I am." She grinned at that empty threat, only for her smile to fade. "You haven't been yourself lately, Devlin."

No, he was being exactly like himself. More than she would ever know. "I'm fine."

Avoiding the concern in her eyes, he turned back to his reflection and caught his breath at the sight. No wonder she was worried. Lack of sleep and the weight of all the secrets he carried on his shoulders made him appear ten years older than he truly was, complete with dark circles around both eyes, lines edging his mouth, and wrinkles in the corners of his eyes. He raked his fingers through his hair to futilely brush it into a semblance of order.

"We're all worried about you."

He grimaced. *Worried.* That was the very last thing he wanted his mother and sisters to be, what he'd worked so hard for the past ten years to avoid. No. For longer than that. Even before he knew the full extent of his father's crimes, he knew how viciously his father abused his mother, the curses and threats, the slaps and shoves. Even when he was a boy, he'd put himself between her and his father, hoping that Dartmoor would take his anger out on him instead. And he had. Brutally so.

Devlin hadn't wanted to go away to Eton, fearing what would happen to his mother in his absence. But she'd insisted. She'd assured him that Father no longer struck her, that the beatings had stopped even while the ones given to him had only intensified as he grew older. As if the old man feared Devlin would someday grow strong enough to strike back and needed to prevent it by hitting him first. So he'd gone away to school at just thirteen, selfishly glad to be away, knowing Father couldn't hit him all the way over at Eton.

What he didn't know was that his mother had lied to him. The beatings hadn't stopped. Worse—in his absence, Dartmoor had begun hitting Margaret.

She added softly, "*I'm* worried about you, Dev."

He hung his head. "Meg...please."

He couldn't deal with the guilt of that right now, not on top of everything else that was coming at him. She thought he wasn't being himself because he'd once used drink, gambling, and women as a way to survive being Dartmoor's son and was back to doing that again, even at the ripe old age of thirty-two. That last night was simply another drunken incident on a downward slide back toward debauchery.

The farthest thing from it! God only knew how much control it took not to truly ravish that woman in the box when she'd thrown herself at him like that, or not to toss Northrop onto his arse and charge after her.

Just as Margaret had no idea of the truth of what happened all those years ago. She didn't know how close he'd come to killing their father when Devlin came home after graduating from Eton to find the bastard had struck Margaret so hard against the side of her head that he'd ruptured her eardrum. She had been only ten years old. Just as she had no idea that Devlin had been forced to cover up their father's crimes in the years since. Protecting his family was the very reason he'd gone to speak to that woman last night at the opera...and the same reason he'd not returned home until dawn.

But Margaret would *never* know any of that. He would protect her from that, too, until he drew his last breath, just as he'd protected Theodora from discovering exactly what a monster their father had been. The youngest of the three Dartmoor children, Teddy had still been in the nursery and under the constant watch of her nanny when Devlin had put an end to the abuse. She, alone, had escaped the old duke's wrath.

He'd protected Teddy, but by then so much damage had been done, not only to his own family but to countless others across England, that the true extent of his father's evil was simply unfathomable. He thought he'd finally buried those days along with his father.

Apparently, the dead were refusing to stay buried.

A hand gently touched his shoulder. When he turned his head to look at Margaret, tears glistened in her eyes, and she choked out, "I couldn't bear it if something happened to you."

"Nothing is going to happen to me, except returning to bed as soon as you shuffle out of here."

"Devlin, be serious." His attempt at humor did nothing to lighten the grimness on her face. Or the knot her expression twisted in his gut.

She shouldn't be worrying about him. She should have been off enjoying her season, spending an indecent amount of money at shopping, or wasting time with all the men who were pounding down his door to court her. After all, wasn't that why he'd put himself through hell, so that his sisters and mother could have the happy, normal life they deserved?

"Last night was simply a misunderstanding." He tossed the

towel over the basin and turned away from the mirror, unable to stand another glimpse of himself this morning. "I am not returning to old ways."

She frowned dubiously. "Then why is Lucien Grenier waiting downstairs in your study with noon still several hours away?"

A *very* good question. One with answers he had no intention of giving.

Instead, he affectionately tucked a curl behind her ear, the way he'd done since she was a child. He doubted he'd ever be able to think of her as a grown woman. The day when he had to walk her down the aisle and give her away to her husband would simply kill him.

"Meg, you know that I would never do anything to intentionally harm you, Teddy, or Mother." When she turned away, he took her chin and made her look at him. "But you have to trust me when I tell you that last night was not at all as it seemed and that I have everything under control. All right?"

She nodded, albeit grudgingly, her worry for him still visible in her eyes.

He placed a kiss to the top of her head, then strode out of his room before she could ask him any more questions he couldn't answer, or cause her more worry.

Because right then, he had enough worry pulsing through his veins for both of them.

Crewe rarely came to Dartmoor House, which he claimed was too respectable an address for his well-honed blackguard's reputation. When he did, he certainly never came before four in the afternoon. Something was wrong. *Had* to be, to bring Lucien here this early.

He feared he knew what that something was.

"Devlin!" Theodora stuck her head over the banister from the landing above, stopping him halfway to the ground floor. Her pretty face beamed hopefully. "Mama says that Crewe's waiting in your study. When you're done talking to him, can you take me out for a drive? It's too lovely a day to stay inside, don't you think?"

He knew what she wanted, and it wasn't a turn in the fresh air. "I am not teaching you to drive a phaeton, Teddy."

Instantly, her hopefulness changed to irritation, and she scowled. "Why not?"

With a tired sigh, he rattled off the usual litany of objections he gave whenever she raised this topic. Which seemed to be all the time lately. "You're too young, it isn't safe, and it isn't what respectable young ladies do."

"But Princess Charlotte drives a phaeton."

"Princess Charlotte is also going to be Queen of England. Rules of propriety don't apply to royalty."

"That is so unfair!"

"More than you realize," he muttered beneath his breath and continued down the stairs.

She leaned out over the railing to call down to him, "You treat me like I'm still in braids in the schoolroom. But I'm seventeen!"

"Still a miss too young to drive." He reached the entry hall and threw out a peace offering. "Ask me again when you're eighteen."

"When I was sixteen, you said to ask when I was seventeen!"

"I was never good at math." As he walked out of her sight, he heard her give a frustrated cry and rolled his eyes. His life would be so much easier if his youngest sister didn't know how to count. Or how to read a calendar. God help him when she finally grew old enough to have a season and be courted. On the brighter side, he still had plenty of time for Margaret to send him to an early grave before then.

Sixteen. The same age Peyton Chandler had been the night her parents were murdered. The same night she'd nearly been raped. If he'd been slower that night, if he'd arrived just a few minutes later—

Sixteen. *Christ.*

Devlin strode into his study to find Crewe helping himself to the cognac in the liquor cabinet. He gestured at the mantle clock. "A bit early for that, don't you think?"

Crewe shook his head and held out a second glass for Devlin as he walked past on his way to his desk. "Not once you hear what I came to tell you."

Tying his banyan closed, Devlin sank into the leather desk chair and took a swallow of cognac to calm the dread now beating through him like a drum. It was too early for that, too.

Crewe dropped into one of the leather chairs positioned in front of the desk. "I asked around about the rumblings you've been hearing." He kicked out his long legs and slumped down, his casual posture belying the tension Devlin could sense radiating from him. "Seven Dials, St Giles, Westminster, Southwark—I even went as far as Wapping in case the dockworkers or warehouse porters knew anything."

"And?" Devlin sat forward as unease stirred inside him.

"You were right. The old criminal ring is being put back together, piece by piece." Crewe stared down into his glass and slowly swirled the brandy. "Smuggling, fencing, prostitution...all of it, and all being run from a centralized location."

The earth fell away beneath Devlin, and he gripped the edge of the desk to hold himself still. "Where? It's not based in St Giles or Seven Dials like before."

With a grim twist of his lips, Crewe tossed back the rest of the brandy in a gasping swallow. "The rumor is they've gone fashionable and moved to the west side."

"St James?"

"Possibly. No one knows exactly."

"How are they doing it?"

"No idea. But that kind of enterprise takes connections at all levels, great deals of money—and ways to hide the money once they make it. Keeping all that quiet is next to impossible. We'll find out eventually."

"But it can be kept silent." After all, their fathers had done exactly that.

Devlin's eyes lifted to the painting hanging above the fireplace. It was a landscape of Wrentham Hall, the family's main country house in Oxfordshire. He'd commissioned it to replace the portrait of his father that used to hang there, until Devlin took it down and burned it right there in the fireplace.

That was the problem with ghosts. Even after exorcism by fire, they could still come back.

"*Quiet*, not silent," Crewe corrected as he raised his glass to his lips. "Money always leaves a trail."

"So we find the trail. Where is the money coming from, and where is it going?"

Then they would find out who was responsible and shut them down. This time forever.

After all, if someone had the resources and knowledge to put the old ring back together—whether Horrender or someone else—then that person knew what their fathers had done and wouldn't hesitate to blackmail Devlin and Lucien over it. Everything they'd worked so hard to save during the past ten years would be destroyed.

Crewe shook his head and tossed back the rest of his cognac.

Devlin pushed himself out of the chair and began to pace. He ran a hand through his still-damp hair. "Do we know *anything* for certain?"

"Yes." Although Crewe didn't seem happy about it. "I have a name for you, and you're not going to like it."

He steeled himself. "Horrender?"

"Chandler."

His heart stopped. Somehow Devlin managed to rasp out, "Impossible." Then, he uttered the one bit of hope he'd been clinging to since last night, when he'd looked his mystery woman in the eyes and felt a terrible flash of recognition—"They're dead. All of them."

"Not so much." Crewe leaned forward to place a piece of paper onto the desk. "Or at least someone connected to the Chandler family isn't."

Devlin stared at the paper, but he didn't dare reach for it, as if it were a snake ready to strike. Or the devil come to take his soul. At long last.

Crewe stood and returned to the liquor cabinet. This time, he brought the crystal decanter back with him as if it were a portent of what he was about to disclose. "Elizabeth Wentworth...does the name ring a bell?"

Devlin sank down into his desk chair before his legs gave out. "The woman at Barton's." And last night at the opera. *Lady Payne.*

"Patton said that was the name on the title she used to back her bets."

"What a coincidence, then, that an Elizabeth Wentworth has also rented a townhouse in London for the season." Crewe took the liberty of topping off Devlin's glass. "All the money she's used to set up her household, buy a wardrobe, lease carriages, and so on, came from an overseas account in Marseilles." He pushed the glass toward Devlin. "An account where Charles Chandler once kept his money and that is now in the possession of one Elizabeth Wentworth."

"How do you know that?"

"I asked." Dryly quirking a brow, he replaced the stopper on the bottle and set it down next to the piece of paper. "I have very good contacts. A title for an estate like that is bound to leave a trail. I merely followed it."

Devlin picked up the piece of paper and read the direction. Portland Place in Marylebone. Close enough to keep watch on him in Mayfair, yet far enough away so as not to be easily noticed.

"Elizabeth Wentworth appeared out of nowhere six weeks ago when she stepped off a ship from France." Crewe leaned back in the chair. "I think we have proof that Horrender's returned."

"I might have been drinking," Devlin muttered and tossed away the piece of paper, "but that woman is definitely not Josiah Horrender."

"No. Most likely just the woman he's hired to front his return." Crewe shrugged as if the situation were obvious. "If Horrender has arrived back in London as we suspect, he'd need to buy everything to set up his household, along with hiring all new staff. No one can hide that kind of spending. Shopkeepers and merchants talk, so do their accountants. Which means he needs someone to do it all for him so he can remain in hiding. What more perfect person to do that than Elizabeth Wentworth?" When Devlin's expression turned doubting, Crewe added, "Trust me. I know how to live a secret life, which means I also know all the ways to reveal it."

Yes, Crewe certainly did. Yet Devlin shook his head. "That woman is connected to the Chandlers far more closely than simply being Horrender's agent. But how?"

Peyton Chandler had no younger sister, no close cousins, and no other relatives whom Devlin had been able to find in those terrible weeks after the attack when he'd attempted to settle the Chandler estate as a way to ease his conscience. Yet he suspected his mystery woman was somehow part of the Chandler family, someone who resembled them enough that his mind made the connection. Nothing more than a distant relative. *Had* to be.

Because the alternative, that the woman truly was Peyton Chandler, returned from the grave... *Impossible.*

"No idea," Crewe answered, "but I'll keep digging. Should I hire men to watch the townhouse in Marylebone?"

"No." They'd be spotted, and the last thing he and Crewe needed was for Horrender to realize the two of them knew he had returned.

"All right, then. What do we do next?"

"I find her." And God help her when he did.

Chapter Seven

T HE BELLS IN the Chinese pavilion at the center of Vauxhall Gardens struck midnight, and a wave of excitement passed over the park. In the rear of the gardens, where close paths wound darkly through the small wilderness, lanterns were quickly extinguished, plunging the area into darkness and signaling the start of the amorous activities the pleasure gardens had become known for.

Closer to the main gates, the lamps and lanterns strung along the alleys between buildings continued to blaze in dazzling colors, while beneath their light, a plethora of performers danced, played, tumbled, and more—anything to entertain the wealthy aristocrats in their private supper boxes where their parties would continue for hours. The activities there among the lights and crowd were far less scandalous than those in the wilderness but just as playfully surreptitious, thanks to the masks and costumes worn by the attendees.

Peyton checked that her own mask was still securely in place as she slipped down the crowded alley. The entire row of boxes had been rented out by Lord Liverpool for tonight's party, with a goodly portion of the alley roped off to keep out the riffraff.

Or was it to keep the MPs in? After all, most of parliament was in attendance, along with their wives and assorted mistresses, which made it easier than Peyton expected to slip into the party with her stolen invitation.

It wasn't much of a masquerade, if she was honest. Despite the fancy dress, she was able to recognize nearly everyone behind their tiny masks that barely covered their eyes and almost nothing of their faces. Some of the women carried masks on long sticks and didn't even bother concealing their faces, instead using the masks to flirt and hide their gossip, the same way they would have used fans at a ball.

But no one recognized Peyton. After all, no one thought she could possibly be among them. Except for Devlin. He alone would be able to spot her in the crowd. So she slowly circled the avenue in her hunt for him.

She needed to speak with him. Her doubts from last night had only grown stronger in the hours since she'd left the opera. Nothing had been able to ease them. Not spending the rest of the night once more pouring over the evidence she'd spent years collecting. Not even talking to Wilkins and Proctor, both of whom still insisted she was correct in pursuing her revenge.

Yet the more time she spent puzzling over it, the less the pieces fit together, even those she had been so certain about before. Now, instead of the cohesive map that pointed to his guilt, she saw gaps, uncertainties, weak assumptions...none of which had been there before.

Most likely because she hadn't been looking for them. But now...

Before she went on with her plans to destroy Devlin, she had to know the role he'd played that night for certain. The only way to do that was to confront him, and to draw him out, she used herself as bait. But she'd been here for nearly two hours and had yet to find him.

With rising frustration, she approached the attendant at the door of the box who was serving as Master of Ceremonies for Lord Liverpool's party.

"The Duke of Dartmoor," she said bluntly. "Has he arrived?"

The man searched the list of names he held in his hand, the same list he'd been checking off one by one as the guests arrived. The same list that claimed she was Martha Besson. As the mistress of Viscount Houghton, Besson had been easy to track down to her townhouse, where Peyton had purchased the woman's invitation directly from her maid, once again proving that most people didn't hire the correct sort of people for their household staff, nor did they pay them enough to ensure their loyalty. But Besson's oversight was Peyton's opportunity. As the viscount's mistress, the real Martha Besson could never ask for a replacement invitation, nor would anyone here approach Peyton to discover the truth of who she was. Not with Lady Houghton also in attendance.

"No, ma'am." He lowered the list. "His Grace isn't attending."

"He's not?" Desperate disappointment pierced her. She'd been so certain of the information her butler had given her. The duke had been invited and issued his acceptance. His own valet had confirmed it.

"He begged off at the last minute."

"Thank you," she mumbled and turned away.

She walked toward the main gate. She should have stayed and carried out the part of her plan that she'd originally intended when she'd first stolen the invitation—to destroy Dartmoor politically. Only a few well-placed comments and questions would be necessary to have other members of parliament doubting his loyalty and ethics, and a few nights of planting such doubts would have him removed from his Parliamentary committees, one by one, until he had no power left in the Lords except to cast meaningless votes.

But she couldn't do that now, not without indisputable proof of his role in her parents' murders. Apparently, the attack and secret life she'd led since hadn't stripped her completely of her soul. *Yet.*

The same question swirled relentlessly through her mind.

How could Devlin be the same person who had arranged her parents' murders and attempted to rape her? *How?* At the theatre, when he'd kissed her so tenderly, when she'd looked up at him through a cloud of fear and confusion, an icy cold realization had slithered down her spine, and in its blistering wake came a brutal truth—

Because he wasn't the same man.

Devlin had been at the attack, she knew that. But he wasn't the man who had tried to rape her. He couldn't have been, she knew that now. His body felt *wrong* and didn't match the memory of that night that had branded itself onto her mind. He was too tall, too broad-shouldered and slender-waisted, his hands too large to match those of the man who had shoved her to the ground, climbed on top of her from behind, ripped off her dress—

God help her, she wasn't certain anymore. And if she were wrong about his role in that, what else might she be wrong about?

Tonight had been her chance to find out, only for the opportunity to slip through her fingers.

As she left the pleasure gardens, she untied her mask and let it dangle from her hand as she made her way past the line of carriages waiting outside the main gates. Frustration warred with desperation inside her, all of it roiling together with mounting confusion...and with an inexplicable desire to be wrong about him.

She found her carriage, and the tiger held open the door for her as she climbed inside. "Go."

The door closed behind her. She leaned her head back against the squabs, closing her eyes as the carriage jerked to a start and slowly rolled away from the gardens toward the new bridge. The night had not gone as well as she'd—

The door flung open, and a large man swung inside. As he landed on the bench across from her and yanked closed the door, he drew a pistol.

"You need better security," he drawled. "The tigers didn't

even try to stop me."

Dartmoor.

With her heart pounding fiercely, her hand slipped between the seat cushion and the carriage wall. She pulled out a loaded pocket pistol and pointed it at his chest. "Because I told them not to."

DEVLIN LOCKED GAZES with her, not daring to lower his eyes to her pistol. If she decided to kill him, her eyes would give her away first. But he knew she wouldn't. Either of them firing ensured mutual destruction, and she'd already proven herself to be anything but rash.

"I'm impressed," he drawled. "You always keep a loaded gun in the cushions?"

"I keep an entire arsenal in this carriage." Her voice didn't quaver. "You know who I am. Given my history, do you blame me?"

The brutal honesty he saw in her eyes cut him to his core, and he knew then without doubt...

"Hello, Peyton," he said quietly. There was no pretending he didn't know exactly who she was.

He hadn't wanted to believe that a dead girl had come back from the grave to haunt him, preferring to believe she was just another part of Horrender's new schemes. The alternative was less damning. But after watching her tonight, following her through the gardens because he knew she'd come looking for him again, there was no doubt left.

Slowly, he eased down the hammer of his pistol and tucked it back inside his greatcoat. "You have a lot of explaining to do."

"I'm not the only one." Following his lead, she lowered her pistol but laid it on the bench beside her, still within reach. "Where would you like to start? Because I'd like to begin with the night my parents were murdered before my eyes and I was almost raped and killed." She paused, then repeated, "*Almost.* I still have no idea who that man was or why he didn't succeed. But you do. You know because you were there."

"I was." He kept his face perfectly inscrutable. "He didn't succeed in harming you because I stopped him."

The soft inhalation as she caught her breath ricocheted inside the compartment as if she'd pulled the trigger after all. Her lips parted as she stared at him, yet the invisible mask she wore now was as good as the one she'd worn in the gardens for hiding whatever thoughts were swirling inside her head. But it couldn't hide the glistening in her eyes, bright even in the shadows.

Then she whispered, the confession so soft that her words were barely audible over the rumble of carriage wheels beneath them, "I used to believe it was you."

"It wasn't."

She stared at him as the bridge passed slowly beneath them, not moving, not blinking, hardly breathing...as if needing all her strength and will to simply absorb his quiet denial and not shatter like glass. "Then why were you there that night? Tell me what you did...*everything.*"

"If you tell me why you're back in London and pretending to be Elizabeth Wentworth."

Her eyes flared at the name. She didn't confirm his accusation, clinging to a fighting spirit even in the midst of this fresh hell, but she didn't have to. The look in her blue depths confessed everything.

"I came upon your parents' carriage after it had been attacked," he confided gently. He knew she wouldn't trust him with her secrets until he revealed some of his. "Your parents were already dead, but you...you were still alive, lying unconscious at the edge of the street where you'd crawled to get away. The other attackers ran when they saw me, but the man who went after you had his back to me. He was on the ground on top of you, one hand yanking up your skirt and the other fumbling with his fall." Devlin forced himself not to look away from the pain in her eyes. "He was too busy to notice me until I grabbed him by the throat and threw him off you."

"You killed him?"

God help him, he'd wanted to. "He got away."

"They all got away," she corrected in a breathless whisper.

"Yes. But so did you."

"How?" She squeezed her eyes shut against the memories and shook her head. "I clawed at your neck, there was blood beneath my nails—I was certain it was you!"

"It wasn't me. It must have been the man who attacked you."

"But I saw you there! I saw your face..." Her voice trailed off in confusion.

"You woke up for a moment and must have confused me with the man who attacked you." Only a moment in which she'd stared up at him, terrified, before the darkness overtook her again. "I picked you up and ran with you to the nearest surgeon. I left you with him and went to your home to tell the butler and housekeeper what had happened, to find out if there was anyone I should notify. That was the last time I saw you. The next morning, word was sent to Dartmoor House that you'd died. I attended your funeral, put flowers on your grave... You were dead." *Christ.* His shoulders slumped beneath the weight of it all. "Until four nights ago when you reappeared at Barton's." *Like a ghost from the fog...* "I didn't recognize you. Hell, how could I have?"

"That was the point," she said quietly, turning to stare out at the passing city that was dressed in nighttime black, as if mourning. Shadows swirled inside the swaying carriage from the coach lamps and passing gas lights, the darkness alive around them. Fitting, he supposed, since they were both creatures of the night, both living out a hellish nightmare. "Being dead was the only way for me to survive. I had no idea who had murdered my parents or why, or if they thought I was a witness to be silenced. Playing dead was the only way to make certain they wouldn't try to kill me again."

"So you buried an empty coffin in Peyton Chandler's grave and became Elizabeth Wentworth."

"Yes." She absently plucked at the curtain that swayed with the rocking motion of the carriage. "It was my mother's maid who had the idea. Proctor had gone to the surgeon's that night, along with Wilkins, the footman. They'd said men had come to the house searching for me. So the two of them took me to Richmond where I would be safe. I was so distraught, so terrified, in such grief for my parents—Pretending I'd died was the only way to stay safe. I knew that even then, even in the hours following the attack." A single tear slipped down her cheek, but she made no move to brush it away. "In the days that followed, I could barely rise from bed, eat or drink anything... I could barely keep breathing." Her voice lowered until it was little more than a breath itself. "If Proctor and Wilkins hadn't been there for me, I would have truly died."

Devlin could barely believe his eyes as he stared at her, but he remembered the shape of her delicate face, her expressive blue eyes and dark chestnut hair, even if the rest of her had changed completely. Gone was the gawky, shy girl he'd met only a few weeks before his mother's musicale, to whom he'd not paid the slightest bit of attention. In her place had blossomed a woman he couldn't push from his mind.

"We moved to France as soon as I was able to travel," she continued. "My father had placed a good deal of his fortune in overseas accounts and businesses there, under the false name of Elizabeth Wentworth, and Wilkins helped me locate the funds. He also helped me hire investigators to learn everything I could about the attack. But there were always missing pieces."

"Now you're back to find them."

She nodded out the window at the night. "The wars ended, and it was safe to travel again. And I already had enough information."

"Enough for what?"

She pinned him beneath a gaze so fierce it ripped his breath away. "To find the man responsible and punish him."

Suddenly, the events of the past few days fell into place, and he realized what scheme she'd been playing at with him at Barton's, at the opera, and even tonight at Vauxhall. Her unspoken accusation burned into him. "It wasn't me."

"You were there." Her eyes blazed in the darkness, full of hatred and fury, and made even more intense by the quiet control of her voice. "Perhaps you weren't the one who attempted to rape me—"

"I was not."

"But you *were* there. Why would you have been there if you didn't have a part in it?"

"Because I went to stop it." He leaned forward, elbows on knees. "When I learned the attack had been planned, I rode after your carriage as fast as I could, but I arrived too late. Your parents were already dead, and you were on the verge of dying yourself. I did all I could to help."

"No, you helped plan it," she forced out through clenched teeth. "That was the only way you could have known that the carriage had gone the wrong way and stopped in that dark street. That was the only way you could have known where—and when—" Her fury choked off her voice.

"I did *not* plan it," he said as forcefully as possible yet remaining calm. "I had missed the end of the musicale—"

"You were bedding the opera singer."

Devlin paused to keep his composure. "Yes, I was." He leaned back against the squabs and slowly shook his head. "Do you really think me such a monster that I could make love to a woman the same night I'd hired men to kill you and your family?"

Her silence answered for her. She thought him *exactly* that kind of monster.

He shook his head. "If I had planned to kill your family, why would I have gone to such trouble to save you?"

Her lips parted. He knew that look... *Doubt*. He knew she wanted to believe him, but ten years of hatred, grief, and revenge had driven her to this point. It would take more than a few simple denials to make her believe him.

"Go ask the surgeon who brought you to him that night," he challenged quietly. "We can go to him right now, in fact. Rouse him from his sleep, make him look back through his records. Perhaps you'll believe him."

Her lips began to tremble. So did her hands that she tried to calm by folding them in her lap. Even in the darkness of the carriage, he could see her grow pale.

"I am more relieved than I can ever express to know you're alive," he admitted, "because I had nothing to do with your parents' murder."

She swallowed, hard enough that he could hear it across the compartment. "If not you—" That breathless phrase cost her dearly, he knew. "Then who? Who was responsible? Tell me." She paused, and the soft begging that followed nearly undid him, "*Please*, Devlin...tell me."

"So you can punish him, the way you wanted to punish me?" He leaned back against the squabs. "I'm afraid you're too late." He pulled in a deep breath to confide the deepest secret of his life, the one no one else knew, except Crewe. "It was my father. And his grave isn't empty."

BREATHE... OH GOD, *the pain!... Just breathe, damn it!*

Peyton didn't move. *Couldn't* move. It took all her strength to simply sit there, returning his gaze, and remembering to breathe.

All the grief she'd suppressed, replacing it with fury and hatred and determination—all the emotions she needed to focus on maintaining in order to keep living, to keep hunting for her parents' killers, *to simply keep breathing*—rushed back with the ferocity of a storm. She wanted to scream!

Instead, she rasped out in a breathless whisper the question that had haunted her for a decade. "Why would your father do something like that?"

But the carriage had stopped in front of her rented town-house, and the tiger flung open the door to let them out, unwittingly interrupting them.

Peyton couldn't tear her gaze away from Devlin, from the man who for so long had been her most hated enemy. The cold night air rushed inside the compartment like an ill-wind.

"Why?" she repeated. When Devlin didn't straighten from his casual slump against the squabs to tell her, she clenched her fists to keep from reaching for her pistol. *"Why?"*

He slid his gaze out the door toward the tiger. "Invite me inside."

"So you can continue to lie to me?" she bit out. Her head pounded! Everything she thought she knew about that night swirled together until she couldn't sort through it all. She felt as if she were sliding away, and her grasping hands couldn't find any purchase to stop her fall.

"So we can finish this conversation in private," he corrected gently.

Then he held out his hand.

She stared at his extended hand and shivered. *An anchor.* That was what he was offering. A tether to the world that was slipping away from her. She didn't move, not daring to reach out—

"Peyton," he murmured. "Please."

Her gaze flew up to his, and she inhaled a sharp gasp of air. Her breath returned, filling her lungs with deep, steady inhalations, and with each one, the dark abyss around her receded, and the swirling slowed. She could feel her heart pounding in her chest, its steady drum bringing her calm, quiet...

"Trust me enough to let me inside," he cajoled, this time teasing her from the darkness by adding, "and I'll let you keep your gun."

"No need," she answered, her voice raw. "I'll make you check yours at the door."

His mouth softened into a faint smile. "Then invite me in.

We've only just started."

Slowly, she slipped her hand into his and gave a jerking nod, one that matched the same rough breaths that filled and left her lungs in an unsteady rhythm. But she *was* breathing, and she would survive. Just as she had before.

He stepped down from the carriage and helped her to the ground. As soon as her foot touched the footpath, she pulled away her hand. The graze of his fingers across her palm left tingles in its wake.

She hurried up the front steps with Devlin on her heels and past the butler as he held the door open. She ignored the surprised look on the butler's face that she was bringing a man home so late at night, when not one other person from outside her household had crossed the threshold in the weeks since she'd rented the house.

"Elizabeth?"

She startled at the name, the one she'd taken for herself so many years ago, and stopped.

Wilkins emerged quickly from the rear of the dark house. His gait faltered in the doorway of the entry hall as his eyes landed on Devlin. She didn't have to make introductions. From the way Wilkins stiffened, he knew exactly who Devlin was.

Yet he came forward and took her arm to pull her aside. Keeping his voice low, he shot a glance over his shoulder at Devlin. "What is he doing here?"

"I invited him." Wilkins had always been protective of her—in some ways, overly protective—and she knew that bringing Devlin home was not at all part of their plan. But she also expected him to trust her. "He has new information about the attack."

"Of course, he does. He knows everything about that night because he planned it." His brow furrowed with worry. "Bringing him here—letting him know you're still alive—that wasn't at all what agreed to do. We agreed to work in secret."

"He figured out who I was. There's no point in hiding from

him any longer."

"And if he tries to harm you? If he decides to finish what he started? You're the only witness left who can place him at the attack." He pursed his lips with concern. "What would Proctor and I do if anything happened to you?"

"I will be fine." She rested her hand on his arm to reassure him. "The truth will come out, and I'll finally know what happened that night and why."

"We already know. He murdered your parents and attempted to rape you."

She cast a glance across the room at Devlin. "I'm not so certain of that anymore, and I need to be absolutely sure before we continue our plans." When her words of caution didn't mollify him, she affectionately squeezed his arm. "Trust me. I know what I'm doing."

"As long as you don't trust *him*." He touched her cheek affectionately. "Sometimes you lead with your heart, and this time, that might get you hurt. You need to think clearly about this man and not let him deceive you with his charms."

"I won't." She slowly stepped back. "You can go to bed now. I won't be needing you this evening." She turned to Devlin and nodded toward the stairs. "This way."

As she led Devlin upstairs, she caught a last glimpse of Wilkins watching the two of them. The betrayal in his expression was heartbreaking.

She turned away to hurry up the stairs. What else had she expected? Wilkins was her protector and bodyguard, a man who looked after her as closely as if she were his sister or wife. Of course, he would be concerned about her, still viewing Devlin as the enemy. Yet she'd upset him, and that simply pierced her.

But she needed to know what happened that night, why the late Duke of Dartmoor wanted her parents dead. Only Devlin could provide those answers.

Ten years of survival, of struggling to find her way through the darkness—they had all come to this. After tonight, nothing would ever be the same for her again.

Come into my parlor...

She opened the door to her room and stepped inside.

Chapter Eight

D EVLIN HESITATED IN the doorway to cast his gaze around the large bedroom that was lit only by the faint glow of banked coals in the fireplace and the dim moonlight falling through the unshuttered window. There was nothing unusual about the space...a bed, a reading chair, a writing desk, two armoires. There was even a cup of tea, still sitting on the side table by the chair, as she must have left it that evening before she dressed for Vauxhall.

Nothing unusual, except the woman it belonged to, who slowly crossed to the larger of the two armoires. She stopped in front of it and opened the doors.

Sweet Lucifer. Devlin gaped at the armoire. No, not an armoire—an armory. A wall of weapons gleamed in the dim light. Rows of knives of all shapes and sizes, pistols he was certain were loaded, swords, rapiers...for God's sake, there was even a battle axe.

With her hands still on the doors at chest height, Peyton stood unmoving in front of the armoire and stared blankly at the deadly cache.

"I've always wondered what women keep in their dressing rooms," Devlin commented dryly as he came forward. He stopped beside her and reached over her shoulder to take one of the knives. He turned it in his hand, watched the razor-sharp blade catch the red light of the banked fire, and muttered, "Now I know why women always refer to them as unmentionables."

She didn't so much as smile. "I know how to use every one of them, too." For once, she didn't rise to his teasing and throw back a barb of her own. Instead, she added in a murmur, almost as if to herself, "I will never be vulnerable again."

He didn't doubt that, remembering the hidden pistol in the carriage. He mumbled as he returned the knife to its place, "You've been busy."

"I had ten years to learn." A distracted, faraway expression clouded her face as she stood there, her hands still holding the doors halfway open. "Do you know what a *maître d'armes* is?"

"Yes." After all, he'd once had his own master in Anthony Titus.

"I trained under Armand Marchand, who served as one of Napoleon's private guards in the early days of the Republic. But then Napoleon turned against all the ideals of the revolution and declared himself emperor, and Armand turned against Napoleon. He attempted to kill Bonaparte but failed and so fled for his life to the south of France where he found me."

"He taught you to defend yourself," he guessed.

"He taught me how to fight," she correctly. She turned her head to look at him over her shoulder. "I didn't feel safe, not even in France, not even in the countryside, so I hired Armand to serve as my bodyguard. But he became so much more to me than that." She turned back toward the weapons, as if seeing Marchand there. "He helped me to heal, made me strong, taught me how to protect myself... Eventually, he became my lover and taught me how to protect my heart as well."

Jealousy pierced him—but not of her lover. What struck him was that Marchand had been able to protect her when Devlin had failed to do just that. That was all it was. Any other sort of jealousy would have been absurd.

But he also hadn't seen any man around her, no one he

would have suspected to be a *maître d'armes* turned bodyguard. Not any of her carriage tigers, although he was certain all of them carried weapons beneath their uniforms, and not the butler, who seemed more muscular brawn than fighting brains. And certainly not the older Englishman who had confronted them in the entry hall.

"Then you need to find yourself a new guard," he drawled and stepped back to lean his shoulder casually against the wall beside the armoire. "He's not doing a very good job if he's allowed you to be alone with me in your bedroom."

"Armand isn't in London," she murmured. "He disappeared last year and is most likely dead."

Devlin felt like a damn fool. "I'm sorry."

Her only acknowledgement of that was a faint nod. "But he taught me the most important lesson of all."

"Which is?"

"That those men didn't kill me that night. And if they didn't kill me, then…"

"Then?" he prompted.

She shoved the armoire doors open wide. She dropped her arms to her sides and stepped back to take it all in.

"Then they made a huge mistake," she finished, her voice icy cold.

Devlin pushed himself away from the wall and stared. He'd thought the weapons were stunning. But this—*Good God.*

On the inside panels of the two wide doors were pinned bits and pieces of writing, notes, newspaper clippings, bulletins, and pages torn from account ledgers. Each grouping was connected to the others by pieces of string, all of it forming web-like circles of information. The pin holes in the wood suggested she'd worked it over and over, moving around pieces and adding to it until the puzzle was complete.

"I've spent ten years collecting every bit of information I could about that night, putting it all together, making connections." Her eyes swept over it as his did, as if trying to see what he saw. But Devlin simply couldn't fathom it all. "I hired investiga-tors—Bow Street, private detectives inside France, the occasional random thief-taker. They brought me bits and pieces of infor-mation. So did Wilkins. He knew about the funds my father had hidden overseas, how to find the properties and claim them."

Unease curled up Devlin's spine. How close had Wilkins come to learning about her father's criminal enterprise? "He was the footman, you said?"

"Yes. And footmen overhear everything, including what they're not supposed to, which is how he knew about the overseas accounts," she mumbled as she stepped forward to examine the information she'd pinned to the door. "You saw him downstairs. He's not happy about having you here."

Undoubtedly. "Because he thinks the same way you do—that I was responsible for the attack."

"Yes."

He waited for her to say she'd changed her mind about that—about him—but that absolution didn't come. Instead, she reached for a keepsake box sitting on the fireplace mantel and set it on her desk in front of him.

"What's that," he asked sardonically, "your gun powder sup-ply?"

"My heart," she whispered and opened the lid. Random items lay inside—a piece of lace, an amethyst bracelet, a brass sealing wax stamp, a snuffbox, other pieces of jewelry—not weapons. "These belonged to my parents. It's all I have left of them." She reached into the box. "And this."

She held up an old silver button, heavily tarnished until it was almost black. But his heart jolted as he recognized it. It was one of his.

"I ripped it off your waistcoat that night. It's proof you were there." Her eyes glistened with pain even as she lifted her chin into the air. "Tell me what happened that night. *All* of it. I've been trying to put it together for so long..."

She turned back to the armoire and ran her fingers down the

left panel's trail of information.

"We were at Dartmoor House for your mother's musicale." She tapped her finger on a drawing of the townhouse. "Everything was normal and fine, except that you surprised everyone by being there."

"I'd recently returned from fighting on the Continent," he explained. "And my mother still had hopes I'd find my way into proper society."

"The performance had finished," she continued, "and guests were having refreshments in the drawing room. Others lingered in the music room. My father, yours, and the late Duke of Crewe had gone into your father's study, which they often did after dinners and other soirees. I was with my mother in the drawing room, while you had slipped away upstairs with the opera singer. I saw you leave with her." Her voice lowered into a disapproving grumble. "Not very clandestine of you."

He fought back a grimace.

She murmured thoughtfully, "About half an hour later, the men in the study ended up in a fierce argument...raised voices, angry threats, pounding fists."

His eyes narrowed on her. "How do you know that?"

She slid him a chastising glance. "Servants know everything that goes on inside a house. Your father should have paid your footman more to keep his loyalty." She turned back to the door panel as she added, "Or at least not to spy on him from the servants' passage behind the bookcase."

Damnation. Devlin would block that passageway himself tonight.

"What did they fight about?" Devlin knew. But did she?

She shook her head. "The footman heard the fighting but couldn't make out the words." She tapped a finger on a blank block of paper pinned to the townhouse drawing. "But when my father returned to the drawing room, he was shaken and upset. He told Mama we had to leave and hurried us outside into the carriage. Your mother gave us her goodbyes because your father and Crewe remained in the study, and you were still upstairs with the opera singer."

He was too preoccupied by her map of events to let that barb register. He plucked at a piece of string that ran from his name to a black edged sheet of paper in the center of the door that represented the attack on the carriage. "What's this twine?"

"Your path that night. You ended up at the attack."

"I did," he mumbled. "I came back downstairs a few minutes after your carriage left and headed to the study. Dartmoor kept his best cognac there, and I wanted a drink before returning to the party." Dark memories swirled back to him. He'd never forget what happened that night, ever as fresh as if it had happened yesterday. "Dartmoor and Crewe were still there, still furious at your father, who had decided to end his business relationship with them." Charles Chandler had threatened far more than that, but Devlin wouldn't share that information with her unless he had to. What good was there in hurting her even more? "But your father knew too much about their affairs, so they'd sent men after him to deliver a warning to keep his silence." He paused before admitting quietly, "That warning got out of hand."

She stared at him, blinking rapidly as the reason for the attack sank through her. "They went to such lengths," she whispered, barely louder than a breath, "just to protect their business interests?"

"Yes." But Horrender had wanted far more than that. He had wanted the attack to be a warning to anyone who thought about crossing him and his criminal ring, and he'd sent that message by killing not just Chandler but also his wife and daughter.

His eyes swept over the doors, yet he saw no mention of Horrender. Did she not know about him? Or worse—did she think that evil bastard was on her side?

"I chased after you, but I arrived too late." He didn't dare glance at her, keeping his gaze fixed on the door. "When I came upon the carriage, your parents had already been murdered, and you had been dragged out onto the cobblestones. You were trying to crawl away, but one of the attackers had gone after you."

She said nothing for a long while, and when her voice finally came, the desolation and unbearable anguish he heard in it cut him to the quick. "The last thing I remember is someone throwing me to the ground. I tried to get away, fought against him—" The pain in her eyes strangled the breath in his throat. "I punched and kicked—I clawed his neck." She looked down at her hands, as if still able to see the blood beneath her nails. "I drew blood, going deep enough to scar his flesh. I heard him yell, felt him hit me and crawl on top of me... Then I saw your face. I knew it was you—Dear God, I *knew* it was you!"

Without warning, she shoved him against the wall. She yanked his coat and jacket out of her way, then halfway ripped off his cravat as she pulled it aside and tore at his shirt to bare his neck to her eyes.

Her gaze burned into his flesh as she searched for any trace of scars, any mark she'd put there ten years ago. But there was none, and her fingers trembled as she ran her hands over his unblemished skin.

Then the truth struck her, so fiercely she flinched. A terrible sound rose from her lips, a howling mix of pain, grief, and relief so intense, it left her shuddering. *Good God.* He'd never before seen a woman simply...*shatter.* The sight of it nearly broke him.

Her arms dropped to her sides as she stepped away from him. "It wasn't you," she whispered, so softly the words were barely audible. "For so long, I thought..." She swallowed hard. "What...what do I believe now?"

Her words stabbed into his heart like daggers.

Defeated, her slender shoulders slumping, she stared at the doors. Her eyes glistened brightly with thick tears, and an expression of complete incomprehension marred her beautiful face.

"Everything I thought I knew..." Desolate tears of anguish

slipped down her cheeks. She no longer had the strength—or the will—to hold them back.

Devlin pulled her into his arms. She didn't fight him.

"I have nothing left," she breathed out, grasping at his waistcoat with her hands and burying her face in his shoulder. "Nothing…"

He tightened his arms around her as ten years of pent-up grief and agony poured from her. "You have everything." He nuzzled his cheek against her hair and promised, "You still have the chance for a future, for the happy life your parents wanted for you. They took your parents from you. Don't let them take your future, too."

She sagged against him, her body boneless in his arms, as the last of her strength left her. She didn't reply, and her silence felt almost as damning as her earlier accusations.

But she tilted her face toward him, parted her lips…

With a groan, Devlin lowered his mouth to hers. He felt the soft hitch of her breath beneath his lips, yet she remained pliable in his arms as she welcomed the kiss he desperately needed to give her, one he desperately needed to claim in return. This wasn't a kiss of lust, not even one of shared grief or healing. What she sought in him was forgiveness.

He cupped her face between his palms to temper the growing need he felt in her as he continued to give her gentle, impossibly tender kisses. Yet she pressed harder against him, her breath growing quick and shallow, until an unbidden whimper of need escaped her.

The soft sound undid him, and he tore his mouth away from hers, then rested his forehead against hers, keeping her face between his hands. If she continued to kiss him like that, to beg with her body for him to quell the aching inside her—

God help him.

"You're never going to find the answers you're looking for," he rasped out, his eyes squeezed shut against the soul-steeling temptation of her and the bitter truth of what he was telling her.

Even now, he wanted to protect her and his family from Horrender—and from himself. "No matter how many connections you attempt to make, how long you search, you will never be able to punish the men who hurt you and your family. Let it go, Peyton." He tilted his head to place one last kiss to her lips. "Let go of the dead and find a way to live."

She tensed, then slowly straightened away from him. Her face slipped out of his grasp, and his hands fell to his sides.

When he opened his eyes to look down at her, the emotion in her eyes ripped through him. He had never seen a woman look so vulnerable in his life, so...*lost*. Yet a fire burned deep inside those watery blue depths and gave him hope that she might eventually be all right.

"Go back to France," he urged her quietly. "Live out a very long life as Elizabeth Wentworth. Find a French lover, perhaps a husband to give you a proper home and family of your own." He paused to drive home his point. "Stop looking for answers that you will *never* find."

"I can't. I can't surrender..." She shook her head as the breathless confession tore from her and grabbed for a chair to steady herself.

He knew what she meant. She'd been driven by a need for justice and revenge for too long. If she gave that up, what would replace it? What would she have to keep living for? How well he understood that! And yet...

"And I can't surrender my family," he told her quietly. "I won't stop protecting them."

Confusion darkened her face, but in the dim light, he could still see the tracks of her tears on her cheeks, the glistening of her eyes, and the soft parting of her lips, still warm and moist from his kisses. "What would you need to protect them from?"

He hesitated. Speak of the devil... "Josiah Horrender."

"I told you before—I don't know who he is."

Devlin believed her. Not even a Drury Lane actress could feign a lack of recognition like that. "He's the man who carried out my father's orders to attack you," he said gently. "A criminal from London's underworld who Dartmoor and Crewe hired to handle the less polite aspects of running their enterprise."

Peyton pressed her fist against her chest, as if physically urging her heart to keep beating, her lungs to keep breathing...just as she must have done countless times over the years. "Like murder."

"Among other things." Beatings, kidnappings, blackmail, theft...rape. Horrender had hired the thugs who had attacked the carriage and killed her parents, as well as the one who'd attempted to rape her, Devlin knew that. His father had admitted as much that same night when Devlin returned to Dartmoor House and threatened him into telling the truth. "Horrender oversaw the daily operations of the various businesses—No, not businesses. A criminal ring, full of all kinds of illegal activities. My father and Crewe used their power and influence to hide their crimes, but Horrender carried them out."

"And my father was their banker." She drew herself up straight, visibly steeling herself. "That's why they argued that night. He must have discovered what they were doing and threatened to go to the authorities to stop them."

He was so much more than merely a banker. Your father knowingly provided the means to make it all happen, then hid their profits. And he was killed because he knew too much... But Devlin didn't have the heart to tell her that, not after all she'd been through tonight. Her father was dead and buried. She didn't deserve to be haunted even more by the truth of what he'd done.

So instead, he said, "Horrender fled London the night of the attack. When I stopped hearing any rumblings about him from my contacts, I was certain he'd died overseas." He rubbed at the ache behind his forehead. "But now there are whispers that he's returned." He slowly closed the distance between then, noting that her hand had tightened on the chairback so fiercely, he saw her white knuckles, even in the shadows. "It can't be a coincidence that those rumors began when you returned to London."

"It has to be, since I had no idea about him. If I had, I would have killed him myself long ago."

He fought down a dour grin. At least her fighting spirit was still strong. "I won't risk that my family might be targeted, or Crewe's." Lucien Grenier had just as much to lose as Devlin if the truth ever emerged about the secrets their fathers had hidden from the world. "Or you."

Her lips parted, stunned. "Why me?"

"For all I know, Horrender has followed you here to kill you, to make certain you can't connect him to your parents' murders." His gaze softly held hers. "So go back to France and let Elizabeth Wentworth live out a very long life, because all you're doing here is putting yours at risk."

"What good is a long life," she objected, "if it's lived doubting everything I thought I knew?"

She held his gaze, as if daring him to contradict her. But he couldn't. God knew he carried enough of his own doubts to understand that.

"It seems we both want the same thing," she ventured. "To find Horrender and put an end to him. We have the chance to finally find justice for what happened that night."

No. There would never be justice for that. But perhaps, to-gether, they could prevent more innocents from being harmed.

"Make no mistake, Peyton." His voice brooked no misunder-standing about what he was about to agree to. "My primary concern is finding Horrender and figuring out why he's returned. Uncovering answers for you is secondary. Understand?"

Not answering, she slowly swept across the room to the armoire, closed its doors, and leaned back against it. Her eyes gleamed intensely in the shadows. "Where do we start?"

Chapter Nine

PEYTON STOPPED ON the footpath in front of the grand townhouse and stared up from beneath the hood of her cape at its stone façade, shadowed by early evening. Five bays wide, four stories tall, fronting one of the most exclusive squares in Mayfair... Dartmoor House.

She frowned. When she'd asked Devlin where they should start to find Horrender, she certainly hadn't expected *this*.

The butler stood at the front door, holding it open for her. "Miss Wentworth?" he called out to her with a bemused bow at her hesitation. "His Grace is expecting you."

Of course he was. But was *she* ready for this?

When Devlin sent a footman to her townhouse the morning after their confrontation in her room, he'd invited her for an informal dinner with his family. She'd laughed. He was mad, surely!

But he was also her only way to Horrender. If that meant walking through the fires of hell itself—or sharing three courses with his family, which might end up being the exact same thing— she had no choice but to do it.

She pulled in a deep breath and lowered her hood with shaking hands as she slowly made her way to the front door.

She pulled loose the tie at her neck and slipped off the velvet and silk-lined cape to hand it to a footman. Her gaze drifted around the entry hall and took in the gilding that decorated the walls and the black and white marble checkerboard floor. She didn't remember any of it.

The butler gestured her deeper into the house. "This way, if you please, miss."

She followed him through the stair hall with its cantilevered stone steps, its walls painted a delicate robin's egg blue to contrast with the elaborate white plaster work on the ceiling. Various rooms led off the central stair hall, but the butler led her to the front reception room and paused to rap his knuckles on the open door before stepping into the room.

"Your Grace," he announced. "Miss Wentworth has arrived."

Devlin stood at the drawing room fireplace, with his forearm resting across the marble mantel and a glass in his other hand as he stared down into the fire. He looked up as she entered, and for a moment, his gaze fixed on hers before slowly lowering over her with such deliberate scrutiny that she trembled.

Then he straightened, set down his drink, and came forward to greet her with a small incline of his head.

"Thank you, Jennings," he said to the butler, yet his eyes never left Peyton. "Please wait ten minutes, then tell the duchess that our guest has arrived."

"Yes, sir." The butler nodded and retreated from the room.

Peyton cocked her head. "Miss Wentworth tonight, then, am I?"

"If you want to be." He paused. "Or I can introduce you as Miss Chandler. The choice is yours."

"And how exactly do you envision that conversation with your mother going? 'Hello, Your Grace. Yes, it's really me. Life is full of surprises, isn't it?' Although by then, she'll have most likely fainted."

An amused smile crooked at his lips. "It takes a lot more than that to frazzle my mother."

Peyton arched a brow. "More than a dead woman appearing

in her dining room?"

Wisely, he ignored that. "Tonight can be whatever you want it to be." He crossed to the sideboard and the drinks tray and poured a glass of claret. He carried it back to her and extended it like a peace offering. "And you can be whomever you want to be."

She nearly laughed. "Your mother will recognize me the moment she sets eyes on me!"

"No, she won't. *I* barely recognized you." He lowered his voice. "Even after I was close enough to kiss you. You've changed, Peyton. No one would recognize that shy, gangly girl in you now." He took another long look at her, from head to slippers, and everywhere he looked, heat shivered across her skin. "You look lovely."

She should have known better than to trust a flattering duke, yet she accepted the claret with a murmured thanks. Then she asked, "And what reason did you give your family for inviting me to dinner?"

"The truth. That you're an old acquaintance who has recently arrived in London and doesn't know anyone else here."

She narrowed her eyes at him. "What are you scheming at?"

"What do you mean?" He retreated to fetch his glass of cognac from the fireplace mantel.

"*This.*" She gestured with her drink to indicate the house around them.

"There's no scheme." He gave the fire a jab with the iron poker for good measure before returning to her. "If you're determined to remain in London to carry out your revenge, then you'll need to ease your way back into society to make the contacts you'll need." His mouth grimaced. "There are better ways of doing that than half-undressing me at the opera and fleecing me of thirty thousand pounds."

"Thirty-*one* thousand," she corrected. "Don't expect me to give it back."

He said nothing as he took a slow drink of brandy, but his

eyes gleamed. *Good.* Perhaps he'd realize they were still foes at heart. He might not have been involved with the attack, but he was still his father's son. A countless number of family dinners could never make her forget that.

"Consider tonight a stepping stone," he explained. "An evening of normal, polite conversation about the most mundane of topics."

"A test, you mean," she countered. "To see if your mother will recognize me or not." She tilted her head slightly as she called him out on his plotting. "Because if *she* does, then others in her social circle will, too, and I'll be no good to move within proper society. Visiting Barton's and the opera is one thing. But moving in respectable venues is something completely different. If anyone recognizes me, I won't be able to uncover any information for you."

"Yes, a test," he agreed. But no guilt registered on his face at being caught. Instead, he turned somber, "Of *us*, to let you know you'll have the support of the Raines family no matter what you decide for your future—if you choose to reveal your true identity or return to France."

"And when your mother learns that we've lied to her tonight?" she asked quietly against the rim of the crystal glass as she raised it to her lips to cover any stray emotions on her face.

"She'll be too overjoyed that you're alive to care."

"Dear Lord, you *are* mad," she muttered and shook her head. "Why are you doing this if not to tell your mother the truth about that night?"

"My mother can *never* learn the truth about that night," he warned, his voice low but firm. "Neither can my sisters."

The harsh realization hit her. "Your family knows nothing about what your father did, do they?"

"No, and I plan on keeping it that way."

"How…?" The word emerged as a breathless rasp. "How can she not have known what your father was doing? She lived with him. How could she not have suspected what he…?" Her voice trailed off beneath his grim gaze.

"Because my parents stopped having a true marriage long before that. They lived under the same roof but led separate lives." He finished off the cognac with a long swallow. "They did the best they could to have nothing to do with each other."

A typical society marriage, then, except…was that *pain* she saw in the hazel depths of his eyes? "Where did you fit into a home like that?"

"I didn't." He stared into the empty glass. "I was sent to Eton when I was thirteen. I stayed away at school as much as possible and spent holidays with friends whenever I could, then kept to myself whenever I had to return home, either here in London or at Wrentham Hall, our family's estate in Oxfordshire." He paused and turned the glass, as if imagining golden liquid against the crystal. "Oxfordshire," he mused, half to himself. "Which is why I went to Cambridge."

"But you didn't stay."

"University life was not for me."

She studied him closely. "But you thought being a mercenary for the Prussians was?"

"Well, when you put it like that…" With a grimace, he set the empty glass onto a nearby table. "My three best friends wanted me to go with them, and we all thought fighting in the wars would give us purpose."

"Did it?"

"Not all of us." He glanced at his glass as if considering whether to refill it. "Some of us realized we were needed more back here at home." He shrugged, although whether at the empty glass or at the past, she couldn't have said. "That's why I returned to London. My mother and sisters wanted me here."

Remorse tightened her chest. All this time, she had assumed he'd left the wars because he was too soft and spoiled to succeed at a military career. She'd been wrong about him in that, too.

She murmured, "That's why you were here at Dartmoor House that night."

"Mother made me attend her musicale. I think she was still attempting to hold together the last tendrils of what she thought a family should be."

"Yet you left with the opera singer."

He quirked a stiff grin. "She was beautiful and accommodating." When she started to give him the cutting reply that deserved, he interjected, "I was twenty-two, remember? Show me a bored, self-entitled twenty-two-year-old man who wouldn't have done the same, and I'll show you a priest."

She blinked at his blunt audacity. Then a small bubble of laughter fell from her lips, and her shoulders relaxed as part of the unease of being here ebbed away.

"I was nervous about tonight," she confided, slowly circling her finger around the rim of her glass. "For the first time since…" Her voice trailed off.

"I know," he said quietly.

She took a deep breath and nodded, then exhaled slowly as she looked around her. "But the house is different from what I remember."

"Because my mother redecorated it from top to bottom when Father died. She wanted to purge his presence from the place." He leaned against the sofa back and glanced around the room, as if attempting to see it through her eyes. Then he drawled, "Exorcism by wallpaper and chintz."

Her hand flew to her lips to stop the burst of laughter, but she couldn't help it. It also felt too good to suppress. She smiled at him from behind her fingers, only for her smile to fade.

She set her drink aside and took a hesitant step forward. "Tell me exactly what your father and the Duke of Crewe were—"

"*Devlin!*"

A high-pitched cry echoed through the ground floor rooms, followed by running footsteps. Moments later, a young girl bounced into the room, her long blond hair flowing loose around her slender shoulders, and her pink dress accentuating the excited flush in her fair cheeks. In her hand, she carried a notecard.

She saw Peyton and halted, and her eyes—the same dark brown as Devlin's—grew round like saucers.

"Oh—apologies!" the girl said, a bit breathless from racing through the house. "I was looking for my brother. I didn't realize you'd already arrived."

A strong urge to flee pulsed through Peyton. She might have done exactly that if Devlin hadn't stepped to her side and taken her arm. Margaret and Teddy had never met her before. Although Peyton had heard stories about the two girls from her mother, who had been close friends with theirs, they had been too young when the attack happened to be in her social circle. But that didn't stop fresh fear from gripping her.

She was playing with fire, and Devlin seemed determined to stoke it.

"May I introduce my sister?" Devlin gave her arm a brief squeeze of reassurance. "This is my youngest sister, Lady Theodora. Teddy, this is…"

He paused, giving Peyton the opportunity he'd promised for her to reveal her identity.

But she couldn't. Instead, she forced a wide smile for the girl and said, "Elizabeth Wentworth. It's a pleasure to meet you."

Devlin lowered his hand away.

"How do you do, Miss Wentworth?" His sister bobbed a curtsey. "Welcome to Dartmoor House." Then, hostess pleasantries over, she turned directly to her brother. "Devlin, you'll never guess what arrived this afternoon." She held out the card. "An invitation to my friend Matilda's ball! It's her introduction. Oh, please say you'll let me attend!"

Devlin cast an apologetic glance at Peyton as he took the invitation and read it. His face remained carefully inscrutable. "You're only sixteen, far too young for a ball."

Theodora's shoulders deflated like a balloon. "I am not at all too young. All my friends will be going, and they're mostly all my age. *Their* parents think it's perfectly fine for them to attend. Besides, I've been taking dance lessons for the past year."

Disappointment colored her voice even as she fiercely argued with him. "I know how to behave myself."

Devlin's brows rose at that.

"It's a *ball*." She dragged out the word to five syllables, as if her brother had no idea what one was. "I couldn't possibly come to any trouble at a crowded ball."

At that, his brows nearly shot off his forehead.

Peyton bit her inside cheek to keep from laughing. What *she* knew was that Devlin had caused countless incidents of scandal at crowded balls across London and knew better than anyone what trouble a young miss could come to at one.

"You're too young for Lord and Lady Bannerigg's ball." Devlin handed back the invitation. "You've not even out in society yet yourself."

Hope skittered across her face. "Then give me an introduction? It doesn't have to be grand."

"Next year, as planned."

Her mouth clamped shut and her eyes narrowed as she glared at him, in that way that only younger sisters could give overly protective older brothers. "But Mattie is my dearest friend, and her introduction is *this* season. Waiting until next year does me no good."

"Me either," he grumbled.

Theodora crossed her arms and stared at him for a moment, then coolly reminded him, "You're going to have to let me into society at some point, you know. Because if you don't, I'll never be courted. Which means I'll likely never find a husband." She poked her finger into his chest. "Which means I'll have to live *with you* for the rest of your life!"

"God forbid," he muttered with exaggerated horror.

"Don't I know it," Theodora replied in the same exaggerated voice.

Biting back a laugh at their antics, Peyton moved her gaze between the two. She understood Devlin's desire to protect his sister, but she also remembered what it had been like to be a girl of Theodora's age, so eager to be part of the happenings, so impatient to grow up.

"Perhaps Lady Theodora doesn't have to miss her friend's introduction," Peyton posited gently. "True, she isn't out in society yet, but that doesn't mean she cannot attend if she goes as a guest of her invited family."

Hope glowed on Theodora's face. "I'd merely be attending with my family, not as a true guest...but at least I'd be able to attend. Oh, that might just work!" She looked at the invitation in her hand and bit her lip. "It would require having Mattie change the invitation—"

"To Her Grace, Duchess of Dartmoor, and Her Grace's family," Peyton explained. She might have been away from London society for ten years, but she still remembered how convolutedly it worked. "Then, your mother can attend and bring you with her, claiming she didn't want to leave you at home."

"My first ball!" Theodora bounced in a circle. "Oh, it's going to be grand! The dresses, the chandeliers, the dancing—"

"No dancing," Devlin corrected firmly. "Not for you."

Theodora stopped and stared at her brother, suddenly on the verge of tears, as if he'd just given away her kitten. "No dancing?" Her arms fell lifelessly to her sides. "But—but...what's the point in a *ball*—" This time she dragged out the word to a good ten syllables at least. "—if I don't get to dance? It's not fair."

"Very well." When her face began to light up at winning him over, he added, "You can dance with me."

She glared at him and grumbled, "That is so *very much* not fair!"

Devlin acknowledged the fatalistic wisdom of that with a long sigh. "And so goes the world."

Peyton intervened by taking Theodora's hands and squeezing them. "But at least you'll be able to attend." She leaned forward to whisper into the girl's ear. "And if a respectable young man very politely asks your brother for his permission to dance with you, he might just say yes."

The girl impulsively hugged Peyton, who stiffened at the unexpected show of gratitude. Theodora stepped back but didn't release her hands. She beamed. "Oh, you are very welcome at Dartmoor House!" Then she spun on her heel and raced from the room. "Mama! Mama, I have news!"

"Look at what you've done." Devlin slid his gaze from the door to Peyton. "You've unleashed a monster."

Peyton countered, "But she's right, you know. Her first ball should be special."

"Then you should be forced to attend with us."

He was teasing, she knew. Yet the subtle nudge to put her further into society's embrace spun fear through her. "No."

Before he could say anything more, his mother, the Duchess of Dartmoor, glided into the drawing room, her hands extended toward Peyton in warm greeting. Behind her entered a bouncing Theodora, whose happiness over the ball was overflowing, and beside her came a pretty young woman who smiled but with a bit more trepidation than her younger sister and mother. She had to be Lady Margaret. Her resemblance to the duchess was undeniable.

"Mother." Devlin went to Peyton's side. "May I introduce you to Miss Elizabeth Wentworth?" He looked down at Peyton, but his face was unreadable. "Miss Wentworth, my mother, Her Grace the Duchess of Dartmoor."

The duchess beamed at Peyton. "Welcome to Dartmoor House. We're so happy to have you as our guest." She placed her hand on Theodora's shoulder to calm the girl and make her stop bouncing. "How are you finding your return to London, Miss Wentworth?"

"A bit trying, Your Grace." That was the God's truth. "The city has grown so much since I was last here."

"And when was that?"

The duchess was attempting casual conversation, but Peyton found it fraught with pitfalls. "A very long time ago." She dodged the specifics. "I was only a small girl then."

"Well, I'm so glad we're able to welcome back one of Devlin's old acquaintances. Aren't we, girls?"

Margaret smiled and murmured her agreement.

Theodora was too focused on the invitation she still clutched in her hands to notice that her mother had said anything at all.

"Miss Wentworth has spent a good deal of time in France," Devlin commented as a way to start conversation.

"You will have to tell me all about your time there and how it compares to England," his mother insisted congenially, "especially the fashions."

"Of course, ma'am," Peyton answered, "although I'm afraid I'm not very fashionable."

"Nonsense!" The duchess cast an assessing glance over Peyton's dress and hair. Then she stilled, her eyes narrowing on Peyton's face. "You seem so familiar... Have we met before?"

"No, Your Grace." Not technically a lie despite the spike of her pulse. No one knew her anymore.

But the duchess didn't seem convinced. Peyton held her breath, waiting for the woman to remember who she was and what—

The butler came into the room and gave a low bow. "Dinner is ready, Your Grace."

"Thank you, Jennings," Devlin called out, then gestured toward the hall. "After you, Mother."

The group made their way through the house to the dining room, with his mother and sisters leading the way. Peyton lingered behind as she fought to calm her racing heart and steady her breathing.

Devlin briefly placed a reassuring hand to the small of her back as he led her forward. But the touch did little to put her at ease. Tonight was her greatest test of the last ten years, and God help her if she failed it.

Chapter Ten

DEVLIN LEANED BACK in his chair at the head of the table and listened to his mother and sisters deliver a barrage of ideas of what Peyton should do in London during the season. They were finishing the dessert course, although he'd noticed that Peyton had done little more than push food around her plate all evening and was now doing the same with her strawberry cake.

He didn't blame her for not having an appetite. Dinner tonight was proving to be an ordeal by fire for her, if only because it was nothing more than a typical Raines family evening. Embarrassing stories about their childhoods and assorted public faux pas as adults served as the main course, followed by extra helpings of merciless teasing and bickering. At every moment she must have been afraid of being discovered before she was ready to reveal herself—if she would ever be ready. The pallor that had gripped her face since his mother walked into the drawing room to meet her was testimony to that.

Fortunately, both he and Peyton managed to avoid specifics about how they knew each other, although Devlin was prepared to claim she was the sister of a school chum he met during holiday, if necessary.

Yet tonight wasn't about giving Peyton a pleasant evening, nor was it the test Peyton accused him of earlier—to prove she was capable of holding her own in society. Hell, he knew she was more than capable of doing just that, having seen her in action at Barton's and the opera.

No, he wanted to see how she would react when faced with the past. If she could maneuver her way through tonight's reminders of that, then perhaps she could find a way to move into the future.

"And you should attend the picture gallery at Somerset House," Meg insisted. "It's always good for a gawk."

Peyton smiled, seeming to enjoy Meg's company, and drawled almost beneath her breath, "Sometimes even at the paintings."

But Peyton was sitting to Meg's left side, and his sister couldn't hear her comment, even though his mother and Teddy both laughed at the quip. Meg blinked. "Pardon?"

Peyton repeated louder, "Sometimes to even gawk at the paintings."

Meg laughed with them then, the happy sound filling the room.

Devlin glanced up from the table as Jennings stepped into the room and stood at the wall near the door, his well-trained butler's presence as unobtrusive as ever. Yet his appearance signaled that the coffee service was ready in the drawing room.

A lull formed in the conversation as his two sisters searched the corners of their minds to add to the growing list of places and things Peyton simply must do during her visit. Before they could inundate her afresh with questions about whether she planned on traveling to Brighton or Weymouth once the London season was over, his mother placed her napkin on her plate. "Shall we go through, then? Jennings's coffee is not to be missed."

The normally staid butler flushed faintly at the compliment.

"And Cook's chocolate," Teddy interjected as she slipped off her chair and stood. "She makes the best in Mayfair."

"Chocolate is for children," Meg baited her as she rose elegantly from her chair.

As Devlin rose to his feet, familiar guilt pricked him. Meg should have been married by now, but their father's ghost still haunted her. She didn't trust a man enough to marry him.

"Good," Teddy called out over her shoulder as her sister followed her from the room. "Then I'll take your share and enjoy twice as much!"

His mother gave a long-suffering sigh as she followed after, leaving Devlin to escort their guest.

Devlin saw relief drain through Peyton as her slender shoulders sank at finally having a moment's peace—and a moment when she didn't have to be on constant guard that his mother would recognize her.

"You're doing well," he assured her quietly as he slowly circled the large table to her.

"Is this how they used to torture prisoners in the Tower?" she muttered and drew in a deep breath to gather herself.

His lips curled. "Just a typical evening at Dartmoor House. But look on the bright side." He took her arm to escort her from the room. "At least now you have an exhaustive list of places to visit while you're in London."

She narrowed her eyes at him.

"And the knowledge that you won't easily be recognized," he murmured into her ear, "if at all."

"There is that," she grudgingly agreed and walked with him into the stair hall.

Instead of following his family, Devlin tugged her aside into the alcove beneath the cantilevered stairs curling above their heads. His mother had placed a Chinese urn on a small table to give some sort of use to the otherwise wasted space, but shadowed and tucked out of the way, it also gave them a moment's privacy.

"How are you holding up?" he asked. "Truthfully."

"Truthfully?" She gave a long sigh. "If I wasn't already dead, this evening would kill me."

A chuckle rose from the back of his throat. He knew then that she would be fine. *Eventually.*

"How much longer will this evening last?" she asked, glancing past his shoulder at the empty hall.

"Another hour, and then you can feign a headache and beg off. Deal?"

"Deal." Yet his compromise didn't seem to please her. She hesitated before asking, "How long has Margaret been deaf in her left ear?"

Devlin's chest squeezed, although he shouldn't have been surprised that Peyton noticed, not with how keen she was on noting everything around her. "Since she was ten."

"An accident or illness?"

"Neither. It was our father."

Peyton's lips parted in surprise.

"He was angry about something—God only knows what— and boxed her ears, rupturing her eardrum. So no, not an accident nor an illness. The bastard fully intended to hurt her."

"Oh, Devlin...I'm so sorry." Then she guessed, "He hit her other times, too, didn't he?"

"Yes. And my mother."

Her eyes locked with his. "And you?"

"Only until I learned to hit back." The pity in her eyes nearly undid him. He shook his head. "It's all in the past now."

The pursing of her lips told him she didn't agree, yet she wisely let the subject drop. He took her arm to lead her into the drawing room.

But she placed her hand on his bicep and stopped him, looking at him with trepidation. "Devlin?"

"Yes?"

"I'm sorry for ending your engagement with Lady Catherine."

His gut tightened at her remorse. "It wasn't official. We were still hammering out the details of the marriage contract." He blew out a hard breath and admitted, "It was probably for the best anyway."

She searched his face. "You didn't love her?"

"No." In fact, he was damnably surprised he felt so little regret over the incident. What bothered him more was the way Peyton had orchestrated it so effectively to maximize the public humiliation for him. He was certain all kinds of fresh allegations that he was an unscrupulous rake were now flowing through London as fast as the Thames, but what bothered him about that wasn't what people thought of him but what damage it might do to his family. "I courted her because her family was respectable and she was pleasant."

"Pleasant?" Peyton repeated as if she couldn't possibly have heard him correctly. "The notorious Devlin Raines prized a woman because she was *pleasant*?"

He grimaced. "I haven't been notorious in a very long time."

"Then the duchess was right," she murmured. "London *has* changed a great deal since I've been gone."

More than you realize.

"Well, then," she corrected herself, "I'm sorry for ending your potentially pleasant match." When he began to give that the reply it deserved, she added, "But I'm not sorry for besting you at cards."

"*I* am," he murmured, "given our wager. I was very much looking forward to winning."

He heard her catch her breath at the reminder of what he had expected to claim from her. "Then you must be extremely relieved now that you know the identity of the woman you were playing with." Her voice emerged as a throaty purr, and he wondered if she realized it...or the heated effect it had on him. "You'll never want to kiss me again."

"I wouldn't say that," he murmured with a glance over his shoulder to make certain the hall was still empty. When he looked back at her, his gaze fell to her ripe lips, which parted beneath his stare. He couldn't resist the temptation of her softness and slowly swept his hand along the side of her body, over the curves of her hip and waist to her ribs, then over the outside swell of her breast.

She trembled.

"Devlin! Miss Wentworth!" Theodora called out from the drawing room. "We've convinced Meg to sing for us. Hurry before she changes her mind!"

He dropped his hand and stepped back.

For a moment, Peyton didn't move; she simply stared at him, eyes bright with confusion. Devlin couldn't help but wonder—who was she seeing…the man standing with her or the one she remembered from ten years ago?

"We should join them," she whispered huskily.

Without another word, he led her into the drawing room.

They took their seats, with Peyton joining his mother on the settee, Devlin slumping into a chair, and Teddy perched on the chair arm beside him, mostly so she could annoy him by loudly slurping her chocolate until he poked her in the ribs with his elbow. Then she slunk off to her own chair.

At the pianoforte, Meg shuffled through her sheet music before finally settling on a piece she loved—a recent composition by Beethoven that Devlin had purchased for her a few months ago for her birthday. Her fingers danced over the keys, and the soft music floated through the room on the candlelight.

When she finished, they applauded.

"Sing, Meg!" Teddy called out. "You promised."

Margaret's cheeks flushed slightly, but she did as requested and accompanied herself in an old song about unrequited love.

"Lovely," Devlin said as she finished.

She hunted through her music portfolio. "Come join me."

Teddy set down her chocolate and jumped to her feet to run forward to the pianoforte. She gestured excitedly back at the others, and Devlin reluctantly came forward with his mother, leaving Peyton on the settee. Devlin shot her an apologetic glance. She didn't deserve to be caught up in this. Hell, neither did he. But he loved his sisters and would do anything to make them happy, including embarrassing himself by singing.

Embarrass himself he did, although Meg had always claimed he had a good voice. They sang together, with his mother harmonizing with Meg and with Teddy and Devlin left to carry the main melody. But soon, the teasing and baiting from dinner overcame them, as it always did, and the sing-a-long became a free-for-all, with Meg finally throwing up her hands in surrender.

Across the room, Peyton stood stiffly. A white pallor gripped her face, and even from so far away, he could see the glistening in her eyes and the trembling in her limbs.

"I...I can't..." she mumbled. "It's all too much...I thought—but I can't!"

She turned and hurried from the room, leaving his family staring silently with confusion and concern. Devlin chased after her.

He stepped into the entry hall just as she snatched her cape from the footman's hands at the door and raced out of the house, down the front steps, and toward her waiting carriage. He chased after and caught her on the footpath, his hand on her elbow stopping her.

She wheeled toward him, and for a split second, he worried she'd hidden a knife in her skirt. But it wasn't a weapon in her hand that ripped the breath from his lungs. It was the startling look of anguish on her face.

Dear God... He laid a gentle hand on her arm. "Peyton, are you all right?"

"I couldn't bear—I couldn't stay." She glanced over her shoulder at the house as if expecting a monster to emerge and devour her. "I need to leave."

"What's happened?"

"You—your family—all this!" Her eyes turned dark in the shadows of the dimly lit street, and the clouds of her breath against the cold air made her seem even more vulnerable. "The way you are with them, the way you all interact with each other—the way you love each other..." A tear glistened in the light of the door lamp as it slid down her cheek. "Why would your father risk his family and all their love and happiness?" Her shoulders slumped in confusion. "Why would *you*?"

Her eyes searched his face, and he knew the time had come to tell her the truth. *All* the truth, no matter how much it hurt both of them. She would never be able to heal until the entire wound had been revealed. And cauterized.

He gently took her arm and led her toward the carriage, calling back over his shoulder to Jennings as the butler stood on the steps in the cold evening drizzle. "Jennings, inform the duchess that Miss Wentworth has taken ill. I'm escorting her home." He was breaking all kinds of propriety and not giving a damn that he was. "Then I'm going on to the clubs. She isn't to worry. I'll see her in the morning."

"Yes, Your Grace."

Devlin helped her into the carriage and climbed in after her. The door closed, and he knocked against the roof to signal to the coachman to drive.

The carriage swayed on its springs as the wheels splashed through the puddles left on the pavement by earlier rains. Outside, the night was cold and wet, and the light of the scattered lamps on the main avenues reflected in the shimmering black water. There would be heavy fog by midnight, but now the gathering whiteness served only to cocoon them together and muffle the sounds of the nighttime city around them.

Devlin studied Peyton through the moving shadows. He was certain her face was still as pale as it had been in the drawing room. But there was no help for that, not now. Not when what he was about to say would only make her pallor worse.

"When my father and the Duke of Crewe became business partners," Devlin began quietly, his low voice matching the depth of the shadows around them, "they kept what they were doing secret from everyone. They'd been partners for years, ever since I was a boy at Eton, and no one had any idea how far their ventures ran or what comprised them."

"Not even you?" she asked quietly.

"Not even." He'd certainly punished himself over the years for not investigating sooner. "I had suspected my father was skirting the edge of legality, but what peer doesn't influence peddle in Parliament or use Whitehall connections for his own financial gains? But I had willfully turned a blind eye to my father, avoiding him whenever possible and tolerating him only for my mother's and sisters' sakes. Truthfully, I didn't want to know what he was doing and did my damnedest to treat him as if didn't exist."

"But that night..." Her voice faded into the darkness.

"That night I stumbled into a viper's nest. I was too late to stop the attack, but I made certain they wouldn't be able to harm anyone else ever again. Lucien Grenier happened to be on leave in London. I told him what happened and what I'd learned about our fathers, and together we decided to put an end to their criminal enterprise."

"You let them get away with all they'd done," she accused in a rough whisper.

"Because we had no other choice. Publicly bringing them to justice would have destroyed both our families, both dukedoms, and all the lives of countless innocent people who depended upon those dukedoms to survive. Servants, tenants, farmers, villagers... *If* their fellow lords in Parliament would have found them guilty in the first place. We had no certainty of that."

He still lived with the guilt of that decision, even knowing he'd made the right one. So did Crewe, although he had even more to lose than Devlin if their fathers' secrets were uncovered.

"So we ended their ability to harm anyone else. Horrender was a different matter, but he fled England before we could make him swing for what he'd done." The familiar taste of acid formed in his mouth. "From that point on, Lucien and I dedicated ourselves to cleaning up after our fathers, to destroying the enterprise they'd built, and to hiding what we couldn't destroy. We chopped up the businesses, destroyed records, and forged others to counter the ones we couldn't destroy until we'd erased all traces of their illegal operations. Our fathers were both dead shortly after, and the last of the bad business was buried with them."

He leaned forward, elbows on knees, and fixed his gaze on her through the shadows.

"You asked me why I would risk my family and all their love and happiness," he reminded her. "Because it wasn't enough to simply end their criminal enterprise. They'd ruined countless lives—including women and children—and restitution had to be made. *All* the restitution I could."

He and Crewe had taken their own money to fund new lives for the innocents their fathers had hurt. Prostitutes were given new lives away from London. Low-level smugglers and thieves were given legitimate jobs. As for the children, those tore at Devlin's heart the most, but he did what he could for them. Those who had family were reunited with their relatives, while orphans and foundlings were placed into domestic service or the navy if they were old enough and into kind homes for the youngest.

Most of all, Devlin had worked in secret to create Brechenhurst, a place of refuge for street children who had no safe place to spend their nights. He didn't want them to fall prey to men like his father, so he used a large part of the money he'd inherited to found the place and keep it running. He'd named it after a mutilated mishmash of the German he'd learned while fighting with the Prussians. *Brechen herz*...broken heart.

Like his father's crimes, it, too, had to remain secret.

"Why did my father risk everything?" Repeating her question, he settled back against the squabs, his gaze not leaving hers. "Because he was a cruel, selfish, heartless son of a bitch who wanted money and power at all costs, no matter whom he hurt to get it."

For a long while she did nothing more than return his stare, her lips parted as she tried to fathom all he shared with her.

"And no one else knows?" she finally asked, her voice so soft it was nearly lost beneath the rumble of carriage wheels. "Not even your family?"

"No one but Crewe." Not even Shay or Chase, both men who were as close as brothers to him. Not even Anthony Titus, the man in whom he'd confessed all his other secrets, who had left England for Spain during the final years of the wars and taken those secrets with him. "And now you."

But she didn't know all the gruesome details and never would.

"Then you need to tell them," she urged, her voice suddenly bright with intensity. "You said that Horrender might have returned. If their lives are in danger, then they need to be warned."

"No." He and Crewe would take this secret to their graves. He hoped Peyton would do the same. "Their lives would be destroyed, not ended."

"Is that why you told me, then? Because my life is at an even greater risk than theirs?"

"No. I told you because you're the same as Crewe and me. Part of the next generation who needs to atone for their fathers' evils."

She stiffened. "My father had nothing to do with this. Not like that."

"He did." He kept his attention on her hands, folded in her lap, to make certain she didn't decide to reach for the gun in the cushion. "He was their third partner."

She shook her head. "My father was a banker and accountant who—"

"Who knew exactly how to hide all their profits and make certain no money trails could ever be traced back to them. They couldn't have built their business without his skills. That's why Charles Chandler spent so much time with two dukes whom he would otherwise never have associated with." He paused to make certain no pity was audible in his voice. "You know how society works. Bankers are middle-class. They work for a living, and high-ranking peers never sully themselves by associating with workers, even ones as successful as your father, and they would certainly never issue invitations to soirees at their homes to a banker's family."

She said nothing, simply continued to stare at him across the dark compartment as the shadows cast by the lamps swirled around them.

"You weren't ignored by everyone the night of the musicale because you hadn't yet been introduced to society," he said as gently as possible, knowing how much the truth would hurt. "You were ignored because you were the daughter of a banker."

Her eyes glistened in the darkness.

"The Dukes of Crewe and Dartmoor used your father the same way that lots of bankers were used during the early years of the wars, to help with smuggling and fencing goods. Lots of men did the same. High-powered and important men, and not just for illegal cognac either but for basic food stuffs, many of which were sold to the working classes. That's how the three of them started. But when they brought in Horrender to oversee the day-to-day operations, their business became more than just smuggling. Horrender made their enterprise far-reaching across England and into France, which was why you were able to access the money your father hid there." He faintly shook his head. "All those businesses and bank accounts, all that property purchased under false names and identities—how did you think it all got there if not through criminal means, in a country embroiled in war for the past two decades?"

"My father was *not* a criminal." But her voice lacked conviction.

He wisely knew not to argue with her. Not yet. Instead, he kept his face calm and his voice steady, and continued, "The night you were attacked, the carriage was purposefully ambushed by men lying in wait. Your father had threatened to speak out against Dartmoor and Crewe—they had finally done more than he could stomach—if they didn't curtail their enterprise. The two dukes wanted to silence your father, but Horrender decided to use the attack as a message, to show everyone who dealt with him the lengths he would go to if anyone dared cross him. That's how you and your mother were caught up in it."

"My father wouldn't have had anything to do with men like Horrender. He wouldn't have entered any kind of business arrangement like that."

Devlin had lost the argument before it had even begun. She'd believed him a villain for so long that she would never believe him about this.

So he would have to show her.

He pounded his fist against the ceiling to signal to the driver to stop. When the carriage slowed, he opened the door and stood up in the doorway to give new directions to the coachman, then dropped back into the seat across from her. He closed the door as the carriage started forward again, but instead of rolling on toward her townhouse, it turned toward the city.

"Where are we going?" she asked.

"To Seven Dials." He glanced out the window at the dark city and mumbled, "Back to where it all started."

Chapter Eleven

P EYTON LOOKED OUT the carriage window at the old tavern where they'd finally stopped. Fear tingled the backs of her knees. "What is this place?"

"The Plough," Devlin answered. Then he popped open the door and called out to the driver. "Drive around the corner and stop there."

The man did as ordered.

"Wait here," he told her.

He jumped to the ground and gestured to her tiger, who hesitated before stripping off his black jacket and handing it over to Devlin. Then he called up to the driver, who tossed down his caped greatcoat a few seconds later. He handed her the driver's coat. "Put this on and button it all the way. It will cover your dress well enough not to draw too much attention."

As she slipped on the tent of a coat and buttoned it as he wanted, she watched him exchange his jacket for the tiger's. The jacket was too small across his broad shoulders, but at least it wasn't the fine blue cashmere he'd been wearing.

When he helped her to the ground, instead of letting go of her hand, he held tighter to her fingers and led her back toward the tavern. The coat covered her from neck to ankle, with only her slippers giving any indication of the fine dress she wore beneath.

"What are we doing here?" she asked as he held the door for her.

"I want you to meet someone," he returned in the same low voice as she slid past him.

Once inside, he took her arm and walked her through the tavern, past tables crowded with men in rough workmen's clothes and women in coarse dresses. The stench of rotten ale stung her nose, so did the scent of burnt stew coming from somewhere inside the smoky, musty building. Devlin threw a coin to the barkeeper but didn't slow his pace as the man called out something to him that Peyton couldn't understand.

They reached a door at the rear of the tavern. Devlin rapped his knuckles against the wood panel.

The door opened, and a man the size of a mountain peered out. "Eh?"

"Caxton."

The mountain stepped back. Before Devlin could enter, the man ran his hands down Devlin's body, patting down his jacket sleeves and waist. Devlin passively held up his hands.

When the man reached for Peyton to conduct the same weapons check, Devlin stepped between them.

"Touch her," he warned in a low growl, "and I'll kill you where you stand. You know I can."

The guard hesitated, then nodded and moved back to let them pass. He closed the door behind them.

"You've a keen ability for making friends," Peyton muttered to Devlin in a low voice. "Has anyone ever told you that?"

He said nothing but slid her a warning glance and led her forward, down a set of stone steps into the cellar.

Peyton stopped just inside the doorway to a long basement room and realized why a mountain-shaped guard protected it. This wasn't a tavern cellar where they stored sacks of grain and casks of ale. It was an illegal gin palace—well, as much of a palace as a dark and dank cellar filled with cobwebs and mold could be.

Not that anyone who was there cared how the place looked, based on the way men and women in working class clothes sat drunk on wooden benches lining the walls, while others hunched over small tables scattered throughout, playing at cards and dice in the smoky light of tallow candles. A few were too drunk to even sit and instead lay on the dirt floor where they'd collapsed.

Devlin guided her slowly through the cellar, slanting glances at the men at the tables and keeping his face inscrutable. When they reached the far end, he stopped at a table in the corner, pulled out a chair without invitation, and helped Peyton to sit.

Across the table, a man in a rough brown jacket glanced up from his cards. His gaze went first to Devlin, then fell to Peyton, where it remained for a long time before returning to his cards. He threw in his hand and gestured for the two men with him to leave. They collected their coins and walked away.

Devlin sat on one of the vacant chairs, looked at the small pile of coins in the center of the table, and threw in a couple of his own to make up for the profits he'd cost the man on the hand. The gesture wasn't one of kindness or remorse, she knew. It was a bribe.

"You're here awfully early," the man rasped out in a gravelly voice. Then he signaled for one of the bar maids to bring him a new cup of gin.

"I could say the same of you, Caxton."

"Cards are better played before the crowd's dead drunk." He tossed the bar maid one of the coins. "And bets best collected 'fore they're just plain dead."

Peyton wanted to crawl out of her skin. So that's how this gin cellar worked. The poor workers came here for a ha'penny dram of gin to forget their troubles for the night, and men like Caxton preyed on their vulnerabilities. Some of the imbibers would drink themselves to death before dawn. Yet the authorities would do as they'd done for the past century—turn a blind eye. Thank God the guard at the door seemed to keep the children and babies away, at least, although the same God only knew how many of the women slumped on the benches had left their children and babies at home alone.

"Why are you here? And with such a pretty little taste in tow, too." Caxton gestured his tin cup of gin at Peyton, then lifted it to his nose and sniffed. "Can't be for the drink."

"You've heard the same rumors I have, I'm sure." The wooden chair squeaked angrily beneath his weight as Devlin shifted on it. "Horrender's back and rebuilding his business."

Caxton set down the gin without taking a sip. He played with the cards in his fingers, turning the ace of spades across his knuckles, again and again. "That's all they are so far, too, only rumors and grumblings. Nothing known for certain 'bout who or what…or why." He nodded at Peyton, then let the card fall from his fingers to the table. "You think it's a good idea bringing her here?"

Peyton stiffened. "I can hold my own in a fight."

His lips curled faintly as he looked at Devlin and jerked a thumb at her. "Does she know about the old business?"

"She knows enough," Devlin answered and rested his arm across the back of her chair, like a territorial guard dog. "Horrender," he said, moving the conversation away from Peyton. "Do you think he's returned?"

"Can't say for certain." He spat on the floor. "Haven't seen him with my own eyes if he has. But someone's been contacting the old players and trying to start up the businesses again, following in his footsteps. If not Horrender, then one of his cronies and one high up enough to know where the bodies are buried."

Peyton knew he didn't mean that figuratively.

"Why now after all these years?" Devlin pressed.

Caxton shook his head. "The wars are over, laws are changing, and the old guard is gone. You think anyone in Whitehall cares a damn what happens to us rats?" He scooped up the coins from the center of the table and stacked them in front of him. "A new brothel opened in Wapping just this past month, run by

Horrender's old manager. The same with a second in Clerkenwell. A store front opened on Petticoat Lane, fencing the same kinds of goods as before. And I've heard children have started to come and go, just as they used to."

Devlin stiffened, not so much that Caxton or anyone who happened to be watching would have noticed. But Peyton knew. She *felt* the change in him.

"Don't mean it's Horrender, though," Caxton considered, rolling one of the coins over his fingers the same way had the ace. "Could be one of his lieutenants who's finally feeling his oats enough to try to put the businesses back together. A man who *thinks* he's Horrender."

"What do you think?"

He nodded at Peyton. "I think it's no coincidence that of all the tasty bits you could have brought along tonight, you brought *her*."

Peyton felt her blood run cold. "What do you mean?"

Caxton palmed the coin and leaned across the table. "I know who you are, lass," he told her, his raspy voice low so the drunks around them wouldn't overhear. "That is, I know who you're related to. You're the spitting image of Eleanor Chandler. That means you're one o' her kin."

"How did you know Mrs. Chandler?" she asked carefully, keeping her voice even, her face blank.

"I worked for her husband." He set the coin spinning on its edge and leaned back in his chair. "I collected his money."

No, that couldn't be possible... What this man was saying, what Devlin had told her—she wanted to scream!

Yet she only stared across the table at him, not moving a muscle, refusing even to blink.

"So who are *you* to Mrs. Chandler?" Caxton leveled a hard gaze on her, and she prayed he couldn't see her relief that he hadn't assumed the truth. "Sister? Niece? Cousin?"

She ignored the weight of Devlin's hand slipping down to her shoulder in silent warning and answered, "Something like that."

"If you're thinking of tryin' to gain any money from the old business, you're mad to try it." Caxton took a long sip of his gin. "Whatever information you might have about Charles Chandler's role with the business won't do you a lick of good. The man was the devil with money. The best I've seen when it comes to hiding it and brushing away all traces of where it came from. That's why he and the old dukes made such a good partnership."

Her stomach roiled sickeningly, and she thanked God that in the dim light of the cellar Caxton couldn't see the blood seep from her face. Her chest felt as if a raw wound had been sliced into it, but her foolish heart somehow kept beating.

"If there's any blunt left, you'll never find it." Caxton leaned forward again, his eyes boring into hers. "And if Horrender has returned and you plan to blackmail him, God help you. I've seen what that man's capable of." He slipped a finger under his neckcloth and pulled it down so she could see his throat and the long knife scar that ran from ear to ear. He traced a finger across the scar to follow the path of the blade. "He'll do worse than this to you, pet. Count on it."

Pushing his neckcloth and collar into place, Caxton leaned back and signaled to his two fellow card players that his conversation was over and to return to their game.

"Take that tasty bit home now," Caxton ordered Devlin. His cold eyes swung to Peyton. "And forget everything you know about the old business, lass, if you want to grow old yourself."

He turned back to his cards and coins, dismissing Devlin and Peyton completely.

Devlin stood and took Peyton's arm to help her to her feet. She didn't have the strength to pull away and leaned against him as he led her out of the cellar and back to the surface, then out of the tavern to the waiting carriage. She heard his muffled orders to the driver, all of her numb as he opened the door and helped her inside, then sat across from her and closed the door.

She deflated against the squabs and stared down at her hands as they rested on her lap, trembling unstoppably. The blood

pounded so hard through her ears that the echo of it drowned out
the noise of the horses' hooves over the streets and the turning
wheels beneath them. She couldn't think, couldn't feel—could
barely remember to breathe!

She squeezed her eyes shut to block out the terrible realiza-
tions that swarmed over her, threatening to consume her. Her
father hadn't been an innocent victim of the attack. He'd been
part of the evil. He'd worked to make it happen, hadn't said a
word to stop it before that night, and even then...

In the past few days, everything she thought she knew and
could depend upon had been destroyed. Her world had inverted,
and she was certain about nothing now. *Nothing.* What was left
now that she could believe in?

"Peyton."

Oh, the pain! How did she make it stop? She pressed her fist
against her chest as if she could will her damnable heart to stop
and finally end the misery. But it only kept beating, as if it didn't
realize her world had just ended a second time. It took everything
she had to crawl out of the ashes last time and survive. Oh God,
how would she ever be able to do it again?

"Peyton. Look at me."

She gasped a trembling breath over numb lips and opened her
eyes. Her gaze stung with hot tears as she stared at Devlin, who
was little more than a dark silhouette in the shadows. For a
moment, neither of them moved, letting the night press in
around them in the cocoon of the carriage.

Then, slowly, he held open his arms.

A soft cry escaped her, and the last of the fight seeped away.
She didn't have the strength to refuse the comfort and strength he
offered. He was the only anchor she had left.

She carefully slipped from her seat and went to him.

He took her onto his lap and into his arms as she let the
tremors overtake her. No sobs came as she clung to him. She was
long past the point of tears, either for her father or herself, and
her body felt like an empty shell with a hollow void in her chest

where her heart had been. All she knew at that moment was Devlin's solidity, his strength and warmth, and she pressed herself against him to absorb as much of him as possible.

"It's going to be all right," he murmured as he nuzzled his cheek against her hair. "The past can't hurt you anymore."

Oh, he was wrong! She couldn't escape it. Tonight proved that. Every time she was certain she'd put a ghost to rest, another rose from the darkness. How many more ghosts would be unleashed to haunt her? "You don't know that."

"I do." He pulled back only far enough to look up at her and tucked a stray curl behind her ear. "Because I've been through what you're going through right now, learning what my father had been part of, discovering the web of lies and abuse he'd created…and I survived." He caressed her cheek. "So can you."

Peyton desperately wanted to believe that, as much as she craved the certainty and strength Devlin possessed. Slowly, she lowered her head and brought her lips to his.

He froze, except for the quick catch of his breath. For a moment, neither of them moved, and her heart beat off the agonizing seconds.

Then, his lips moved beneath hers, so softly that the movement was barely more than a featherlight caress, so faintly, she wasn't certain he was even kissing her back. But her numb body realized what her mind didn't and allowed his determination to seep inside her, and achingly, his tenderness filled the empty hollow inside her until she trembled.

He lightly trailed his fingers along her jaw to her ear, then down her neck to the collar of the coachman's greatcoat still engulfing her. His sensuous lips bestowed on hers a string of kisses that weren't quite kisses, light nibbles that weren't quite bites, and all of it stirred more feelings of reassurance and trust than desire. She knew the pleasure a man could bring to her and where such kisses could lead.

But tonight, what she needed wasn't physical release but absolution for the past, and only Devlin could give her that.

She slipped her hand to his nape and ran her fingers through the silky hair at his collar, not to titillate but to simply touch. She couldn't fight the urge to scrape her nails slowly over his scalp and revel in the solidity of him beneath her hands even as she drank in the wonderfully spicy taste of him on her lips. Her heart began to pound so hard against her ribs that she feared he could feel it…then didn't care if he did.

He slipped free the first button at her neck, and she didn't stop him, not even when he slowly undid the next one…and the next. The coat gaped open a little more with every inch his hand moved down her front. She stilled when he reached the button lying at the top of her legs as she remained perched on his lap, but he did nothing more than slip it free as he had done all the others and moved down to the last of the buttons above her calves. Acute disappointment gripped her that he'd not dared to take a more intimate touch. But when his warm hand slipped beneath her hem to rest on her stockinged knee, the resulting thud of need landed between her legs with a shudder.

Devlin broke the kiss and rested his back head against the squabs to gaze up at her. With both hands, he gently took the greatcoat and slowly stripped it off her shoulders and down her back, until it draped over his legs. She still wore her evening dress and all the layers of undergarments, yet she now felt strangely bare, and when his gaze raked over her, from lips to lap, she felt downright naked.

"Trust in me, Peyton," he cajoled in a husky voice that twined around her like a ribbon, tying them together.

"I do," she breathed and meant it.

The soft sound was lost beneath the rumble of carriage wheels, but the faint flare of his eyes told her he'd heard.

When he rose up to kiss her, there was none of the tender reassurance of before. This time, she tasted his desire, and she welcomed it, parting her lips and sinking against him with a deep sigh.

The tip of his tongue outlined her lips before slipping between them. Long licks across her inner lip alternated with smooth glides across her tongue and matched the unhurried sweep of his hands to the short row of buttons on the back of her bodice. Her dress loosened with each pearl button he slipped free, and electricity pulsed across her skin at his touch.

She leaned into him, pleading for more. For once, she wasn't confused about him. She trusted him; he hadn't harmed her before, she knew that, and she instinctively knew he wouldn't harm her now.

Her eyes closed with sweet surrender.

He continued to kiss her as his hand slipped beneath her dress to untie her short stays. Desperate for the breath he was stealing away by removing even less clothes than her own maid would have before bed, Peyton tore her mouth away. But she didn't shrink from his persistent kisses that found her neck and made her flesh shiver. His lips rested tantalizingly against the pounding pulse at the base of her throat even as his hands brushed lightly beneath her dress and corset. Her chemise might have not been there at all given the way the heat of his hands warmed through it and into her skin.

"Devlin," she murmured, although she couldn't have said if his name was meant in protest or encouragement. But when he rubbed his palms over her breasts and made them ache for more, the mewling that fell from her lips was all pleasure.

"You are alive, Peyton." He lazily strummed his thumbs over her nipples and made them harden against the soft cotton of her chemise. His dark gaze watched his hands as they languidly teased her breasts, as if he had all night to do nothing more than this. God help her, she would have let him. "You're warm and humming with life, pulsating with it...and so very beautiful because of it."

She didn't stop him when he tugged down her bodice and placed his mouth to her breast—she didn't *want* to stop him. His lips closed around her nipple through her chemise and sucked. At first, the sensation was so light she barely felt it, only for the pull of his lips to increase its intensity, little by little, until he'd taken her nipple completely into his mouth and was laving it hungrily with his tongue. A wet circle formed in the cotton fabric. When he blew a stream of cold air through it and onto the nipple beneath, she let out a startled gasp that transformed into a low moan when he closed his warm mouth over her again.

A liquid heat bubbled low in her belly.

Then he moved to the other breast and began the sweet torture all over again. The heat in her belly sank lower and lodged achingly between her legs.

"Can't you feel it?" His deep voice rumbled against her breast and into her chest. "All that life in you, all the promise of wonderful things to come... Embrace it, Peyton. Take comfort in it."

She couldn't find her voice to respond. All she could manage was a breathless, "Show me how..."

He placed a kiss to her lips that was so filled with reassurance that her eyes stung with emotion.

His hands slid tantalizingly down her body to the hem of her skirt and slipped beneath. When his palm changed directions and moved back up her calf, a shiver stirred in its wake that blossomed goosebumps over her bare thigh above the lace of her stocking. His fingers stroked along the curve of her calf and teased at the back of her knee. As with his kisses, he was in no rush, and the desire he roused inside her wasn't so much a flaming need but a decadently slow burn. He emphasized that by the unhurried sweep of his finger beneath her garter and a torturously slow circle around her leg.

She knew he didn't want to frighten her, didn't want to hurry in this first encounter after all the secrets between them had been revealed. But she *needed* his touch in a way she'd never needed another man's comfort before. She wanted exactly what he'd promised—*to feel alive again.*

"Devlin," she whispered and shifted on his lap to part her legs as far as possible beneath the confines of her skirt in invitation to be touched.

Even then, though, he didn't rush. The slow brush of his hand up her inner thigh was simply torturous, compounded by the ever-gentle assault of his lips on hers in featherlight kisses that were barely kisses at all, in whispered words only slightly more than mere breaths.

A whimper fell from her lips. He lightly squeezed her inner thigh in a wordless urge to be patient. His hand drifted upward in slow caresses toward the throbbing ache at her core, moving so agonizingly slowly... The anticipation aching inside her became unbearable.

"Please," she whispered and closed her eyes as she rested her cheek against his.

When his fingertips finally touched her core, she shuddered against him. He caressed her as gently as he had kissed her, the tease of his fingertips as light as his lips. Thank God it was, or she might have shot right out of her skin from the sheer joy of it. Good Lord, he was barely touching her! Yet desire pulsed through her with a wanton need that left her panting.

He leisurely stroked the length of the damp cleft between her legs, fanning both heat and wetness beneath his fingertips until her folds were silky smooth and slippery. With every pass, his fingers delved slightly deeper, until one slipped inside her tight warmth.

The gasp on her lips faded into a throaty moan. She knew he could feel her wetness with every slow, slippery caress in and out of her tight core, knew he could feel her aching arousal, but she simply didn't care how wanton he thought her. He was right—she felt alive. For the first time in years, she could feel her blood coursing through her body and reveled in the pulse of electricity out to the ends of her hair and the tips of her fingers and toes, and she didn't want him to stop.

When she was a girl, when she'd been so infatuated with Devlin that she turned scarlet if he did so little as glance in her direction, she never would have imagined him doing such a thing to her. But now…oh, now she wanted this—wanted *him*—with every ounce of her being.

Her body shamelessly bore down on his fingers as they continued to thrust inside her, coming faster and harder now to feed her growing desire. Soft mewlings of yearning and encouragement rose from her lips, and she arched herself against him to meet each wonderful slide inside her.

"More," she begged, her arms wrapped fiercely around his neck and her fingers grasping at his soft hair. "Oh, please, Devlin…more!"

A second finger joined the first and stretched her intimate lips wider. The sensation of being filled shivered deliciously through her, and she writhed against his hand, unable to sit still. Biting down a cry of pleasure, she rolled back her head as he pumped harder and faster into her.

She was barely aware when his second hand slipped down between them and spread her folds open wide, exposing her most sensitive place to his touch. His thumb teased the hard bead he found there, flicking against it lightly like the flutter of butterfly wings, then squeezing—

Her hips bucked as a jolt of electricity sparked through her so intensely that she gasped for breath. She was so close to shattering in his arms that a begging whimper for just that fell unbidden from her trembling lips. She could do nothing more than cling to him as he gave her what she so desperately craved and stroked her a second time, this time holding her open wide as he simultaneously rubbed the hard heel of his hand against her clitoris and thrust his fingers deep inside her.

A fierce cry tore from her. As blinding pleasure rushed over her, she threw back her head, and her body spasmed uncontrollably against his. He held his fingers deep inside her tight heat while her folds quivered around his hand, drawing out her sweet release even longer. She collapsed against him and panted hard to catch back her breath. Only when the tide of pleasure began to fade and the roar of her heartbeat in her ears faded did she realize that he was whispering sweet words of reassurance into her ear.

She shifted back only far enough to stare down into his eyes as they looked back at her in the shadows, as filled with desire as her own must have been. There were so many more pleasures they could give each other, so many more intimacies to share. She craved exactly that. She wanted nothing more at that moment than to continue to feel alive. With him.

When he slowly slipped his fingers from her warmth, the loss of him flooded through her and left an emptiness in his place, and she realized for the first time that the carriage had stopped. Her desired-fogged mind faintly registered that they had arrived at her townhouse and that he was now buttoning up her bodice and fixing her dress so she could look presentable to leave the carriage.

But leaving him tonight was the very last thing she wanted.

Come inside with me, come to my bed… She brushed trembling fingertips along his jaw. *Make love to me in every possibly wicked way you can imagine.* She rested her palm against his chest and felt the fierce pounding of his heartbeat beneath her fingertips. *Make me burn with need for you, then bring me to tears with agonizing release, over and over…*

She threw all caution to the wind by whispering, "Devlin, I want you to—"

An ear-shattering explosion tore through the townhouse. The carriage team startled and bolted a few feet down the street until the coachman could wrestle them back under control, tossing both Peyton and Devlin to the floor. But Peyton didn't wait for the carriage to stop before darting out the door and racing toward the house.

Chapter Twelve

DEVLIN LET OUT a curse and charged from the carriage after her. But she was too fast and had raced into the burning house before he could catch her.

"Send for the fire brigade!" Devlin ordered the tiger, who stood on the footpath and stared dumbstruck at the building as flames quickly engulfed it. As Devlin ran toward the house, the butler stumbled out, coughing and hacking to clear his lungs of the black smoke. "Organize buckets," he called out to the butler. "Now!"

Then he leapt up the front stairs and rushed inside.

Black smoke and heat from the growing flames eating their way forward from the rear of the house engulfed him. He pulled his cravat over his mouth, bent down to keep away from the thickening smoke overhead, and hurried on.

"Peyton!" he yelled above the noise of the flames and the creaking beams damaged from the initial explosion. If he didn't find her soon, they would both be dead in a matter of minutes.

He ran from room to room, searching for her. The dark rooms were lit by the licking flames racing through the townhouse yet further darkened by the thickening smoke, but it was enough for him to see she wasn't there.

"Peyton!" *Where the hell are you?*

Then he heard her—her voice calling out above the noise of the fire from the rear of the house, but not for him. She was screaming frantically at the top of her smoke-choked lungs for Wilkins and Proctor.

He ran to her and grabbed her arm to stop her just as she was about to start up the rear steps toward the floors above. The fire from the explosion had already engulfed the back of the house and was lapping at the walls and floors, and the stairs groaned beneath the weight of the flames from the cellar below. If she tried to go down them, they would have collapsed beneath her.

"Let me go!" she cried, her voice hoarse from inhaling smoke and coughing. But Devlin held fast and refused to let go of her arm. "I've got to find them—Proctor! Wilkins!" A new fit of coughing gripped her lungs. "I've got to make certain they're safe."

A window exploded from the heat. Devlin instinctively shielded her with his body and his face with his arm. The sound reverberated through the house like cannon fire and tore a soft scream from her.

"And I have to make certain *you're* safe," he countered.

Without asking her permission, he scooped her into his arms and tossed her over his shoulder, then ran back with her through the house toward the front door. She angrily swung her fists and kicked her legs, only to capitulate after just a few feet's progress through the smoke that was now as black as pitch and so thick that each hot breath seared his lungs.

Just as they reached the entry hall, the ceiling groaned angrily beneath the weight of the flames and gave way. Plaster, lath, and beams crashed down upon them in a shower of debris and bright sparks. A piece of wood hit his arm, and he stumbled, nearly dropping Peyton to the floor. But there was no time to hesitate, so he grabbed her hand and ran with her through the door and out into the street.

They paused at the bottom of the steps to fill their lungs with fresh air, with Devlin bent over nearly double as coughs racked his chest.

"You're hurt," Peyton rasped out between coughs as she reached for him. "Your arm…"

He glanced down. A long rip had torn through his left jacket sleeve and into the muscle beneath, and already bright blood had seeped into his white shirtsleeve. But he dismissed it with a gritting of his teeth and laced his fingers through hers.

"Come on," he ordered and pulled her along with him. "We can't say here."

"But—Wilkins—and Proctor—" She glanced over her shoulder at the townhouse, not strong enough to halt his steps and make him go back. "We have to save them!"

"It's too late." He hurried her through the small crowd of curiosity-seekers already gathering on the footpath. He had to take her away from here. *Immediately.* "If they're not already out—"

"No!" She yanked his arm and dug in her heels. "I have to help them!"

He stopped and leaned toward her, his voice low and deadly serious. "And who helps you if the person who set that explosion realizes you weren't inside when it went off?" He could afford no misunderstanding about this. "Townhouses don't explode like that unless someone wanted them to. They tried to kill you tonight, and they'll try again as soon as they realize they failed."

Her face paled even in the moving shadows cast by the flickering flames of the inferno raging behind them.

"There are enough people here to help those who might still be inside." He glanced over her shoulder at the gathering crowd, then narrowed his eyes on her. "You are my primary concern, understand?"

"Yes," she whispered, clearly unconvinced.

But he didn't have time for more persuasion. He took her elbow and pulled her along with him as his long strides hurried away from the house, down the street, and around the corner. Then around another corner. Only then did he slow his pace and let her catch her breath. Finally, they emerged onto a wide avenue. Devlin stepped to the edge of the footpath and waved an arm to signal for a hackney.

When a small carriage stopped beside them, he yanked open the door and helped her inside. "Brownlow Street in St Giles," he ordered the driver.

The jarvey pulled at the brim of his rain-dampened beaver hat, flicked the ribbons, and started the old horse forward.

"Where are we going?" she asked as he settled onto the seat across from her.

"To a refuge." He let that be enough answer for now. "You'll be safe there."

Thankfully, she didn't press him for more information. Instead, she asked, "Why didn't we take my carriage?"

"Because I don't trust your coachman or tigers."

"I hired them myself." Her words were forced out between rapid breaths. "They can be trusted."

He glanced out the window at the rainy night and muttered, "I don't trust anyone around you."

He saw the cold realization finally seep over her that tonight had been an attempt on her life. "Why would anyone want to harm me? No one knows who I am."

He turned back to her. "And yet, in the few weeks you've been here, you've managed to make yourself visible to half of society at the opera, the gamblers and courtesans at Barton's, and nearly every member of Parliament who was present at Vauxhall. Quite noticeably, too."

"Only to gain your attention," she admitted quietly beneath the loud squeak of the hackney's wheels, looking small and vulnerable. Even in the darkness, he could see her hands shaking as they rested in her lap. "It didn't matter what anyone else thought as long as I was able to get close to you."

"Then disappear as secretly as you'd arrived." *Not* a question. "Looks like your plans have changed."

She silently turned to stare out the window, although he

knew she could see nothing of the dark city except black shapes and moving shadows.

Half an hour of silence later, they arrived in St Giles, and the carriage horse let out a shudder of relief as the jarvey reined it to a stop. Devlin helped Peyton to the muddy ground and did his best not to notice that she was still trembling. He tossed up a coin for the old driver, who was most likely thrilled to be on his way out of the dangerous neighborhood and back toward the safety in the west.

"This way." Devlin led her toward a small warehouse halfway down the street. Thankfully, for once, she didn't fight him.

He rapped his knuckles against the door and waited. He frowned at Peyton who stared at the wet ground, her face lowered into the shadows. Unable to resist, he caressed her cheek with his knuckles.

She lifted her face to look at him.

"It will be all right," he assured her.

"You don't know that," she argued breathlessly. In the dim light he could see the watery glistening of her eyes. "Proctor, Wilkins…what will I do without them? They're all I have."

You have me. But he couldn't utter that aloud.

A few minutes later, the small, square-shaped inset window in the door opened, and the soft glow of candlelight lit a round face as it peered out. Wide eyes blinked with surprise and sleep. "Mr. Hunter? Is that you, sir?"

Devlin squeezed Peyton's arm in warning to say nothing. "Sorry to disturb you so late, Mrs. Martin. Can you let us in?"

"Of course!" The window snapped closed, and behind the door came the fumbling sound of dangling keys and the clank of metal in the lock.

The door flung open and revealed an older, plump woman in a flannel dressing robe cinched tightly around her wide waist and a large night cap over her graying hair. Her sleep-blurred eyes blinked rapidly, this time to clear away the fog of interrupted sleep, as she stepped aside to let them pass into the house.

She glanced into the street, taking long looks in both directions. "No children with you?"

"Not tonight. Just me and a friend." He gestured at Peyton. No other introduction would be made, certainly no explanation given for why Peyton looked so distraught. And her clothing singed at the hem.

But the older woman understood and nodded as she closed the door behind them and locked it securely against the night. After all, in the past five years that Devlin had employed her, she'd grown used to not asking questions. Beginning with his real name. Certainly she knew he wasn't Mr. Hunter.

Devlin couldn't have been blessed with a better partner in running Brechenhurst than Mrs. Martin. An experienced former housekeeper at an orphanage in Twyford, she kept an orderly house, supervised a maid of all work and a property caretaker, and took excellent care of the two dozen or so children who appeared on the property's doorstep every night, seeking shelter from the streets. But what the children needed most was simply a piece of bread, a cup of clean water, and a safe place to sleep out of the elements and away from harm. From the last midnight clang of St Giles-of-the-Fields until the bells sounded again in the morning, the front door was locked tight, the children safe inside. They were all given a bit of food to take with them for breakfast when they were turned out in the morning so the house could be cleaned and readied for another batch of small visitors come nightfall. Mrs. Martin somehow managed to squeeze them all into the beds on the floors above that had been turned into dormitories without turning any of them away, and the only complaint he ever heard from her was her frustration at not being able to provide help to even more children.

"We'll spend the night downstairs," Devlin told her. "No one is to know we're here, not even Miss Smith and Mr. Hobbes." He glanced at Peyton and frowned. *I don't trust anyone around you.*

"Of course, Mr. Hunter." Mrs. Martin paused. "Do you want me to bring food and drink for you?" Her eyes flicked to his wounded arm, but she knew her place and didn't comment directly, instead asking, "Or anything else?"

"No, thank you. But I will need your help delivering two messages." He held out his hand for her candle. "May I?"

When she handed it over without question, he stepped to the small desk positioned near the door from where Mrs. Martin manned the entrance from sunset until midnight every night. He took two note cards and picked up the quill, then quickly scrawled out two messages, folded, and sealed them with a drop of wax. He wrote the direction on the front of each and snatched up a second candle and holder sitting on the desk. He lit the stub and carried all of it back to Mrs. Martin.

He handed over her candle and the two messages. "Have those delivered immediately by one of the older boys staying here tonight." He gave her a coin. "Give him this for his troubles. Tell him that each man to whom he delivers the message will pay him another coin when they read it."

"I know just the boy. Albert can be trusted."

"Thank you." Devlin nodded, took Peyton's arm, and lifted the candle to guide their way. "Good night."

"Good night, Mr. Hunter. Sleep well."

He glanced at Peyton with concern. Sleep? *Impossible.* Yet he nodded his gratitude and escorted her across the large front room that served as dining hall, common room, and reception for the children who sought refuge here and toward the wide wooden steps in the center of the building where porters had once stomped up and down to store goods in the old warehouse.

"Mr. Hunter?" Peyton murmured, her voice as soft as shadows around them.

"You're not the only one with a false identity, Lady Payne."

"Yes, but you're a duke. I'm dead to the world." She paused for a beat before adding in her grief, "And now the world is dead to me."

"Oh no, it's not." But the firmness with which he said that did nothing to lessen her anguish.

Instead of leading her upstairs, he guided her down into the cellar. He unlocked the door barring their way at the bottom of the steps, and she stopped and stared at the room beyond when he pushed open the door.

Her hand dropped away from his arm. "What is this place?"

"It was used to store casks of wine," he explained as he closed and locked the door behind them. He paused to take a look around what could be seen of the long, narrow cellar in the dim candlelight. It was filled with fighting equipment and a separate living space at the far end where he could collapse from exhaustion after a long night of training or haunting the city streets...or from being haunted. "Now its purpose is the same as the three floors above."

Her gaze fixed on a dummy target made of burlap sack, sawdust, and reed layers that had seen too many days at the end of his sword. "Which is?"

He acknowledged quietly, "A refuge."

She arched a disbelieving brow.

He took her arm and led her through the room in the soft light of the candle so she wouldn't trip over any unseen apparatus in the dark that he had left strewn across the floor after his last visit. "I use this place to hone my fighting edge," he explained vaguely. And where he could physically take out his frustrations and lingering resentments. Here, he could let loose the pent-up anger that he hid from the rest of the world. Anthony Titus had taught him that. *Control.* The problem wasn't when a fighter succumbed to his emotions; that always needed to happen in the end, one way or another. No, the problem was when those emotions couldn't be controlled until they could be dealt with.

Here, he could control them.

He guided her to a separate room in the rear of the cellar. Although calling the room a bedroom was a stretch, it did hold a small bed...and nothing else except a worn leather reading chair where he usually tossed his clothes and a bedside table that held a bottle of brandy, which he often needed far more than the bed. A rickety old Franklin stove sat in the corner, its pipe sticking up thorough a hole in the foundation and emerging in the sliver of the rear yard tucked behind the building.

"We'll stay here for the night," he explained as he closed the door and set the candle on the stove. "You're safe. No one knows to look for us here." He added in a mutter as he knelt in front of the stove and began to build a small fire inside its metal belly, "Not even my family."

"And Mr. Hunter?"

He pushed the candle inside the grate to light the tinder. "He's a very private patron who owns the building and funds the services it provides."

"What exactly are those services?"

His lips curled slightly as he concentrated on the fire. She was asking questions, if quietly. That was a good sign. "We take in homeless children who have nowhere else to go for shelter and security. We ask no questions, give them a small meal and a clean bed, and provide a safe place for them to spend the night, with a locked door between them and whoever might want to harm them. From dusk to dawn, we provide a temporary reprieve from the streets."

When the flame caught, he tossed in a few lumps of coal and stirred them until a small but growing warmth emanated from the stove.

"Sometimes we're able to find work for the older ones, positions on ships or in households. A few want to go to school. Some come for several nights in a row. Others stay once and never come back." He rocked back onto his heels and flipped shut the front grill. "Mostly, though, we address the most pressing needs of food and shelter from the weather."

She nodded toward the training room. "Something tells me Mr. Hunter does far more in this place than just write cheques."

"As I said, it's a refuge." Devlin pushed himself up to his full height. "Sometimes Mr. Hunter finds children on the streets himself and sends them here."

"And sometimes he goes out looking for children to help, I would wager," she added quietly, still standing by the door but not yet entering.

"Sometimes," he admitted, carrying the candle to the bedside table. "Only children on the streets know about this place, and even then, most children who hear about it think it's a fairytale. They can't bring themselves to believe that someone might care about what happens to them."

"And why does Mr. Hunter care?"

If he had to explain that, the night would be very long. Instead, he poured a glass of brandy from the bottle sitting on the table. He took a long, calming swallow, then held it out toward her.

"Until we can learn more about the explosion," he said, bluntly changing the conversation, "this is the best place for us to hide. I've sent word to two friends to ask for their help...Lucien Grenier and Chase Maddox." Neither man had any idea this place existed. By morning, his two old friends would learn the last of his secrets. "We can trust them with our lives."

With a silent sigh that drooped her shoulders, she came into the room and took the glass from his hand. She took a long drink, then rested the back of her hand against her lips as the liquor seeped down her slender throat.

"Thank you," she whispered between her fingers. "For...everything."

He gestured for her to turn around. "I'll undo you, if you'd like, and then we can go to bed and try for sleep." *Try.* Precious little would come tonight for either of them.

"In my experience," she said, forcing a thin smile, "going to bed precipitates the undoing."

He knew she was aiming for the same flirtatious sassiness she'd engaged in with him at Barton's, but the attempt fell flat. Still, she was trying, and he took hope in that. Perhaps her grief wouldn't overwhelm her after all, no matter what Lucien and Chase learned about the explosion or whose lives it had claimed.

"And in *my* experience," he returned, matching her attempt at playfulness, "an undoing doesn't require a bed at all."

She tossed back the rest of the brandy and held the empty glass out to him. "Then you shouldn't mind at all if I take the bed while you spend the night on the floor." She turned her back to him and warned over her shoulder as she gestured at her bodice, "Don't stretch the fabric."

With a chuckle, he set the glass aside. He slowly unfastened the short row of buttons until her bodice sagged over her breasts. His fingers brushed over her bare skin as he pushed her capped sleeves off her shoulders and down her arms, and her dress puddled at her feet, leaving her in her shift and stays. Removing her dress should have been difficult, far too much of a wanton temptation to strip her completely bare and have his way with her. But he managed to hang on to his control...until he dared to remove her hair pins and take down her hair. When he brushed his fingers through her dark tresses until they hung loose around her slender shoulders, the sweet torture of touching her nearly undid him.

He pulled in a deep and silent breath to steady his hands as he unlaced her short corset, slowly loosening it one long pull at a time. Whenever his knuckles caressed the thin shift and felt the warmth of her skin beneath, he had to fight the urge to place his mouth against her nape and lick his way down her spine, to peel away every layer of clothing until she was breathtakingly naked before his eyes, quivering with desire—

Christ. He was losing his mind.

The corset dropped away, and he stepped back to snatch up the glass and pour himself a very full drink. Of course, it didn't help that her warm curves were covered only by a thin shift and stockings. For the first time, he thanked God that the room had a dark stove instead of a fireplace that would have silhouetted her curves through the thin cotton as if she wore nothing at all.

"Your arm." Her soft voice curled around him like a ribbon. "You hurt it."

He glanced down at his torn and bloodied sleeve, then took a long swallow of liquor and welcomed the burn down his throat. "It's nothing."

"Liar." She waved her hand at him. "Take off that jacket so I can look at it."

"It's only a scratch." Yet he shrugged off the tiger's poorly fitting jacket he still wore from their visit to St Giles and dropped it to the floor. "It doesn't need nursing."

She said nothing, but determination flickered in her eyes. He was thrilled to see it instead of the grief she'd been wearing for the past hour. Yet his breath strangled in his throat when she reached to unbutton his waistcoat.

He took her wrists and stilled her hands. "What are you doing?"

"Undressing you so I can look at your arm for myself." She tsked her tongue. "Surely, Devlin Raines doesn't mind being undressed by a woman."

"Well then." He held his arms out wide and gave her his best rakish grin. "Who am I to stop you?"

She slid him a cutting look, yet she carefully removed his waistcoat and only lightly scraped his wounded arm as she slid it off his shoulders and onto the floor. Truthfully, though, the dull throbbing in his arm was nothing compared to the throbbing at his crotch.

She untied his cravat and slipped it off his neck, then turned away and crossed the room to the wash basin near the stove. "Take off your shirt."

"Yes, ma'am." He grinned to himself as he pulled down his braces to let them dangle around his hips. The shirt slipped over his head and off. With his left arm completely bare, he could see the wound now and assess it for himself. Perhaps it was more than a mere scratch. So for a better view, he turned toward the dim light of the candle burning on the bedside table next to the bottle of cognac.

"Do you think we should send for a surgeon?" She frowned

into the water pitcher and set it back down. "Empty." She glanced over her shoulder at him. "I can go upstairs for water unless you…"

Her voice trailed off as she stared at him, eyes wide and stunned.

He froze. He didn't have to look over his shoulder to see what had startled her. He knew. *Christ.* For the first time in his life, he hadn't remembered to hide his back, too caught up in the sweet temptation of her nearness. Shame and humiliation pulsed through him.

"Dear God," she whispered, her eyes scouring over the rough scars on his back. "What on earth happened to you?"

Chapter Thirteen

PEYTON WAS BARELY able to keep hold of her breath as she stared at Devlin. The lines across his back and shoulders, crisscrossing unevenly at angry angles… *Good Lord*. She'd never seen so many scars on one man before, except for a soldier she'd met in France who had been whipped for deserting his regiment. That man had received two hundred lashes and barely survived.

Had Devlin been…*whipped*?

Her heart lurched into her throat. "Devlin…?"

He shrugged as if it were nothing more troubling than a sunburn and turned his back away from her as he refilled his glass, the loose braces bumping dismissively against his hips. "It's nothing to be concerned about."

"Truly?" She arched a brow at his indifference and returned to him, empty-handed. No cloth to clean the wound except for his cravat, no water to wet it… "Because to me, it looks like you've been beaten." She dunked the neckcloth unceremoniously into his glass of brandy. "Repeatedly."

"If you're going to answer your own questions, there's no point in asking me." Frowning at the cravat in his glass, he slowly pulled it out of the brandy and dangled the long piece of cloth in the air. His mouth twisted as he watched it drip onto the floor. "That was a waste of perfectly good cognac."

"No, it wasn't." Taking back the soaked cloth, she brought his arm toward her. She dabbed as gently as possible at the long, bloodied wound sliced into his forearm.

He sucked in a harsh breath through clenched teeth at the sting of the liquor, and his arm flexed, the muscle tightening. But to his credit, he didn't pull away. He might be keeping secrets of his own, but at least he wasn't running away from them. Or from her. She admired that.

The dried blood slowly washed away to reveal a long but clean cut. It would be painful until it healed, certainly, but he was in no danger of bleeding to death or losing his arm. She would have said he would have an ugly scar, but... Well, one surreptitious glance at what she could see of his back told her he cared little about that.

"It might need stitches." She wound the neckcloth around his forearm as a makeshift bandage and tied it off as gently as she could. It would do for now. "We should send for a surgeon."

"No need." He glanced down at his arm. "I've had worse."

"So I see." She dared to step behind him and run her fingers over the hard ridges of the old scars. His muscles quivered beneath her touch, yet he didn't walk away. Something dark and unspoken told her he needed to reveal them as much as she needed to see them. Whatever had put them there, it wasn't an accident. "Who did this to you?"

"You've been studying my family for years." He turned his head to ask her quietly over his shoulder, "Don't you recognize my father's handiwork when you see it?"

Her hand froze. "Dartmoor did this...to his own son?" Her fingertips curled into his back muscle as shock and revulsion surged through her. She whispered in little more than a breathless rasp, "I knew he was despicable, but this... Oh, dear God." She swallowed down the bile rising in her throat. "When?"

"For years, starting when I was just a boy, still in the schoolroom."

He took a slow step forward and moved just out of her reach.

Her empty hand fell to her side.

"He had flares of anger he would take out on whoever—or whatever—he could." Devlin set down his empty glass and reached for the bottle itself to raise to his lips for a long drink. Although he now carefully kept his front turned toward her, he didn't meet her gaze as he quietly continued, "Horses, dogs...me, Mother, Margaret...or whatever servant was nearby."

"Not Theodora?" *Please God, not Teddy!*

He shook his head. "She was too young and still out of his reach in the nursery."

Relief eased down her shoulders, yet she nodded in the direction of his back. "It wasn't hands that did that."

"No. This was the work of switches, straps, an occasional riding crop." He shrugged in macabre acceptance. "At least the fireplace poker never broke the skin."

She placed her hand on her belly. Good heavens, she was going to be sick! "And your mother—*she knew?*"

Despite his attempt to keep his face inscrutable, Peyton could see his pain. "There was nothing she could do to stop it. She tried, only for him to turn his anger onto her. So she protected me the only way she could by sending me away to Eton, where I learned to fight." He set down the bottle on the bedside stand and faced her, his arms crossed over his bare chest and unknowingly calling attention to the size and definition of his biceps and shoulders. "When I was eighteen and returned home from school, I was finally able to stop him."

"You did more than that, though, didn't you?" She closed the distance between them. With her eyes never leaving his, she reached a trembling hand to his cheek. Even now, so many years after the event, she felt the fury still lingering inside him.

"I told him that if he ever touched any of us again, I'd kill him. I meant it."

He turned his head to place a kiss to her palm, but there was nothing desirous about the gesture. It wasn't a kiss. It was a promise...to protect her from her father's ghost just as he'd protected his family from his father.

But he couldn't protect her from the past. That was a battle she had to win on her own.

She cupped his face between her hands and rose up on tiptoes to bring her lips to his. She blinked hard to keep the stinging tears at bay as she tenderly moved her mouth against his.

Slowly, the tension faded from him, and she felt him relax, even when she slid her arms around his waist and stepped into his embrace. She buried her face against his shoulder and closed her eyes to absorb this moment within the solid circle of his arms. She needed his strength and resolve, now more than ever.

"You had your family and friends to help you," she whispered against the bare skin of his neck. "Even now you have them." Her arms tightened their hold on him as she dared to whisper the thought that now tortured her. "How will I go on without Wilkins and Proctor to help me?" Her voice was little more than a rasping breath. "If they were killed tonight…"

"You don't know yet that you've lost them. The explosion came from the rear of the cellar near the service yard. Your butler got out, so did the maids and footmen. If they all got out, Wilkins and Proctor might have, too. You have to hold on to that hope until we know more."

She nodded, her chin rubbing against his shoulder with each bob of her head. Yet she remained wholly unconvinced.

He stepped back with a tender caress of his knuckles across her cheek. "Now, you need to rest." He pulled back the covers of the bed, then held out his hand. "I can't offer you a hot bath to wash away the night, but I can provide a soft mattress and clean sheets."

She looked at the bed and shook her head. She wouldn't be able to sleep a wink, no matter how physically and emotionally drained she was.

"Why are you doing this?" She didn't mean giving up his bed.

He knew that, too, based on his somber countenance. "Because we both want the same thing—Horrender brought to justice."

Nodding slowly, the last of her energy draining away, she removed her stockings and laid them over the footboard. Then she slipped her hand into his and allowed him to help her into bed.

Her body tingled from the slide of the coverlet over her bare legs and up to her shoulders. She nearly laughed. No man had ever tucked her into bed before. That it was Devlin, a notorious rake and the man who now permeated her thoughts, made it all the more ludicrous. Deliciously, temptingly ludicrous.

When he moved away from the bed, she reached for his hand. "Where are you spending the night?"

He tossed a glance toward the battered leather reading chair. "I've done it before."

Now knowing the ghosts that haunted him, she held no doubts that he'd spent many a tortured night here, training until he wore himself into physical exhaustion, then collapsing into the chair and hoping for sweet oblivion. She'd done the same countless times herself in France.

"Stay," she cajoled. "You can sleep here with me."

He didn't move, except to stare down at her with the same expression as a child with his nose pressed against the sweets shop window—a desperate longing mixed with the grim realization that it would not be his for the taking. Not tonight.

Then, reluctantly, he nodded, and a quiet thrill darted through her. He pulled the bedding up to her neck, then blew out the candle and lay on his back on the mattress next to her, on top of the coverlet that separated them.

In the silent darkness, the small room lit only by the dim glow through the stove grill, they both stared up at the floor overhead. Neither moved, but Peyton could feel the steady rise and fall of his breathing, just as she could feel the weight of his large body sinking into the mattress and gravity slowly nudging her toward him.

With a grimace, she rolled on to her side, putting her back to him. There would be no more intimacies tonight. At least not physical ones.

"You said we'll know more in the morning," she whispered into the shadows, repeating his earlier words. Even with his comforting presence next to her, her worry returned with the silent shadows. "Are you certain?"

"Yes." He turned toward her and slipped his arm across her over the coverlet to hold her close. He hesitated, then his deep voice tickled the back of her neck as he murmured, "Your father was willingly part of it, Peyton. You need to accept that, or you will always be in danger."

She nodded against the pillow. He was right, she knew. But... "How could he have done something like that? He was a good man, a wonderful husband and father. How could he..."

When her voice trailed off, the deep silence once more enveloped them, until Devlin murmured, "He wasn't evil. He was simply ambitious, and to his credit, he didn't know all that Dartmoor and Crewe—and especially Horrender—had been doing. He was part of the smuggling, the brothels, the stolen goods, all of that. But he didn't know about the children who were—" When his voice broke, she knew he was suffering just as much as she was over what their fathers had done, the lies that had been told, the lives that had been destroyed. "Who were forced into slave labor and offered up to the highest bidders for...God only knows what exactly."

That bit of self-censorship was meant to protect her, but horrifying images filled her mind of terrible possibilities until she had to bite her inner cheek to keep from crying.

Sensing her anguish, he nuzzled his mouth against her hair. "Dartmoor and Crewe had funneled those profits through the fencing operations and the brothels so Chandler wouldn't know the truth. When he discovered what they'd been doing, he felt they'd gone too far. It was one thing to smuggle French goods and sell them to their friends or profit from prostitution that was already happening, but it was something else altogether to exploit children. In your father's eyes, the entire enterprise had to be shut down."

A tendril of hope rose inside her, and she clung to it, praying her memory of her father could still be redeemed.

"So Chandler gave them an ultimatum. He would inform the authorities if they didn't stop their criminal activities by year's end, changing the illegal operations to legal ones where possible, shutting down the rest completely." Devlin's arm tightened around her as he pulled her back against his front and nestled her against him. "He gave them until the night of the musicale to make their decision."

Her mind raced back through the years to that night, and she fought to bring back into focus every detail she could, no matter how small. She could hear the music flowing around her, smell the floral scent of beeswax candles, taste the bitter-sweetness of sugared orange peels and the unexpected bite of her first glass of claret. In her mind's eye, she could see the women in their fine dresses, the men in their kerseymere jackets, and all of them glittering beneath the chandeliers and floating along as if in a dream. She'd had no idea that darkness lurked among such bright rooms.

At every moment of that night, her silly girl's attention had been fixed someplace else. Somewhere not important. While her father had been dealing with matters of life and death, she'd sat in the corner and pouted because Devlin had never noticed she was even there.

"That's what they'd fought about that night," he continued quietly. "Dartmoor and Crewe refused his demands. Your father stormed out, collected you and your mother, and you all started for home."

She rolled over to face him. Even in the darkness, she could see his resigned expression. But then, he'd had a decade to process everything that had happened that night, while she was still fitting together bits and pieces into a desperate puzzle.

"But Dartmoor and Crewe panicked." Now facing each other

on the bed, he brushed his fingertips lightly over her cheek, as if they were lovers sharing a tender moment rather than what they truly were—two people who barely trusted each other. "They were both peers and could have claimed privilege to have the charges dismissed—they hadn't yet committed murder—but the scandal would have ruined them." He tenderly traced his fingertips along her jaw to her ear, but she knew he wasn't looking at her. He was lost in that night ten years ago. Just as she was. "Charles Chandler had to be removed as a threat. He knew how all the money had been earned, where it had been hidden, and exactly how to link it back to them. If your father was silenced, no one would ever be able to prove what they'd been doing."

"So they sent Horrender after us."

"Only as a warning." He shook his head. "They didn't think Horrender would kill any of you, just threaten your father. Horrender was supposed to have stopped the carriage, dragged Chandler out and beaten him to within an inch of his life, then threatened to kill him and his family if he dared breathe a word of what he knew. But Horrender decided to issue his own kind of warning and attempted to murder all of you."

She pulled in a deep breath, afraid of the answer yet needing to know. "And you? What did you do that night, exactly?"

"I walked downstairs into the study and straight into the hornets' nest. The two dukes were arguing, and I overheard their plan." He rolled onto his back and hooked his arm beneath his head. "I rode out after your carriage to stop the attack but arrived too late. Your parents were already dead, but I stopped the man who had gone after you. You were unconscious. I picked you up and raced with you to the nearest surgeon. When I was handing you over to him, you woke up for only a moment, grabbed at my waistcoat—that must have been when you ripped off the button." He paused. "I left you there and went to your home, to inform the household of what happened. The next morning, I was told you had died. Lucien and I attended your funeral three days later."

Slowly, fighting back tears, she slid her hand across the coverlet to take his as it rested on the mattress between them and laced her fingers through his. She now knew everything he could tell her about that night. So many pieces of the puzzled snapped into place that she could barely comprehend it all, yet she also knew some bits were still missing and most likely always would be.

But she wasn't alone any longer. They were in this together now.

When his fingers reassuringly squeezed hers, a single tear slipped down her cheek and soaked into the pillow.

"Thank you, Devlin," she whispered.

He'd given her a gift tonight. Her father hadn't been completely innocent, and his behavior could never be fully absolved. But she knew now the limits of his criminality and could begin to come to terms with the man he had truly been.

She also knew exactly how much Devlin blamed himself for not stopping the events of that night, how much guilt he still carried over what their fathers had done.

"That's why you created this place, isn't it?" Her voice was no louder than a breath. "To atone for what our fathers did."

"Yes."

Peyton doubted that anything the two of them did could ever be enough to provide the kind of restitution those crimes deserved. Yet Devlin proved to her that they could try, and hope fluttered in her heart. For the first time in too many years to count, she could finally believe that the future might help right the past, that she might have a way forward.

"I will help you, Peyton, however I can, to remove you from danger and stop whoever is targeting you. I promise you that." He lifted her hand to his lips and kissed it before resting it on his chest. His slow, strong heartbeat pulsed against her fingertips. "But what happened that night—what our fathers and Crewe's did all those years ago—none of that can ever come to light. Understand?"

Dread tightened her chest, squeezing the little bit of hope from her heart, and she slipped her hand free of his. "No, I don't. We're on the verge of stopping Horrender from harming anyone I care about ever again. If that means shouting out from the rooftop what our fathers did, then I am all for the shouting."

He rolled away from her and slipped off the bed. With his braces still dangling around his hips, he snatched up the bottle of cognac and collapsed into the leather reading chair. His gaze burned darkly into hers.

"What good would it do to reveal it all now?" he asked, contemplating the bottle.

"It might stop Horrender from—"

"*Might* stop," he repeated her words. "*If* it's even Horrender who's after you now, and we don't know that." He leaned forward, elbows on knees. "I can't accept the risks for what will happen if people find out, including revealing your existence to the world."

Her existence… The thought terrified her, but she also knew she couldn't continue to live in a ghost world. "I'm prepared for that."

"Are you? Then get dressed." He waved at the pile of her clothes on the floor. "We'll go back to Mayfair, and you can properly introduce yourself to my mother."

Damn him. He knew she wasn't ready for that. Yet she lied in an attempt to convince herself as much as him, "If it means keeping people safe, I'll do it."

"But it won't keep anyone safe. You can't fathom the lives that will be ruined if the past comes back."

"You mean your family."

"And others."

"I don't want to hurt anyone." She pulled the coverlet up to her shoulders to cover herself, feeling suddenly bare and vulnerable. "But I can't keep living this way. I am so very tired of the uncertainty, the hatred, the fear—of losing people I love." Her shoulders slumped beneath the unbearable weight of it all, and she pressed the heal of her hand against the pain in her forehead at the thought of Wilkins and Proctor. "I've suffered enough for crimes I never committed, and so have the people around me."

"Should more people suffer for crimes they don't even know happened?"

"If it means bringing to justice the people who killed my parents, who attempted to kill me and who—" *Who attempted to rape me.* But she couldn't utter that last out loud. She clenched the coverlet in her hand, desperately needing something solid to cling to now that he sat on the other side of the room. "Who deserve to pay for the evils they've done. *All* of them. If the only way to do that is to be public about what our fathers did, then that's what we have to do."

"At what cost? The destruction of two dukedoms and all the people who depend upon them to survive, both our families, all our servants and employees, our tenants, hundreds of villagers, and everyone their lives touch in turn…all the millers, carpenters, brewers, innkeepers—my family's main estate is eighty-five thousand acres by itself and supports nearly half the county. Should cottagers who have never been more than ten miles from the village be punished if we reveal the truth about what our fathers did?"

"Innocent people are still being hurt," she whispered, barely louder than breath. "I lost Wilkins and Proctor tonight."

"We don't know that for certain."

She looked away, too overwhelmed by confusion and uncertain—and grief—to accept what he was saying. Too much had happened, so many people had been lost… How could she turn her back on all of them?

He rose from the chair and slowly walked back to the bed. When he sank onto the edge of the mattress, he gently took her chin and turned her face until she looked at him. Thankfully, there was no judgment or condemnation in his expression. Only concern.

"Until we know more," he continued, "the best plan of action is to do nothing." He held out the bottle to her, and she could just see in the dim light from the stove that one final drink remained. "Lucien and I agreed a long time ago that we would keep secret what our fathers had done. Now I ask the same of you."

She took a deep breath and tried to sort through the barrage of thoughts and emotions assaulting her from every direction. She knew so much more now about that night, but her heart also knew justice wouldn't come as long as secrets were kept.

She blinked hard to keep the hot tears at bay. Not tears of grief but frustration. She was so close to finding the men responsible, so close to making them pay—*so close!* "What you're asking of me...I can't say silent."

"Just for now," he conceded. "Until we find another way forward."

She repeated so he would understand, "Just for now."

From his frown, he wasn't pleased about that concession, but it was all he'd gain from her tonight. She'd come too far and fought too hard to let justice slip through her fingers now. Especially after tonight.

With watery eyes, she grimaced at the bottle. "That's a sorry attempt at a peace offering."

"Fitting, then. Because it's a sorry attempt at a peace. And brandy." His expression softened. "But it's also all I can offer."

All he could offer... She had no choice but to accept his terms. *For now.*

Grudgingly, she took the bottle and helped herself to the last of the cognac. It burned as it seeped down her throat, and she wiped the last drops from her lips with her fingertips as she handed back the empty bottle.

"Now come back to bed," she urged. "We both need sleep."

He set the empty bottle aside on the night stand. "I can't do that."

"Why not?"

He placed his hands on the mattress on either side of her and leaned in, bringing his dark brown eyes level with hers. "Because if I joined you in this bed—"

His mouth captured hers. Gone was any of the sultry slowness that had marked his early kisses. This time, he seized her lips with a fierce intensity that burned through her, as if he wanted to do nothing more at that moment than devour her. God help her, she wanted exactly that, and when his tongue plunged between her lips in a gesture both passionate and possessive, a low moan of surrender rose from her throat.

He shifted back just far enough to finish whispering against her lips, "It wouldn't be to sleep."

He flopped back down into the leather chair, kicked out his long legs, and lay back his head, his eyes closed. The posture of a gentleman perfectly at ease. But she knew better. Even from this far away she could see the fast rise and fall of his chest as he fought to steady the breath she'd taken from him.

She lay back in the bed and stared up into the darkness. Sleep wouldn't come tonight for either of them.

Chapter Fourteen

DEVLIN HELD OPEN Brechenhurst's door as Lucien Grenier, Duke of Crewe, stepped into the building for the first time. He hadn't wanted Crewe to learn about the place this way—Hell, he hadn't wanted Crewe to learn about the place at all—but it couldn't be helped. The enemy had attacked, and Devlin needed to rally his forces.

"So this is where you've been hiding," Crewe said as he swept his gaze around the ground floor common room and took in the converted old warehouse. "Never figured you for the estate development—"

He froze as his eyes landed on Peyton as she stood next to the long dining table, her hands folded demurely in front of her. His face paled.

His shock was understandable. After all, he was staring at a ghost.

For a long moment, neither moved. Then Crewe blew out a hard breath and muttered, "Demme... It's true, then. You really *are* alive."

"So they tell me." She shrugged a slender shoulder. "I'm surprised you remember me."

"Barely," he admitted. This time, the look he gave her scoured over her from head to toe. "But then, innocent misses fresh from the schoolroom weren't exactly my concern in those days." Then Crewe added in a mumble, because it was expected from the rake he so carefully cultivated himself to be, "They still aren't."

Devlin remained by the door and watched as Crewe approached Peyton and held out his hand to her. Their gazes remained locked as she slipped her hand into his. Instead of bowing over it as he should have, Crewe folded both of his over hers and held it, as if he needed to feel her to discern for himself that she was corporeal and not just a figment of his imagination.

It was also a silent acknowledgement of all the wrongs his father had done to her family.

He released her hand with a nod and stepped back. He couldn't help but rake a second, unbelieving look over her, even as he asked Devlin over his shoulder, "She knows, then?"

"She knows everything about the criminal enterprise." His carefully phrased answer put Crewe at ease. Lucien's secrets, at least, were still his own.

"Then she can hear what I have to share with you." Crewe crossed to the long dining table where trays of leftover food still sat after the children had filed out that morning and took with them their share of sausage rolls, apples, buns—foods that could be easily put into a pocket and kept for later. He helped himself to an apple. "It's exactly what you suspected." He shined the apple on his jacket sleeve before crunching out a bite. The casual move hid his own concern over the news. "Horrender's back. He wants to reassemble the old network, and this time, he'll make certain to pick peers or officials for protection whom he can better push around than our fathers."

Devlin glanced at Peyton to see her reaction. But her face remained calm. Like him, she wasn't surprised.

"Are you certain?" Devlin pressed.

"Have I seen him in the flesh with my own eyes?" Crewe asked around chews. "No. But my contacts claim he is, and I believe them." He swallowed and gestured the apple at Devlin.

"Someone with inside knowledge is attempting to put the old enterprise back together. If not him, then who? Who else would know so much about the management of their scheme?"

When Crewe's gaze slid to Peyton, Devlin bristled at the implication. "She doesn't know as much as that."

"Nor would I willingly participate in anything like that," Peyton confirmed.

Crewe's eyes assessed her coldly. Then he wordlessly took another bite of apple.

A knock sounded from the half-open door behind Devlin, and he turned to find a tall figure in the doorway. The morning sunlight from the street behind the man darkened his face and front, but Devlin would have recognized him anywhere.

Chase Maddox, Duke of Greysmere. Former mercenary with the Prussians during the War of the Fourth Coalition. One of Devlin and Lucien's oldest and dearest friends from Eton. A dedicated student who had gained more from Anthony Titus's guidance than simply learning to fight.

And the most troubled man Devlin knew.

Chase stepped into the converted warehouse and slowly moved his gaze around the room to take it in, his face inscrutable. Dressed in all black, wearing a greatcoat over a tunic and loose-fitting trousers, Chase greeted Devlin and Crewe with slaps to their backs as each man came forward.

Devlin had been best friends with Chase for nearly twenty years, yet since the accident that claimed the life of Chase's toddler son two years ago, his old friend had been completely out of contact. Immeasurable grief and anger at himself for letting the accident happen had driven him to the Continent in pursuit of Anthony Titus. He needed to study under his old mentor once more to learn how to exorcise the new demons that haunted him. Devlin had heard rumors that Chase had returned to England and sent word to Greysmere House that he was needed, but he hadn't been certain until that moment that Chase would appear.

Then his eyes fell on Peyton. Chase cast a careful look over her from head to foot. It was the same measuring glance he would have given any opponent—or any enemy on a battlefield. Since his son died, that was exactly how Chase saw the world, Devlin knew. As a battlefield filled with enemies.

Peyton tensed under Chase's scrutiny.

Devlin went to her side to put her at ease. "Chase, this is Miss Peyton Chandler, the woman I wrote to you about. Peyton, may I introduce Chase Maddox, Duke of Greysmere, and one of the best men to ever enter battle?" He squeezed her elbow. "You can trust him with your life."

"Thank you for coming to help," she said and held out her hand to him. He bowed over it with all the stiffness one would expect from someone who had been well out of society and living like a monk for two years.

With a sharp nod, he released her hand. "I went to your townhouse at dawn to investigate and found evidence of gunpowder in a rear cellar storage room. The explosion and fire were intentional."

Her face darkened with worry. "Who was hurt?"

"Most of the servants escaped unharmed. Your man Wilkins is recovering at a nearby inn. He wants to see you, to make certain you're safe. I told him you'd contact him later today, if you were feeling up to it. Hearing from you will put him at ease."

Devlin frowned as he watched his old friend. Chase's voice was low, deep, and controlled, as was every aspect of his presence. *Now.* Two years ago, the loss of his son, then his estrangement with his wife—and with her, everything he'd wanted for his future—had left him little more than a ruined shell. Titus had managed to do the impossible and bring him back to the land of the living. *Partially.*

Peyton nodded. "I'll send a message to him immediately." Then she pressed, "And Betty Proctor?"

Chase grimly met her gaze. "She's still unaccounted for."

"Unaccounted for," Devlin repeated to reassure her. "That doesn't mean dead."

Chase agreed. "Especially since the rest of the household seems to have escaped without harm, and no remains have yet been found in the debris. We have to assume everyone made it out safely."

She nodded stiffly, as if willing herself to believe that. "And everything else…is gone?"

Devlin knew what she was asking—did anything from her past survive the blast and fire, anything from her childhood or of her parents?

Chase understood the grief of such a loss, and empathy softened his voice as he answered, "The fire destroyed everything."

Except for a faint tremble, Peyton showed no outward sign of how devastated she must have been. Good God, the control she possessed to stand there and accept news like that, how hard-won that restraint must have been, and all she'd gone through to gain it… It broke his heart.

So Devlin turned the conversation to another concern and asked Crewe, "And Horrender?"

With that, he passed a faintly apologetic glance in Chase's direction. Their old friend had only learned that morning about what their fathers had done with Horrender's help, when Crewe had taken it upon himself to tell him with Devlin's permission. There would be feelings of betrayal at not being confided in sooner, Devlin knew, but he also knew that Chase understood the need to protect family at all costs. Even at the price of keeping secrets from old friends.

"Horrender—or someone pretending to be him—is taking credit for it," Crewe answered. "But then, he would. If he's putting back together the old enterprise, he would see it as an opportunity not just to destroy you and whatever evidence you have linking him to the attack but to also send out a warning to Dartmoor and me to leave him alone and to others not to cross him. Just as he wanted to do when he murdered the Chandlers." He tossed the rest of the unwanted apple into the stove and slapped closed the front grill. "But he didn't do it alone."

"What do you mean?" she asked and reached for Devlin to steel herself against the answer.

"He gained access to your house and was there long enough to plant several casks of gunpowder. He didn't do that by himself. Someone helped."

Her face paled. "Who would do something like that?"

Crewe shrugged. "Who else wants you dead?"

"No one. I'm already dead, remember?"

"Well, someone knows you're not but wants to keep you that way," Crewe persisted. "Permanently."

She shook her head. "No one in London knows who I am except you three. Even the Duchess of Dartmoor doesn't—" She cut herself off and turned toward Devlin, clutching at his sleeve. "That man last night in St Giles recognized that I was a Chandler. If he recognized me, then someone else could have, too."

"Only because he saw you in person," Devlin reminded her. "Unless you've been frequenting quayside taverns, no one else from that world would know you're alive."

From her dubious expression, she wasn't convinced.

"You met him last night in St Giles?" Chase interjected.

"Yes," Peyton answered. "For a few minutes around midnight."

He shook his head. "Then whoever set the explosion wasn't anyone you saw in St. Giles. They wouldn't have had time to plant the gunpowder before you arrived home."

"Then who?" She stepped away from Devlin and began to pace.

"No one else in London knows your true identity?" Crewe pressed. Then he hesitated before asking, "Not even one of your servants?"

She bristled at the implication that someone in her own household had attempted to kill her. "Only Wilkins and Proctor, but I trust them with my life." She must have seen doubt in Devlin's face because she stopped pacing and indignantly put her hands on her hips. "I've been with them for years. Why would they attempt to kill me now—here—when they could have done it in France years ago?"

Crewe shook his head. "*Someone* knows. If I could discern the truth about a mysterious woman named Elizabeth Wentworth and her connection to the Chandler fortune, then so could anyone. And whomever he is, someone gave him access to your house."

"But why?" Her face paled as her watery eyes rose to meet Devlin's, her voice emerging raw and raspy, "What threat am I to Horrender?"

Devlin rested his palm on her shoulder to reassure her. "We won't know for certain until we catch him," Devlin muttered.

Peyton stepped away from Devlin to pace again. "How?"

Devlin rubbed at his nape. Damn that it was far too early to open a bottle of drink. "We use his fear against him."

"Yes. By letting him know he didn't succeed last night," Peyton murmured. "By telling the world that I'm alive and well."

An icy realization of where her thoughts were heading poured through Devlin. She was planning to offer herself up as bait.

"No." He locked eyes with her, brooking no misunderstanding about this. "I won't put you into further danger."

"We don't have a choice," she argued. "This has to stop. *All* of it. If revealing my identity is the only way to bring him to justice, then so be it."

"And in the process expose all our fathers' crimes?" Crewe shook his head. "I don't mean to be cruel, Peyton, but your family's gone. If we reveal the past, then both the Raines and Grenier families will also be destroyed by it." Determination sounded in his voice. "I won't let that happen."

"Then place the full blame on my father." She approached him and put her hand beseechingly on his arm. "Keep secret what the Dukes of Dartmoor and Crewe did and protect your families by letting my father take full responsibility." Her mouth twisted with irony. "As you said, the Chandlers are all dead and can't be hurt."

Guilt darkened Crewe's face. "I didn't mean to imply that you—"

"My father was neither innocent nor naïve. He was willingly involved. Let the tarnishing of his name and reputation be his punishment." She paused to pull in a shaking yet determined breath. "Let him find some sort of absolution by stopping all this before anyone else is hurt."

Crewe cast a questioning glance at Devlin, who grudgingly nodded. Yet Devlin's chest tightened with dread. Peyton was wrong. This wouldn't end with only her father. All their sins would be dragged out into the sunlight.

Peyton turned beseechingly to Crewe and pressed, "Can you manipulate the proof you have against Horrender to mention only my father's name?"

Crewe grudgingly nodded. "Yes."

"Then we stop Horrender and blame my father for creating the enterprise," she said firmly. "We have him arrested, tried, convicted—We put an end to his criminal enterprise once and for all before anyone else is harmed." She straightened her spine, and Devlin recognized her expression. He'd seen it on the faces of countless men in the wars as they prepared for battle. "We need to come up with a plan. What can we do?"

"We set a trap," Chase said. "We offer up a bait he can't refuse, then surround him with men and capture him when he arrives."

"What would draw him out?" Crewe asked.

"Me." Peyton instantly drew all three men's attention. "That is, the *real* me."

Devlin didn't like the sound of that. "What are you suggesting?"

She slid a look at Crewe. "Can you disseminate a message to Horrender through your contacts in Seven Dials?"

Crewe nodded. "What do you want the message to say?"

"That I'm alive and back in London—"

"No," Devlin interrupted.

"—and that I have proof he attempted to kill me."

"*Hell no.*" Devlin folded his arms. "Are you trying to get yourself killed—again? We need to find a different way to lure him out." Preferably one that didn't dangle Peyton in front of him like meat before a beast.

"She has a point," Crewe countered. "If we're going to get his attention, we need to make a grand gesture."

"Not that grand." Devlin refused to back down. What she was proposing was far too dangerous.

"I will do whatever it takes to make him pay for harming the people I love." She said that so calmly that Devlin couldn't help but feel a jolt pierce him. This was the same resolute woman he met at Barton's who would have done anything to precipitate his downfall. "Including killing him myself, if necessary."

"Demme," Crewe muttered, clearly stunned by what she'd just said and the coolly dispassionate way she'd delivered it. "No wonder you beat Devlin at cards."

She said quietly to no one in particular, "It's easy when you have nothing to lose."

Devlin knew she didn't mean her gambling wagers.

"Your message won't be enough," Chase interjected.

They all turned to stare at Chase, who folded his arms over his chest and widened his stance. It was the same position he always took right before a fight.

"You need to make a public announcement, one revealing your identity to everyone of importance in London. He can't put together the old enterprise without protection from members of the aristocracy," Chase explained. "If the men he's working with think they're in danger of being exposed, they'll send him after you immediately. When he does, we'll spring our trap."

The blood drained from Peyton's face. The false identity she'd hidden behind for the past ten years would be completely stripped away. There would be no going back then, no other name to hide behind. What Chase was asking of her...Devlin wasn't certain she was up to it.

Apparently, neither was she. "I don't—I don't know if—" Her voice faltered, and she glanced warily between the three men, as if looking for any means of escape from their plan but finding none. So she jerked a nod and said, as if to convince herself as much as them, "If that's what it takes, I'll do it." She paused, then put voice to her fears. "But can we be sure it will work? If I reveal who I am, and he doesn't come after me…"

"He will," Chase assured her.

"But if we fail to capture him," Devlin added, giving her yet another bleak reason to back out of their plan, "he won't stop coming after you until you're dead. You won't be safe anywhere."

"Then let's not fail, shall we?" Despite the pallor of her face, her lips twisted in a grim smile. "I'd prefer not to die a second time."

Chapter Fifteen

PEYTON SAT AT the table where she, Chase, and Crewe had been working out the arrangements for their trap and taking notes of all that had to be done in the short time they'd given themselves to enact it. After all, delaying only gave Horrender more time to make another attempt on her life.

In only two days, their plan would be put into motion. She offered up a silent prayer that she had the strength to carry out her end of it. If all went according to plan, Chase, Crewe, Devlin and a half dozen of their men would be there to rush in, save her, and capture Horrender. But if it went wrong…

No. That was not an option. She'd come too far to fail now.

"That's it then," Chase announced.

He slid the top sheet of paper toward Crewe and gave a second set of instructions to Peyton. Devlin had already left them, to go downstairs and work out his frustrations there.

She folded her sheet. "We know what we have to do."

"Then best to get started on arrangements." Crewe pushed himself away from the table, and with a nod at both Peyton and Chase, he walked to the door. He paused and turned back, meeting Peyton's gaze across the room and confided, "I still place flowers on your grave, you know."

She forced a smile. "Hopefully, you can stop doing that

soon."

With a grim nod, he left, closing the door behind him.

When she returned her attention to Chase, she found his dark eyes watching her. "You're more than strong enough to do your part," he said gently.

Her shoulders sank under his quiet compliment. "Thank you." She paused, then admitted, "I lost my parents, my friend Armand...now I've lost Betty Proctor." She swallowed hard. "If anyone else is lost because of me..."

"Then no blame will fall on you." He rested his hand on her shoulder. "Please understand. We don't do this for you. Well, not only for you," he corrected when she arched a brow to call him out on that statement. "I'm doing it for Devlin and Lucien, and they're doing it to protect their families."

"But you have no stake in this, yet you're willing to risk your life?"

"I'm a soldier at heart." He dropped his hand away as he shrugged. "It's what we do." He stood and picked up his black gloves resting on the table. "You'll be well-protected. My men will have the building surrounded and will keep you in sight at all times. We'll capture him when the moment is right. You need to trust in that."

She nodded, yet she wasn't completely convinced.

Neither was Devlin, apparently. When they had begun to plot out their plan, he'd excused himself from their planning and went downstairs to leave it to the three of them. His absence bothered her.

"Devlin said you trained with him," she murmured.

"Yes, at Eton under Anthony Titus."

"And you know why Devlin wanted to learn to fight?" she asked carefully. "So he could...harm his father if he had to?"

"No." His eyes grew somber. "He studied with Titus so he wouldn't."

Cold understanding fell through Peyton. *Control*—that's what Chase meant. Devlin needed to learn to control himself so he wouldn't kill his father. Just as he had needed to be anywhere but here when the others were planning the trap. For their plan to work, he had to cede control to Peyton, and apparently, he didn't like it.

"Thank you," she whispered. "For everything."

He nodded, not meeting her gaze. "If you'd like, I can hire some men to discover what happened to Mrs. Proctor, to find out if anyone saw her leave the house or if she's been reported staying at any of the nearby inns."

"You think she might still be alive?" Peyton whispered, hopefully.

"I think too many people have come back from the dead lately to write her off so soon."

"I would appreciate that very much." Her voice choked. "Thank you."

Without another word, he left, following after Crewe to carry out his part of the plan.

Peyton locked the door after him, then leaned back against it to give the troubled thoughts spinning through her head time to settle. But none did. Even in the quiet stillness of the old warehouse, her pulse pounded with an anxiousness she couldn't ease, and her skin tingled as if from the electricity of an approaching storm.

Wasn't that exactly what their plan was—a storm ten years in the making? On the distant horizon, she could hear the first low rumbles of thunder.

She pushed herself away from the door and went downstairs to find Devlin.

Stopping in the doorway of his training room, she leaned against the doorframe and watched as he methodically moved through a series of footwork and arm movements with a foil in one hand and a long dagger in the other. His body was bare except for a loosely fitting pair of trousers cinched tightly at the waist. The sheen of sweat covered the hard muscles in his chest and shoulders, and the muscles in his back rippled as he swung both foil and knife in deliberate movements. He moved fluidly, every position controlled, every breath carefully measured.

He turned and saw her, and he froze mid-step, the foil extended in his right arm and the dagger poised behind his head. Slowly, he lowered both weapons and straightened from the lunge.

"All done planning, then?" He set the weapons back into the rack along the stone wall. "Chase and Crewe have left?"

"Yes."

His shoulders remained as stiff as before, even though he'd ended his training session. He reached for a towel and began to wipe at the beads of sweat covering his torso, and she shamelessly watched him. She'd always remembered him as good-looking whenever she'd thought of him ten years ago. But the reality of the man he'd become...*breathtaking.*

"You're not happy with our plan, are you?" She noted the rough edge to her voice, and that her words weren't a question so much as an accusation.

He yanked off his gloves and stuffed them into a hole in the rack. "I'm not happy with what we're using as bait."

The pointed gaze he scoured over her from head to toe tingled her skin everywhere he looked.

"Are you certain you want to do this," he asked, "to reveal yourself to the world like that?"

Not at all. And yet... "It's the best chance we have of stopping Horrender," she said, as much to convince herself as him. "It's a good trap. I'll be protected."

She came forward to his side, took the discarded gloves from the rack, and slipped them onto her hands. The warmth of him lingered on the leather, and the musky scent of him, pungent with sweat, filled her senses.

He stepped up behind her and murmured, "Not if it exposes you to unnecessary risks."

She could feel the heat of him warming her back, and she trembled, suddenly hot and achy. To be in his arms, she simply had to lean back. That was all, just bring herself against him and surrender... The anxious swirl of anticipation that shadowed her before now simply engulfed her. It was all she could do to remember to breathe as she ran gloved fingers along the blade of the foil hanging on the rack. "I know how to take care of myself."

"That's what worries me." He caressed his knuckles along the side of her face, and her breath hitched. "You take too many risks."

"Because I know what I'm doing."

He gave a soft sigh that rumbled into her. "Because you won't let go of the past."

"I am letting go of it." In the grandest, loudest, most stunning way imaginable. "But you're not. You refuse to let the evils your father did come to light."

"I won't let him hurt any more people, including you." To punctuate his point, he touched his lips to her nape, and she shivered. Not a kiss of seduction, but a promise. "Not even from his grave."

She took one of the blunted training foils down from the rack and turned around, pointing the tip at his bare chest. "You can't stop me from doing this." His face remained frustratingly inscrutable as she tapped the foil against his breastbone. "Moreover, once Horrender is no longer a threat, there's no reason to keep secret what our fathers did."

"So many reasons you'll never know," he corrected beneath his breath.

Slowly shaking her head, she turned the thin blade and watched the metal glint in the lamplight. "One way or another, this has to end."

"Your life doesn't have to end with it."

"Actually, that is *exactly* how it has to end. Elizabeth Wentworth dies, and Peyton Chandler rises from the ashes. It can't happen any other way, and we both know it."

She stepped away from him, needing air to breathe and distance to think. Her skin tingled from his nearness, and her belly twisted from the masculine scent of him and the solidity he presented. It would be so easy to surrender, in every way... But he also represented all the secrets that had ruled her life for the past decade. She would never succumb to those.

She held up the foil. "Spar with me." Not a request. An order. She was determined to prove she could take care of herself.

"You'll lose."

"Probably. I'm in a skirt." She removed his ill-fitting gloves and tossed them to the floor at his feet, as if throwing down a gauntlet. "But I'll still give you my best go...unless you're afraid of losing to a woman—again?"

His lips curled at the challenge, and he kicked the gloves aside. "All right, then. Best two of three. Saber rules."

Saber rules weren't the finely executed moves of foil fencing. With sabers, contact with any part of the body above the hips counted as a touch, including glancing blows with the side of the blade. In other words, it was anything goes. "All right."

He snatched up a second foil from the rack and pointed it at an old but large rug covering most of the room's floor. "The rug serves as the *piste*. No touches outside its edges count."

"Agreed." She moved to the center of the long rug which was about half the length of a normal *piste*. Yet she didn't care. She planned on giving him the fight of his life. *"En garde."*

He took his position in front of her and raised the blade in front of his head in salute to her.

"Prêts?"

He lowered into his stance, and she mirrored his, despite her skirt. A simple dress wouldn't stop her from besting him.

"Allez!"

Peyton feigned an attack, only to catch Devlin off guard with a parry into thin air. He retreated a step, his eyes flashing.

"So that's how we're playing, is it?" he muttered.

"Saber rules." She shrugged. "Anything goes."

She attacked, this time coming full-on with her foil and easily parrying his defensive thrusts. His might be bigger and stronger, but all those broad shoulders and taut muscles took longer to move, leaving him constantly a half-step behind, which evened out the disadvantage of her skirt.

Only a few lunges and retreats later, she ascertained that they were equally matched in skill. She wouldn't win unless she found a chink in his armor. Easier said than done, too, since he wore no armor. He barely wore anything at all.

His foil slapped her shoulder. "Touch!"

With a faint curse at her lack of focus, she retreated a few feet so they could reset for the next volley. *Concentrate!* But she also needed to change her mode of attack. She'd never win by simply fencing.

She needed to attack his control. If he lost control, he'd lose the match.

They both took their ready positions, and she called out, "*Allez!*"

Devlin rushed at her, but she retreated, not because she needed to but because she wanted to draw him in closer.

"Titus taught you to fence?" she asked, expertly parrying his thrusts.

"And others here and there." He lunged. "That's why I'll win."

She thrust at his chest, only for her foil to be knocked away at the last moment. She laughed at how easily she'd set up the parry. "Not if you keep fencing like that."

She saw his eyes flare. *Good.* She needed to prick him, and not just with the foil, although she promptly did, right in his broad shoulder.

"*Touché,*" she purred and demurely flexed her foil on the floor at her heel, as if she'd just noticed she held a weapon in her hand and didn't know how to use it. "If you want to quit now before you lose, I'd be happy to accept your forfeiture."

This time when he smiled at her, his expression was tight.

A dangerous thrill raced up her spine. When she was with him, she often felt like a mouse being played with by a lion.

It was the mouse's turn now to taunt.

"What do I get when I win?" he asked.

"What do *I* get when *I* win, you mean," she corrected and took her *en garde* position. "Any opponent who bends his wrist when he parries shouldn't be hard to defeat."

He lowered into his stance. "I don't bend my wrist."

"No? Apologies." But the glance she shot to his wrist wasn't at all mistaken. Or apologetic. "So it all comes down to this next go, then. Do try to concentrate. I would hate to be able to tell everyone that Dartmoor was bested in both cards and fencing by a skirt."

The heated look he cast over her was scalding. "I don't mind being bested by a skirt," he purred in a husky voice that tingled through her like liquid heat. "I find it exhilarating when a woman comes out on top."

That turned the tingle into a pulsating ache. She pushed from her mind the unbidden, and thoroughly wanton, images his words created but didn't give him time to center himself. *"Allez!"*

She charged. They met in a flurry of thrusts and parries, charges and retreats, and the metallic clang of metal foil against foil reverberated against the cellar's stone walls.

Peyton side-stepped his slashing thrust. Had he been a real foe, she would have run him through with her foil or dropped to the ground and taken him out at the knees. Instead, she closed the distance between them, pressed the hilt of her foil against his, and pinned both foils between them. Neither could move back without losing the advantage to the other.

"You've trapped us both," he told her.

"But I know the way out, and it isn't by hiding." Emotion tightened her chest. "I've hidden from the past long enough. Soon, I won't be able to hide any longer."

"And you think I am?"

She gazed at him between the crossed foils. "As long as you keep secret what our fathers did, you're doing exactly that."

He let out a fierce growl and shoved her away, disentangling their foils and sending her staggering back a few feet until she regained her balance.

But he didn't claim the advantage and attack. Instead, he waited at the edge of the rug for her to regain her stance before charging. His control was snapping, his thrusts and parries less carefully measured than before.

She was winning the fight. Now she had to win the war. "I've lived too long with their secrets. So have you. I've made up my mind. I don't want to live in secrecy any longer."

The clash of foils punctuated her words as he went on the attack, never giving ground, never retreating. All Peyton had to do now was wait for his guard to slip, for just enough room in the movement of his arm to expose a vulnerable space—

"What you want isn't to reveal secrets. It's to continue your revenge against my father," he huffed out between rapid breaths. "But you can never have that."

She skillfully parried his thrust. "Dartmoor shouldn't be allowed to get away with what he's done."

"He's dead!" he half-shouted, his control slipping more with every passing moment. "You can't punish a dead man, but you *will* hurt the ones who are still alive. Give up your revenge before you're hurt again."

He lunged, and she retreated another step, then ground out, "Haven't I already surrendered enough to the dead?"

"But you're *not* dead, and you owe a debt to the living." He paced her around the room, relentlessly on the attack and seemingly not caring that they'd long ago left the boundaries of the rug. Each thrust was less controlled than the one before. "Is that the kind of revenge you want, Peyton—the kind that harms innocents? Then you'll be no better than our fathers. Including yours."

She halted in mid-retreat, stunned at his accusation. She froze for only a moment, but a moment was all he needed to knock her foil from her hand. It clanged against the stone floor at her feet.

Instead of taking the winning touch, Devlin locked eyes with her and threw his foil away. When he stepped forward, she retreated again, this time hitting her back against the wall behind her. But he closed the distance between them, placed his palms flat on the wall on both sides of her shoulders and leaned in until his blazing eyes were level with hers.

His mouth was so close that his warm breath tickled her lips. "You are *not* that person."

"You don't know that."

"I do." His rough voice trembled with the same intensity that shook his body. "Because I would never want someone like that as much as I want you."

Her pulse spiked, sparking a fierce ache between her legs. "You...want me?"

"God, yes."

Beneath his hungry admission, all the anger, retribution, and doubts she'd carried about him for the past ten years vanished, leaving her nothing in this moment but the man standing in front of her. A desperate need blossomed inside her, one she could no longer fight back. She ordered on a soft breath, "Then take me."

He lunged forward and seized her mouth beneath his in a blistering kiss that left her boneless. Heat sizzled her skin everywhere his front touched hers, and she returned the kiss as fiercely as he gave it.

When she tore her mouth away to gasp back her breath, the final threads of his control snapped. He dropped to his knees, yanked her skirt up to her waist, and buried his face between her thighs.

A cry of raw need tore from her, and she grabbed onto his hard shoulders to keep from falling to the floor as he kissed her intimately with the same intensity he'd captured her mouth only moments before. His tongue plundered her folds, licking and flicking against her. Just when she'd regained her breath, he spread her intimate lips wide with his fingers and then plunged his tongue deeply inside her.

She shuddered against his mouth, and the little muscles inside her wickedly tightened around his tongue to draw him even deeper. The pulsating ache he stoked inside her with each hot, wet thrust overwhelmed her. But she didn't want him to stop— *please, don't stop!*—and silently begged for more by wrapping her leg over his shoulder and opening herself wide to his wanton kisses.

His answering groan of pleasure thrilled her. She pushed herself back against the wall for leverage and tilted up her pelvis to bring his mouth as hard against her as possible. Oh, heavens, how wonderful the sensations he flared right there beneath his lips! How desperate she was for even more of him. A string of senseless encouragements fell from her lips, and she fisted his silky hair in her hands. The same man who was making the earth slide away beneath her was also her only anchor, and she clung to him to keep from losing herself completely.

His lips closed around the little bead of her clitoris and sucked.

"Devlin!" Her hips bucked shamelessly against his mouth.

Giving her no quarter, he slid his hands up the backs of her legs to cup her bottom in his palms and keep her pulled tightly against him as she arched out from the wall behind her. He sucked again, longer and harder, relentless in his pursuit to drive her over the edge.

Sheer joy shattered her as she found her release. Too quickly, *far* too quickly, the cry of bliss on her lips faded to a whimper of disappointment as residual waves of pleasure lapped at her toes. She didn't want the encounter to end, not this soon. She wanted him inside her, filling her completely, bringing her sheer bliss.

Knowing what her body craved, he lifted her in his arms as he rose to his feet and deftly unfastened his fall. He wrapped her legs around his waist and stepped forward to plunge himself inside her.

The cry of surprise on her lips transformed into a shuddering moan as he pinned her between the wall and his body. He began to move inside her in fierce, hard thrusts of his hips, his thick, hard length buried deeply inside her. Right where she longed for him to be.

"Let go, Peyton," he cajoled, his soft words contrasting against the hard thrusts that rocked her to her soul. "Stop fighting...for once, surrender."

Peyton wrapped her arms around his shoulders and held on tightly, shaking uncontrollably as each plunge and retreat of his body into hers brought her both new pleasure and new anguish. She knew what he wanted from her was total capitulation, and not only physically but emotionally. He wanted her to free herself from the past, but she couldn't. What he was asking of her—what he was begging of her with his body—she simply *couldn't* give him that.

"Devlin," she whispered and buried her face against his neck, his name a plea for mercy.

"Let yourself live again," he murmured hotly into her hair.

"I can't!" She clung tighter to him and summoned all her strength to keep from falling over the edge. "I don't...know how."

"Then trust me to show you."

But she refused this last surrender, with all her body, heart, and soul. What would she be if she let go of the only things that had sustained her since she lost her parents? What would she cling to then to simply keep living?

Not leaving her tight warmth, he wrapped his arms around her and carefully lowered her away from the wall. The red rug beneath her back softened the floor as he laid her down, then spread his tall body over hers.

The soft kerseymere of his breeches brushed against her inner thighs as he moved inside her. His hips teased at hers with deliberate circles of motion that spiraled raw need through her and left her teetering breathlessly on the edge. Once again, he was in control and carefully measuring each delicious plunge and retreat—for now. He was equally as gentle as he'd been fierce before, and he paused in his rhythm only to kiss her so tenderly that she feared a tear might slip down her cheek.

"Let the past go, Peyton," he murmured as he rocked into her. His rhythm increased, his thrusts growing harder.

The rising tide of pleasure inside her began to lick at the backs of her knees, and she knew he could feel her trembling around him, just as she could feel the shaking of his tense muscles in hard-fought restraint to keep from losing himself inside her.

"Let go." He nuzzled her ear with affection. "Send the past away and accept what's here for you now."

He shifted his hips and rubbed his pelvis against her already sensitized clit, eliciting a plaintive whimper from her.

"Take this moment, Peyton," he rasped. "With me."

He rubbed his hips against her again, and a jolt of electricity shot through her. She bucked beneath him, arching herself hard off the floor as the wave of release broke through her. She cried out, and he kissed her, drinking in the sound, even as he continued to swirl his hips against her to prolong her pleasure as long as possible, to keep the flashes of light dancing before her closed eyes.

Then his movements changed. She could do nothing more than cling to him as her pulse raced and try to catch back her breath at this wonderful melding of bodies and souls as his thrusts came fast and fierce. Just as his body tensed, every muscle hard and shaking, he suddenly pulled out of her warmth and squeezed his length between their bodies. With a groan, his buttocks clenched, and he released himself against her bare flesh just above her feminine curls, then collapsed against the floor beside her, gasping for breath. Completely spent.

Devlin gathered her into his arms and pressed her against him. When his lips lovingly caressed her temple, a single tear slipped from her eye. The terrible mix of pleasure and torture she found in his arms was nearly unbearable. Sheer joy tingled out from her fingers and toes, but it was tempered by overwhelming guilt—that she hadn't yet found her parents' killer, that she should have realized earlier the truth about the attack…that she should take such joy in being alive at that moment with Devlin when her parents were in their graves.

"Peyton?" Concern thickened his voice as he gently brushed away her tear with his thumb. He caressed her cheek. "Is something wrong?"

Everything. Yet she couldn't bring herself to utter that aloud. Instead, she gave a jerky shake of her head and buried her face against his neck where it curved so perfectly into his shoulder.

Silently, they lay together, their limbs entwined, with the heat of him still pulsating deliciously inside her and her scent now covering him. Yet in her heart, she knew they remained in separate worlds—and ten years apart.

Chapter Sixteen

DEVLIN HELD HIS breath and carefully gauged his mother's reaction as she and his two sisters sat on the settee across the tea table from him and Peyton at Dartmoor House. Both her mouth and Meg's had fallen open, their eyes growing wide as saucers.

Then his mother rasped out, "Pardon?"

"I'm Peyton Chandler," Peyton repeated, pulling in a deep and steadying breath. "I'm not dead."

The two women continued to stare at her, saying nothing in their shock. Devlin readied himself to dart forward to grab their cups of tea to keep them from spilling onto the rug.

Beside them, Theodora blinked in confusion. "Well, of course not! We can see that—"

"Hush," Margaret chastised. Both she and the duchess stared as if they were seeing a ghost.

But then, he supposed, that was exactly what they were see-ing.

"But I don't understand," Teddy complained. "If you're here...then who's in your grave?"

"Hush!" Without taking her eyes off Peyton, the duchess slapped her hand gently against Theodora's leg.

"It's all right," Peyton assured them quietly. "I'm certain you all have many questions for me, and you have the right to ask them." She sat forward on the edge of the settee next to Devlin and leaned toward Theodora. "No one is in that grave. The casket is empty. You see, ten years ago, I was traveling home from Dartmoor House with my parents when our carriage was attacked, and they were killed." Devlin was beyond grateful that she omitted the more gruesome details. Teddy didn't need to know any of that. "I let everyone believe that I had been killed, too, because I feared the attackers would come after me again if they knew I'd survived. I left England and only recently returned."

Devlin could tell from his youngest sister's expression that she didn't completely understand, but he also trusted that Margaret would explain it all to her later. For now, they simply needed to confide in his mother and Margaret in order to put the next part of their plan in motion.

"Peyton?" his mother whispered, her shaking hand going to her throat as she searched Peyton's face for any resemblance to the long-lost girl she'd known. "Is it truly…" A strangled sob tore from her throat as his mother finally recognized her. "Oh my heavens—Peyton!"

Devlin dove for the teacup and saucer as his mother rose suddenly to her feet and came forward to sit at Peyton's side on the settee. She cupped Peyton's face between her hands.

"My dear girl." She blinked rapidly as her bright blue eyes glistened in the afternoon sunlight streaming in through the drawing room windows. "I am so sorry." Then the dam of her tears broke, and they fell down her cheeks. "I am so very, *very* sorry!"

She pulled Peyton into her arms and hugged her tightly to her bosom, rocking her like a child in her embrace. Devlin stood and moved away to give the two women a moment's privacy, but over his mother's shoulder, he could see tears at Peyton's lashes and Margaret reaching up to swipe her hand across her eyes.

Finally, his mother released her hold and leaned back. But this time, instead of searching Peyton's face, she locked eyes with Peyton and choked out, "You are not alone, do you understand? You are *not* alone."

Unable to keep her seat, Margaret rose and sat on the other side of Peyton, and both Raines women embraced her again, holding her close as more tears fell from all three of them.

Theodora remained where she was, her mouth falling open at the scene in front of her. Her wide eyes looked up at Devlin for guidance.

I will explain later, he mouthed to her over the three women's heads. He jerked his thumb toward the door. *Go.*

She nodded, scooted off the settee, and slinked quickly out the door.

Devlin pulled in a deep breath. He had come prepared and held out three handkerchiefs. His mother gratefully accepted one, but her attention never strayed from Peyton.

"Tell me the truth now," his mother insisted. "Are you all right? Are you in trouble?"

Thankfully, Peyton knew not to glance at Devlin. Instead, she forced a faint smile. "Nothing to be concerned with."

Peyton covered his mother's hand with hers and placed the other over Margaret's. She squeezed them both to reassure them, then shared with them all that happened to her since the attack ten years ago. *Almost* all. She never mentioned learning to fight or her plot for revenge. Devlin was relieved. One shock at a time… From the way his mother and sister continued to stare at her, he knew it would take a goodly while before they came to terms with this first one. No need to give them apoplexy, at least not until the tea was cold.

"I'm sorry I let you believe I was someone else at dinner." Peyton finally lifted her eyes to Devlin, and his gut clenched at the sorrow he saw in those blue depths. He'd become even more attuned to her since making love to her that morning, and he never wanted to see such grief in her again. "I wasn't ready then to face the past. But I am now."

Devlin nodded with approval. He was so very proud of her for facing down her demons. This meeting with his mother and sisters took only a small fraction of the courage she would need to survive the next few days, but it was a good first step.

"Now you're back in England." His mother smiled as she wiped away the last of her tears. "For good."

Peyton's lips parted, as if she were going to deny it. Then she looked away from Devlin as she equivocated, "I'm not certain what I'm going to do."

"You're going to stay here and let our family become yours," Margaret insisted. "Let us help you, Peyton. You shouldn't have to go through this alone."

Peyton slid off the settee and stepped away, as if seeking out the warmth of the small fire, but Devlin knew she simply wanted distance. Too much familiarity and affection were overwhelming her. He could see it in the way she wrung her hands and fought back the urge to pace.

Peyton straightened her shoulders. "Actually, there is something I need your help with."

Devlin recognized the gesture. It was time to start the next part of their plan.

"I'd like to announce to society that I'm alive and back in London." She added beneath her breath, "For the time being, at least."

Devlin frowned. What the devil did she mean by that?

"But it needs to be done in a very specific way," she explained, "and I can't do it alone."

She didn't dare look at Devlin as she made her request. He hadn't wanted to involve his family at all, and Peyton had come to understand his desire to protect them. But they desperately needed his mother's and sister's help if their plan had any chance of success.

"What do you need?" Margaret asked.

"Help me host a party?" She softened the absurdity of that request with a nervous smile. "I don't want to wait to make the announcement, and I don't want to ease back into existence. It's going to be painful no matter how it's done, so best it be done quickly—and softened with drinks and refreshments. Many, *many* drinks." She forced a nervous smile. "I want to announce myself, let the room have a good look at me, and then deal with the consequences all at once rather than letting the torture drag out." She paused. "As soon as possible."

"How soon?"

"Is two evenings from now too soon?"

"Two evenings from now?" his mother repeated as if she couldn't possibly have heard correctly.

Peyton nodded, her smile turning sheepish. Devlin knew she wasn't acting. "I know it's a bit rash, and that's why I need your help. I don't think I can wait a moment longer than that."

Devlin said nothing. He hated that he and Peyton were misleading his family, even though not one falsehood had yet been uttered—they *did* need a party, and it *did* need to happen as soon as possible. He simply hated manipulating his mother and sisters like this.

But once the evening was over and Peyton was safe, the truth could come out.

The duchess exchanged dubious looks with Margaret, then asked, "What did you have in mind, exactly?"

"Nothing too grand. I just need an excuse for a big gathering."

His mother blinked. "How big?"

"Everyone in society."

"*Everyone?*"

Devlin had to give his mother credit. She was handling this conversation extremely well, given everything she had been told this afternoon.

Peyton nodded. "Everyone we can squeeze into the party. Everyone in society, Parliament, Whitehall, the army—"

His mother's eyes widened like saucers. "The *entire* army?"

"Just the most important officers based here in London."

Peyton laughed at herself. "After all, we need to leave room for the navy, too, of course."

His mother leaned back against the settee and repeated, deadpan, "Of course."

"But there isn't time." Margaret injected a dose of sanity into their plans. "Our house isn't ready for a party, and we can't issue invitations and receive replies in time."

"That's why I was thinking of having the party somewhere else. I wouldn't ever ask to put you out like that."

Nor would Devlin ever allow his family to be placed in so much danger as to welcome snakes under their own roof. The army and navy be damned.

"There must be somewhere else we could host it." Peyton shook her head. "I've been unexpectedly put out of the townhouse I was renting, so we can't have it there."

"I have an idea," Devlin interjected as if the thought had just occurred to him, although his input had been completely planned in advance. "The Duke of Malvern has given me permission to use his townhouse whenever I have need. I think this counts."

"Malvern?" Margaret asked for clarification. "Seamus Douglass has opened up Malvern House to you?"

"Don't sound so shocked," Devlin drawled with a touch of pique. "I'm not hosting bacchanals and virgin sacrifices. Just the occasional card party."

"It's not that. It's…" She blinked, as if her concern was obvious. "Well, he hasn't opened Malvern for years, if ever. I don't think he even comes to London at all anymore since his brother died."

No, Shay didn't. But Devlin had no intention of weeding through the details of his friend's private troubles. "Which makes it perfect. No furniture to move, no rugs to roll up—the place is clean and empty. We'll have the staff from Dartmoor House work the party, and I'm certain Lucien will offer up his as well, given the circumstances. The Dukes of Dartmoor and Crewe will host." With security provided by Chase and his men, just as they'd planned that morning. "All we have to do is provide the glasses and drink."

"And music and food and candles and lamps..." His mother ticked off each item on her fingers.

"Which is why I need your help." Peyton went to the duchess's side and squeezed her hand beseechingly. "I've never thrown a party before, and I don't know the first thing about it." She glanced at Margaret. "I also need help finding an appropriate dress. I have nothing in the current London style."

She had nothing at all, actually, except the dress on her back.

"Of course." Margaret nudged her mother. "We can help her do this. Isn't that so, Mama?"

Peyton grimaced self-effacingly. "And if it's any consolation, after my announcement, everyone will most likely be too stunned to notice that there's no dancing or supper."

"I suppose." Yet the duchess frowned. "But it won't make a difference if no one shows up because of the last-minute invitations."

"Then we also make a point of calling on everyone we know to tell them about it and assure them that a shocking announcement is going to be made that they need to hear for themselves," Devlin explained. "Tell them to invite everyone they know. We'll start with the biggest busybodies and convince them it's the announcement of the season."

"That is a grand understatement," his mother murmured as she cast an assessing look over Peyton. "Are you certain you want to do this, my dear? *Truly* certain? Once let loose, this secret can never be put back into the bottle."

"I know." She nodded firmly. "I have to do this. It's the only way forward."

Her eyes finally lifted to meet Devlin's, yet only for a moment before looking away. The guilt and grief he saw was undeniable.

"Very well, then." His mother gracefully stood, then helped Peyton to her feet. "We shall throw the biggest, best last-minute party England has ever seen! I'll make a quick list of all we need to do and then set Jennings and Cook right on it." She looked at the mantel clock. "There's yet time to pay visits to several friends today and start the invitations flowing."

"While you're doing that," Margaret offered as she linked her arm through Peyton's, "we'll be up in my dressing room, looking for the perfect dress."

"And I'll contact Lucien to let him know we'll be borrowing his staff for the evening," Devlin added. Although he didn't have to. It had been Crewe's idea in the first place to use Shay's house and send in his servants to man the event.

"Thank you." Peyton hesitated before impulsively throwing her arms around the duchess in a grateful hug. "Thank you so much!"

Then she was gone, hurried from the room by Margaret, who was already jabbering a mile a minute about the current London fashions and how Peyton should style herself. The two women didn't look back.

"Good God…" His mother whispered, finally letting her grief show. "Peyton Chandler is alive."

"Yes, she is." Devlin reached for the tea tray to help himself to a cup. "And she needs us more than you realize."

"I can only imagine. What she went through…" His mother's face lost all color, and she trembled as she sank onto the settee, her knees giving out. "She didn't say… Did she see her parents killed?"

"Yes."

His mother was quiet for a long moment, then she whispered, "She must have been so terrified, not only during the attack but every day after."

Devlin wordlessly stirred sugar into the tea. There was nothing good to say to that.

"To come back, after so many years… Why is she back? What brought her back to London now?"

She wanted to exact her revenge and completely destroy me. In-

stead, he shrugged and dissembled, "Us."

"Then she shall have our help, however we can provide it."

In silent agreement, he passed the fresh cup to his mother. Nothing fortified her better than tea.

But Devlin needed something far stronger. He headed toward the door. He had a new bottle of Bowmore whisky waiting in his study and planned to—

"You like her, don't you?"

His mother's words drew him up short. *Not* a question.

He faced her. "I want to protect her."

She nodded faintly at that explanation, but her eyes narrowed. "Well, yes. But you *like* her, too. More than simply as an old acquaintance."

Christ, he needed that whisky. He leaned his shoulder against the doorway, his casual posture belying the way his heart suddenly leapt into his throat. "She needs us."

His mother eyed him over her cup as she lifted it to her lips. "I think she needs *you.*"

"She doesn't need me." His heartbeat spiked despite his scoffing dismissal.

"She needs the protection of a duke to ease her through her announcement. With you and Crewe at her side, everyone in the room will know to take her seriously and not assume she's attempting some kind of fraud. They'll know she is truly who she claims, and if you accept her return to London—and from the dead—then so will the rest of society. There will be an inquest, I'm certain, and much, *much* gossip and newspaper columns about her. She will need you and Crewe to remain at her side while she weathers the scandal."

They would do exactly that because the weather she would face was going to be one hell of a storm. "As I said, she needs us. *All* of us."

She returned her cup to her saucer balanced on her knee. "And *you* need her."

At that, his foolish heart stopped completely.

"You need someone like her anyway," his mother clarified.

He grimaced, having been through this conversation with his mother too many times before when she'd prodded him in the direction of marriage. The reprieve he'd earned with his pursuit of Lady Catherine was apparently over. He recited the old litany. "Because she's accomplished, refined, wealthy—"

"In pain." His mother's eyes turned somber. "You have suffered so much in your life, Devlin. If anyone can understand that kind of pain, I think she can."

Devlin knew so. That same pain had drawn them into each other's arms that morning.

But he also knew that what stood between them now wasn't ghosts from the past but fears of the future. For both of them. He wasn't at all certain they would be able to help each other through those dark days.

"You need someone who understands you, someone who can be your best friend and companion—"

"You're suggesting I need a dog?" he asked, deadpan. This conversation was not going in the direction he wanted. Best to cut it short however he could, including by impertinence.

Her mouth tightened. "I'm suggesting you need a wife."

Definitely not in the right direction. "And you're suggesting I consider Peyton Chandler?"

"No," she corrected. "Not necessarily." Her second correction made him feel no more assured than the first had. "But you need someone like her much more than you need someone like Lady Catherine."

He bristled at that. After all, hadn't his mother been prompting him for years to find a suitable wife? "Catherine is well-educated, polished, the daughter of an earl—she would have made a fine duchess."

"Yes, she would have. But you need more than just a fine duchess. You need someone who understands you and challenges you. You deserve so much more than a peer's perfect daughter."

He arched a brow. "I deserve a peer's *imperfect* daughter?"

"Impertinent." She set her tea down on the table and rose to her feet. "I'm not disappointed Lady Catherine broke off your engagement, no matter how scandalous the circumstances." When he began to defend himself, she cut him off with a wave of her hand as she approached him. "I have heard the rumors regarding what happened that night. I am assuming the woman you visited in her private box was Peyton Chandler, because if there is a *third* woman caught up in all this, then—"

"There is not," he said firmly and, with that, admitted to far more between him and Peyton than a simple desire to help her.

His mother knew it, too, based on the way her expression softened. "You need a true partner and a kindred soul. I'm not saying that Miss Chandler is that woman. What I'm saying is to let your heart lead you to where you belong." She cupped his face between her hands and emphasized her wishes for him. "Marry for love, not for a perfect duchess. You are under no obligations for the title. *Absolutely* none." She placed a kiss to his forehead, the way she'd done since he was a boy in leading strings. "But I also don't want you to be lonely."

He stepped back with a teasing grin he certainly didn't feel. "How can I be lonely when I'll have Megs and Teddy underfoot for the rest of my life?"

She pursed her lips together at that flat attempt at a joke. She returned to the settee and sank down onto the cushions, letting the subject drop, although he could tell from the determined glint in her eyes as she reached for her tea that this conversation was far from over.

"I will find a wife when the time is right," he assured her, pressing the point to prevent any future discussion of the matter. He knew what a brilliant battle tactician his mother could be. Medieval sieges were nothing compared to her patience in wearing someone down to eventually win what she wanted. "Right now, my concern is simply being supportive of Miss Chandler. That's all."

"Well," his mother murmured against the rim of her teacup

as she took a sip, "I suppose it's a moot point anyway, if Miss Chandler isn't planning on remaining in London."

"No," he mumbled in quiet agreement, knowing Peyton thought her future lay elsewhere, some place far away from the ghosts of her past. "Most likely not."

He turned on his heel and marched out of the room, praying there was enough whisky in his bottle of Bowmore to get him through the next few hours. But a sinking feeling in his gut told him there wasn't enough whisky in all of Scotland for that.

Chapter Seventeen

SEATED AT A small writing desk in the Malvern House drawing room, Peyton darted a glance at Crewe's reflection in the wall mirror as he leaned against the arm of the settee behind her. "You're staring again."

"Can't help it." He nodded toward her and grimaced. "If you saw a ghost wrapped in silks and jewels, you'd stare, too."

"I suppose I would," she sighed.

She turned toward her reflection and swept another look over her hair and the jewels at her throat, at the fine silk of Margaret's dress that had been quickly refitted for her by a very put-out dressmaker just that morning. Appropriate, she supposed. A borrowed dress to finish off a borrowed life. What would she wear tomorrow when she was once again herself?

But she felt dressed for a part in a play rather than an event in her own life. Fitting. Because tonight she played the part of bait.

The Duke of Crewe was currently her guard as she waited, hidden from sight, to make her announcement. Although he and Devlin hadn't admitted as much, that was exactly what they were doing. The two had been inconspicuously trading off the responsibility all night so that she would never be alone, not even with Wilkins, who was faithfully in attendance somewhere in the crush of the ballroom. He'd insisted on being present tonight in order to provide as much support as possible and had come by the drawing room a few minutes ago to grudgingly wish her well...and to unsuccessfully talk her out of appearing at the party.

Her old friend knew she planned on revealing her identity tonight, but he knew nothing of the real reason why. He wasn't at all happy about it, knowing that calling attention to herself would put her at further risk. But Devlin had insisted she keep the rest of their plan secret, and she knew he was right. They needed everyone in the ballroom to be shocked and surprised by tonight's announcement. Including Wilkins.

He would understand in a day or two when the danger was finally over and she could explain everything. He would forgive her for keeping secrets from him, they would find Betty, and together, they would be friends and family again, just as they'd been in France. She had to believe that to maintain her courage, despite the faint accusation of betrayal she'd seen in her old friend's eyes.

She blew out a long sigh. At least the party seemed to be going well.

The duchess had outdone herself tonight. The grand town-house was stuffed to the eaves with hundreds of guests who at that moment were being plied with glass after glass of strong drink and tables of refreshments that an army of kitchen staff had spent the past two days and nights creating. The duchess had also hired a sextet of musicians, although she'd done so grudgingly to concede to Lady Theodora's wishes to dance as part of her reward for being there. The entire Raines family needed to be present tonight in a show of force for Peyton, and every one of them would be at her side when she made her announcement.

Despite the last-minute arrangements, Devlin's mother had thrown herself into the task and pulled off the most-talked about event of the season—and no one yet knew the true reason for the gathering. She and Lady Margaret had done their jobs well by visiting as many friends and influential acquaintances as possible in the past two days and by sending personal notes to others, and to everyone they dangled the same intriguing, tantalizing bit of *on dit*—

"You will not want to miss the evening. It will be the topic of conversation across the empire for decades to come!"

Their strategy worked, and their guests scrambled to cancel previous plans and cram into the Duke of Malvern's townhouse, along with several others who hadn't been invited but arrived on the coattails of others. No one was turned away. The more people who heard her announcement, the better. By morning, news of her resurrection would be flowing through London faster than the Thames.

Good. Peyton wanted this over, once and for all. It was time to put the past behind her and move on.

She rose from the desk and turned toward Crewe as he also came to his feet, as any proper gentleman would. Peyton was beginning to think his reputation as a libertine and blackguard was unfounded. "You don't have to stay here to guard me."

"Guarding you?" He laughed at the idea. "I'm not guarding..." When she arched a brow, his lie trailed off, and his shoulders sagged at being caught. "All right, I'm guarding you. And yes, I have to."

Her chest tightened. She shouldn't have been surprised. She *was* the bait, after all. "Because you're afraid I'll be killed if you don't?"

He fixed her a hard look. "Because I'm afraid Dartmoor will kill *me* if I don't."

A smile teased at her lips, then faded into grim solemnity. Absently, she rubbed her left glove. She'd tucked into it a small piece of lace that Teddy had given her as a good luck charm. Even as she rubbed her fingers over it, though, she knew she'd need much more than luck to survive tonight.

"I am so very sorry for what my father's actions put you through," she apologized to Crewe, "the lengths you've had to go to in order to make right his crimes."

"It wasn't only your father." He added in a sardonic murmur,

"Mine had a little something to do with it, too."

"But my father controlled the money. Without him, none of what they did would have—"

"It wasn't only your father," he repeated, all teasing now gone, and so firmly this time that she knew not to brook any more argument.

The door opened, and Devlin strode inside, carrying a glass of champagne. The sight of him took her breath away. Dressed in Bond Street's finest, he exuded power and privilege. Every inch of him proclaimed him a duke, from the shine of his blond hair to his diamond cravat pin, from the cut of his black kerseymere jacket to his white satin waistcoat.

More—he exuded a sense of trust and solidity that had been missing in her life. How would she be able to live on without that, once their plan was over?

Devlin gestured at Crewe. "Would you give us a few moments alone?"

"Of course. I'll find the duchess and see if she needs my help with anything."

As he turned to leave, Peyton placed her hand on his arm to stop him. "Thank you, Lucien." Her voice hitched with emotion. "For everything."

Impetuously, she rose up on tiptoe and placed a kiss on his cheek.

Surprised by the small show of affection, he gave her a stiff bow and retreated from the room, closing the door after himself.

When Peyton looked back at Devlin, she found him staring at her—and frowning. She knew it wasn't the kiss that bothered him.

"It's almost time for the announcement." He held out the champagne flute to her. "Are you ready?"

More grateful for the drink than she would dare admit, she accepted the glass and nodded as she raised it to her lips to take a long sip.

"You don't have to do this."

The somber tone of his voice turned the taste of the champagne on her tongue to acid. She lowered the flute and stared into the bubbling liquid.

"It's not too late to change your mind. You can wait until you're absolutely certain you should reveal your identity."

"It's the best way we have to bring Horrender to justice," she said, studying her glass. If she looked up at him, the concern in his eyes would undo her.

"We'll find another way."

She shook her head. "What our fathers did... They can't be allowed to harm anyone else."

To seal that promise, she finished the remaining champagne in one long drink.

"But you don't have to endanger yourself to do it."

"If I don't, then your family will continue to be in danger. So will Crewe and you...and me." She admitted, "I no longer want to live in fear of the past."

"Just in fear of the future."

Her heart painfully skipped a beat at his quiet accusation, and her gaze rose to meet his. "If I don't do this, I will never be safe." Then she added in a whisper, "And I can never find absolution for my father."

He paused, as if he didn't believe that would ever be possible, then said instead, "Then your new life will begin."

"Yes." The word emerged as a breathless murmur, barely audible, because Peyton knew it was a lie. *I'm not a phoenix who can rise from the ashes to be more glorious than before.*

From the ballroom, the musicians struck up the first flourishes of a new song. The music was muted, but the tune was unmistakable.

"A waltz." Her shoulders dropped as an inexplicable yet deep sadness of all she'd lost came over her. "I'm a hypocrite. I told Theodora how to scheme her way into her first dance at a ball when I've never even been to one."

"Never?"

She shook her head. "I had to leave London before I debuted." Had she led a normal life, her debut would have been magical, a special evening shared with her mother and father, who would have been so proud of her. That loss pierced her, even after all these years. "The only true society event I attended was your mother's musicale at Dartmoor House."

"Well then." Devlin took her empty flute, set it aside, and held out his hand. "Dance with me."

Her mouth fell open. "You can't be serious!"

"Perfectly so." He gave her a low bow. "May I have this waltz, Miss Chandler?"

She bit her bottom lip. She should refuse. Tonight wasn't a time for play. Yet she couldn't resist another opportunity to be in his arms, and she slipped her hand into his.

He took her into position in his arms, then swept her into the waltz. He led her through the basic steps rather than leading her into more challenging maneuvers, as if realizing her dance skills were rusty. *Rusty?* She bit back a laugh. Nonexistent! Yet they moved together more fluidly than she would have thought possible, every step reminding her of how perfectly they'd moved together when they'd made love.

He shifted her closer. The heat of his body and the masculine scent of him filled her senses until she longed for nothing more than to find a way to crawl beneath his skin and be with him always.

Dear God, how much she would miss him! And not just the joining of bodies, although that had been more special than she'd ever imagined making love could be. No...she would miss *him*. She would miss his strength, his resolve, and most of all his assurances that all would be well, even when she knew it wouldn't.

He lowered his mouth to her ear. "Enjoying your waltz?"

"Very much."

"Yet you don't seem happy." He stopped dancing and reached up to stroke her cheek so tenderly that she had to close her eyes to bear it.

"I could be." She forced a teasing lilt into her voice that she certainly didn't feel. "If you kissed me."

A smile curled his lips. "Who am I to stand in the way of your happiness?"

He lowered his head and brought his mouth to hers. The tenderness of his kiss shivered a low heat through her. Slowly, she wrapped her arms around his neck and leaned into his embrace, pressing her front against his and craving more...more reassurance, more certainty, more determination. More of *him*. But the most she could do at the moment was part her lips and let him sweep inside in a kiss that was somehow both impossibly erotic and sweet at the same time. Only Devlin had ever made her feel this way. She knew in her heart no one else ever would.

For one precious moment, they were frozen in time, completely in the present moment, and for once, not a captive of the past or the future. Peyton wanted to stop time forever and remain right here with him, when nothing from the past could rise up and hurt them, when the fear of whatever the future would bring couldn't yet consume them...when the terrible sense of impending loss couldn't overwhelm her.

But time could never stand still. She knew that better than anyone. Regretfully, she broke the kiss and stepped out of his arms.

Thankfully, he didn't attempt to reach for her and kept his expression carefully neutral despite the visible way he worked to control his breathing. Then he asked the one question with the power to cut her like a knife—"Do you still plan on leaving?"

She allowed herself a single hard blink. "I can't stay."

"You can. You'll have a new life here." He smiled at himself and corrected, "You'll have an actual life here."

But what kind of life would it be, alone even while surrounded by strangers in a city which had become as foreign to her as the deserts of Arabia? Who could she trust or depend upon?

"My mother and sisters have already embraced you. They'll

be upset if you leave."

"And when they learn what my father did, how he enabled monsters to harm innocent people?" Her voice broke, and it took all her strength to force out her fear, "Will they still embrace me then?"

"You need to give them a chance, Peyton. They understand the plight of innocents."

How much she wanted to believe that! But when his family learned the extent of the crimes that had been committed, when everything they'd believed in was destroyed, what would they think of her then? And Devlin...would the past take him from her, too? "Can *you* forgive my father's role in harming you?"

"I don't have to forgive your father, Peyton. I only have to accept what he did." Empathy colored his voice. "You're the one who has to find a way to forgive."

How could she forgive when everything about London reminded her of her father and the price her family had paid for what he'd done? How could she carve out a future here when the past still haunted her?

"I don't know how." Each word emerged from her lips with agonizing hesitation. "I need your help."

"I can't help with that." His eyes were more grim than she'd ever known them. "You have to find a way to do that yourself, or you will never find peace."

She reached for him. "Devlin—"

A sharp knock rapped on the door only a second before it opened, and Margaret rushed inside, all reassuring smiles and glowing excitedly.

Peyton turned away before Margaret could see her swipe at her eyes.

"Mama sent me to fetch you." She saw their grim expressions, pulled up short, and frowned. "Are you all right?"

"We're fine," Devlin answered, and Peyton was glad. At that moment, she couldn't have uttered a word.

"Good." Margaret held open the door. "It's time for your

announcement."

Oh God. Peyton inhaled a deep breath that did little to steel her for what was to come and nodded.

Devlin held out his hand to her. "Shall we?"

Another nod, just as stiff as the first. Yet Peyton allowed him to take her arm and escort her from the drawing room, with Margaret following dutifully behind.

"You don't have to do this," Devlin told her again. His concern devastated her. "It's not too late to change your mind."

"Yes, it is," she replied in a hoarse whisper. *Ten years too late.*

Forgive the past…that's what Devlin wanted her to do, and she could think of no better way to do that than bringing all the secrets out into light. She'd made up her mind. She would put an end to it by doing just that…by telling the world everything.

Tonight.

Chapter Eighteen

DEVLIN STOLE A glance at Peyton as he escorted her toward the ballroom stairs. Her spine was ramrod straight, her head held high. Every inch of her shouted how determined she was to go through with their plan. He prayed they'd made the right decision.

His mother and Crewe waited for them on the stair landing. Devlin felt Peyton pull in a deep breath as he led her toward them.

"You will do fine," Devlin murmured, giving one last word of encouragement before handing her off to his mother. "Just do as we planned. Stand before them and admit your true identity, and Crewe, Chase, and I will take care of the rest."

Her stiff nod did little to reassure him. Neither did the parting look she gave him over her shoulder as his mother linked Peyton's arm in hers and led her toward the wrought iron railing overlooking the crowded ballroom below.

Yet the only way onward was forward, so he nodded at Crewe, and the two men flanked Peyton and the duchess in a show of solidarity. Margaret and Theodora lingered at the side of the landing, their presence reinforcing the Raines family's support. After all, this moment wasn't about making a news announcement. It was a show of power.

His mother gestured to the portly but authoritative master of ceremonies at the bottom of the stairs. The man nodded and signaled to the lead musician to end the song. When the music stopped, he pounded his staff on the marble floor and shouted over the din of conversation to capture the attention of everyone in the ballroom and turn their gazes to the landing above.

"My lords, ladies, and all welcomed guests," he called out loudly with such authority that his face turned red from the effort. "May I turn your attention to Her Grace, the Duchess of Dartmoor?"

With an exaggerated sweep of his arm and a low bow, he retreated to the side of the landing.

The duchess smiled and imperiously raised her hand to wave to her guests, most of whom had lifted their glasses to her in a toast. "On behalf of the Dukes of Dartmoor and Crewe and myself, we thank you for joining us on such short notice, but I assure you that attending tonight will be worth your while."

Confused whispers spilled through the crush, and Devlin knew why. They all thought they'd been invited to a rushed engagement announcement for him. Peyton's beautiful presence only reinforced that notion. But the mention of Crewe dashed all certainties of that.

"There is an important announcement to be made tonight, one which could no longer wait and which I am certain you would all want to hear for yourselves. Now, I have a very special friend I would like you to meet."

She turned her smile on Peyton and stepped back to let Peyton become the center of attention.

Devlin watched her closely. Her nervousness was palpable, as well it should be. While this moment might have been a carefully orchestrated trap, the revelation of her identity was real. So was all the support his family and Crewe would provide in the days and weeks to come. He hoped she realized that.

"Good evening," Peyton called out. Her knuckles turned white as she gripped the railing. "Thank you, Your Grace, for the kind introduction and for hosting this wonderful gathering." She looked from the duchess to Crewe and Devlin in turn, bobbing her head as courteously as possible without releasing the railing. It was her anchor. "Your Graces." She pulled back her shoulders to steel herself and turned toward the ballroom below. "And my deepest gratitude to all of you for attending tonight."

She forced a bright—if wholly disingenuous—smile. He'd never seen her more unsettled, more nervous.

"I'm glad you could all be here to welcome me back to London. You see, I've been gone a long while." Her smile never wavered. "Long enough that I don't expect any of you to recognize me, although you might remember my parents, Charles and Eleanor Chandler." She paused a beat to let that sink in before admitting, "I am Peyton Chandler, and the last time any of you saw me was ten years ago, at Dartmoor House, before our carriage was attacked."

Stunned bewilderment swept over the room, and a dropped pin could have been heard in the resulting silence. Everyone stood as still as statues, doing nothing more than blinking. Including whichever peers were working with Horrender.

"I was hurt and afraid for my life," she continued, "and I had no choice but to leave England and allow everyone to think I died that night." Her lips twisted into an amused smile at the gaping stares and wide eyes. "Yes, I have returned from the dead." Then all her dark amusement at her situation faded. "I understand completely the confusion you must be feeling, and I assure you that I will reveal more in the days to come. But I can also confess that I am very much looking forward to getting to know you. Again." She forced a calm smile. "And I look forward to returning to the old Chandler townhouse tonight...returning once more to my true home."

The room remained in silent stillness. There were no whispers, no flitting of fans, no snide remarks or cutting comments. No one moved. They simply stared at her as they tried to absorb her announcement, taking a moment to dig back far into their memories and remember what they'd heard of the Chandlers and that horrible attack whose grisly details filled the papers for weeks. Peyton stood just as motionless as they, bravely letting them have their long looks, as if she were a lioness on display in the Tower Menagerie—No, a mythical creature they couldn't fathom.

She was exactly that, Devlin decided as he stepped up to her side to commence the second part of their plan tonight. She was a phoenix rising from the ashes of death.

Devlin placed his hand over hers as it rested on the railing and turned to address the crowd. Everything had gone according to plan. Now, they needed to leave the party, set the trap, and wait for—

But Peyton stopped him with a squeeze of her hand and a quick sidestep in front of him. "I have returned now," she continued, loudly and with just as much determination as before, "because I have learned who murdered my parents that terrible night all those years ago."

Devlin's heart stopped. *This* wasn't what they'd planned. All she was supposed to have done was declare she had returned and was going back home. Claiming evidence of her parents' murders was going too far. "Peyton, do *not*—"

"Josiah Horrender!" she called out impulsively, his name loudly echoing through the ballroom.

Devlin bit down a curse. She'd gone beyond dangling herself as bait. This wasn't a simple revelation of her identity.

It was a declaration of war.

"Peyton," he warned under his breath. Beside them, Crewe, his mother, and Margaret stared in bewilderment. "Stop this."

"No," she muttered back, just as low. "I have to do this. It all has to stop—tonight." Then she pulled herself up as tall as possible and called out to the ballroom, "I have irrefutable proof that Josiah Horrender and his men were responsible. That was why I returned to London, to put together the final pieces of the puzzle. Now, I intend to go to Bow Street in the morning to have that murderer brought to justice."

Low whispers rose around the room at the intensity of her voice.

"My father was not a saint. He had gotten involved with men and activities he shouldn't have." She didn't dare glance at Devlin as she said that. "But I plan to put to rights all that happened that terrible night, as my parents would want me to do, and I hope I can rely on your support in the coming days as Horrender and all his associates are rounded up, arrested, tried, and sentenced." She paused to drive home the knife—"*Every* last one of them."

Instantly, like the bursting of a bubble, the ballroom exploded into murmurs of disbelief and mutters of indignation, followed by loud utterings of distrust and a few bits of laughter scattered throughout. But mostly, there was confusion, even as shouts rose throughout the room and demands called up to Devlin and Crewe—

"Dartmoor!" Lord Melville shouted. "What the devil is going on here?"

"Can't you tell?" Baron Thornton shouted down Melville. "It's one of Crewe's bad jokes!"

"Not a joke," another gentleman shouted from the rear of the ballroom. "A fraud! She can't possibly be who she says she is."

That last sent a wave of nods sweeping around the room, now joined by calls from the ladies for explanations. Soon, raised voices called out as loudly as the silence had been deep only a few moments before.

Peyton's face paled, but the brave woman stood firm at the railing, even though she had no idea what to say to defend herself.

But Devlin did.

"Your attention, please!" He took Peyton's arm in his right hand, just in case she decided to bolt, and raised his left to beg their patience so he could explain. "You all know my mother and sisters' impeccable reputations, although I daresay mine is a bit more tarnished. *Only* a bit." A ripple of laughter went up at that, exactly as he'd hoped. He gestured at Lucien. "As for Crewe…well, the less said the better."

More laughter scattered across the room at Crewe's expense. *Good.* But the men working with Horrender certainly wouldn't be laughing.

"I can assure you that all of us can confirm the truth of what you've just heard," Devlin continued. "Tonight is no joke, and Miss Chandler is no fraud. As old family friends and business associates of Charles and Eleanor Chandler, the Raines family swears to the veracity of her identity. I promise you, she is whom she claims to be, and all of us support her."

Peyton smiled gratefully at him, and she mouthed, *Thank you.*

He gave her arm a quick squeeze. "My family and I urged Miss Chandler to reveal herself to those of us here tonight who were friends and business associates of her mother and father." And various hangers-on who came uninvited on their coattails. He would have said the more, the merrier, but there was nothing at all amusing about what they were doing. "Miss Chandler and I decided it was only right that you all learned the truth at the same time. Although more information will be forthcoming in the following days, I now ask that you give Miss Chandler the peace and quiet she needs to settle into her home and re-enter London society."

Crewe stepped forward, taking his cue. "Now, on behalf of Dartmoor and myself—and the overgenerous hospitality of the Duke of Malvern, who has no idea what we have done to his townhouse in his absence—please stay and enjoy your evening."

Crewe signaled to the army of footmen waiting in the wings to ply the room with trays of fresh drinks, then to the musicians to strike up another song. The master of ceremonies nodded and hurried back downstairs to once more take charge of the evening, as if this were any other society party.

Devlin quickly escorted Peyton away before the curious crowd could rush up the stairs to them and overwhelm her.

"Stay behind and be good hostesses," he told his mother and

sisters, knowing they would be the first line of defense. He ordered Crewe, "Keep everyone happy, especially my family."

"Of course." When Crewe protectively moved to the duchess's side, Devlin knew the Raines women would be in good hands.

He led Peyton down the hall, but instead of taking her back into the sitting room, he opened the door of another unused room. The furniture lay covered by ghostly looking sheets, and the only light came from a slant of moonlight shining through the windows whose shutters hadn't been latched against the night. Cool, quiet, dark...the room would do fine as a place where she could rest a moment and catch her breath. He closed and locked the door.

"What the hell were you thinking, naming Horrender like that?" Devlin bit out, his anger rising.

"That it was time to seize the moment." She leaned back against the edge of a square-shaped card table, her relief that the announcement was over visibly washing over her. "Isn't that what you wanted from me—to let go of the past and embrace the present?"

"Do *not* twist my words," he half-growled. "We had agreed to reveal your identity, not make public accusations. What you did was reckless."

"Why?" She lifted her chin in challenge. "Horrender has already tried to kill me twice, and I'd rather not give him time to improve upon his attempts. Best to force him out into the light." Her eyes blazed with determination. "This is what we wanted—a confrontation. All I did was speed it along."

"And if he strikes before we're ready?"

"Then we best be ready because there is no going back now. There's only going forward." This time when her eyes gleamed, it wasn't only determination that lit their depths. He felt that look curl through him, stirring desire all the way down to the tip of his cock. She murmured temptingly, "Embrace the now."

Embrace me *now.* The invitation hung on the dark shadows

around them, as real as if she'd actually uttered it aloud. It was all the permission he needed.

Devlin closed the distance between them with a single step and captured her mouth beneath his.

Chapter Nineteen

PEYTON CAUGHT HER breath at the raw hunger she tasted in Devlin's kiss, coupled with a fierce need that matched her own. They both knew their time together was growing short and that moments alone like this would prove increasingly rare—if they ever came again. She wasn't foolish enough to let this opportunity pass by untaken and shamelessly arched against him.

Years from now, when she lived alone in France and reflected on this time when her life changed forever, she would have this moment to sustain her, this one moment of perfection before her life irrevocably changed again. This last moment with the man she loved.

The tip of his tongue traced the seam of her lips in silent cajoling for her to open, and with a soft sigh, she did just that, allowing him inside. His tongue took long, seductive licks that explored the recesses of her mouth and then transformed into insistent and steady thrusts. She suddenly felt so weak that she sagged against the table behind her. The sensation of falling away completely overcame her, stopped only by the solidity of his hard shoulders beneath her hands.

As she closed her lips around his tongue and sucked, a groan rose from the back of his throat. The low sound vibrated into her mouth and sent a delicious thrill spiraling through her, one that landed with an aching thud between her legs.

"Touch me," she ordered softly and raked her fingers through the silky hair at his nape.

He obliged and swept his large hands up the sides of her body. Heat penetrated her dress and underclothes as if they weren't even there, and goosebumps shivered across her skin in his wake. When he paused to cup her breasts in his hands, her confining stays kept him from giving her the kinds of touches she craved, so she twisted away from him to reach behind her back in an attempt to unbutton her bodice. But her fingers couldn't reach the little buttons, and a whimper of frustration escaped her.

"Let me," he insisted hotly as he moved his mouth away from hers, along her jaw to her ear. The tip of his tongue traced the outer curl as his hands made swift work of unbuttoning her dress. She gasped when his tongue plunged inside her ear with the same swirling motion, for one delicious heartbeat not noticing that he'd pulled loose her bodice and untied her stays until they hung loose between her gown and her shift.

His hands slipped under the back of her gown and slid across the thin cotton of her shift to her breasts, as if nothing at all existed between them and her flesh. He strummed his thumbs over her aching nipples, teasing them into hard little nubs, and she arched her back to bring his hands harder against her.

When he gave her nipples a sharp squeeze between his fingers, Peyton nearly burst out of her skin. "Devlin!"

The frustrating devil had the nerve to chuckle as he tugged down the front of her clothes and revealed her bare breasts to his eyes. Shamelessly, she let him look, reveling in the hungry expression that gripped his face. Finally, he dipped his head to take her nipple between his lips, and the pull of his lips drew a low moan from her. She dug her fingers into his hair as his mouth worshipped at her, licking and suckling and nipping gently with his teeth in a sweet torment that made her shake.

But their clothes were still frustratingly in the way. She slid her hand between them. "Let me," she repeated his words and quickly unbuttoned his fall.

She pushed herself away from the table and onto her tiptoes as she rose up to claim his mouth in a blistering kiss that ripped away his breath—or perhaps he lost his breath because she also slipped her hand into his trousers and cupped him, hot and heavy, against her palm.

She smiled against his mouth as she began to fondle him, her fingers teasing and caressing along his hardening shaft. She gave him a tender yet possessive squeeze, then pulled him free of his trousers. His erection stood thick and hard, and the steely length flexed against her hand as she rubbed her palm over this round head and claimed the wet drop that formed at its tip. He belonged to her, every last bit of him, for now at least. She refused to surrender that.

His thighs clenched as he leaned into her hand, his hands now gripping the table on both sides of her and his eyes squeezed shut. But she wanted him to look at her, for him to remember this wonderful coming together as much as she would. And she knew exactly what to do to make that happen.

Slowly, she lowered onto her knees and took him between her lips.

His eyes flew open, and he uttered a guttural sound of surprise that turned into a shuddering growl as she began to move her mouth over him. In turns, she took him deep and then pulled back to let him nearly slip free of her lips before plunging down over him again. Always, she kept a firm suction around him, even as she lifted her eyes to watch him watching her as she gave him this primal pleasure.

"That feels... Sweet Jesus," he muttered. Unable to find the words, he reached down to stroke his knuckles over her cheek. "So good....so damn good..."

Spurred on by the hot desire she glimpsed in his eyes, she increased the pace of her mouth bobbing against him, of her lips pumping along his length.

Devlin groaned and plunged his hands into her hair. He held

her head still and began to pulse his hips lightly against her.

"Mmm mmm," she purred, her own need for him growing with every pounding heartbeat. The sound vibrated along his length, and he flexed inside her mouth, giving her the first salty-sweet taste of his male essence as a drop escaped him.

Quickly, the intensity grew until he thrust eagerly between her lips, and she thrilled at the electric spark that surged through her. Heat throbbed wantonly between her legs, and she felt herself grow wet, even though he'd yet to touch her there. Bringing him this pleasure stirred her own, and even now, as he closed his eyes and hung his head between his shoulders, she felt herself nearing the edge.

With a lingering kiss to his hot tip, she rose to her feet, brushing her breasts against his chest as she slid up his body to kiss him.

"Take me," she whispered against his lips. She needed him the way she'd never needed any other man, the way she knew she'd never need anyone else. "Here." Her hands grabbed at her skirts and yanked them up. "Now."

With a growl, he grabbed her around the waist and lifted her onto the edge of the table. He guided his erection toward her center, then took her hips in both hands. He thrust forward while his hands yanked her toward him, plunging himself deep inside her tight warmth, filling her so completely that a cry of joy tore from her. The sound transformed into a low moan as he began to thrust inside her, and she could do nothing more than cling to him and fight to keep her breath.

"You are amazing, Peyton," he murmured against her temple as he circled his hips against her, the teasing sensation simply torturous. "Brilliant." He retreated from her body's tight hold on him. "Beautiful." He plunged deep and pulsed a jolt of electricity through her as his pelvis ground against her clitoris. "Utterly delicious in every way."

"Prove it," she taunted breathlessly.

He answered by thrusting into her so hard that her bottom lifted off the table, and stars flashed before her eyes. Never…*never* had she experienced such desire as this before, such raw pleasure.

Yet somehow, it still wasn't enough. He'd freed her from the darkness of the past, and she wanted to show him how much he meant to her.

"Stop," she choked out and placed her hands flat against his chest to push him away. "Devlin—stop."

He halted instantly. Slowly, he stepped back and slipped himself from her warmth, his chest heaving with stolen breath as he stared down at her, puzzled. "You don't want—"

"God yes!" She cupped his face between her hands and showed him with a hot, open-mouthed kiss exactly how much. "But not like that." She slipped off the table and turned her back toward him. "New life, new future…"

She placed her hands on the table, stepped her legs apart, and gazed at him invitingly over her shoulder.

She whispered tremulously, "New everything."

Devlin stepped forward and entered her from behind.

Peyton tensed at the unfamiliar angle. As if he understood she needed a moment to become used to this new intimacy, he stood perfectly still, doing nothing more than holding himself inside her and letting her catch her breath. Then, when she couldn't bear the stillness a moment longer, she began to rock herself back against him.

The teasing little pulses of her bottom against him soon grew bolder, and she pushed away against the table in hard, smacking thrusts of her bottom against his pelvis. A rollicking, rocking rhythm formed between them, and she realized again how perfectly their bodies fit together, their needs and desires matching in a way that moved past the physical and down to their souls.

He reached around her and nestled his hand between her legs.

"Devlin," she forced out breathlessly between thrusts. "What are you—"

His thumb found her clitoris and rubbed it. He caressed her

intimately even as his hard length continued to thrust into her, and she shuddered at the spark of pleasure that heated through her, shooting out to the tips of her fingers and toes. She closed her eyes, licked her lips, and gave over to the sensation that consumed her, a mix of being alive tempered by the overwhelming trust between them. What they were doing was both animalistic and the most tender, loving melding of bodies imaginable, and a choking sob tore from her.

Beneath a rush of emotions, she arched her back and broke with a shuddering cry. He thrust deep into her tight warmth and held himself there. His body tensed against hers, and she felt his thighs clench as the rush of his release surged inside her, as her body quivered around his to milk every sweet drop from him. A second pulse of joy gripped her.

Devlin lay over her, his spent length still buried inside her, as he fought to regain his breath. He gathered her into his arms beneath him and nuzzled the back of her neck.

"I'm sorry," he murmured into her hair. "I didn't mean to come inside you like that." He placed an apologetic kiss to her nape and explained simply, "I lost control."

The happiness that rose inside her at his quiet confession thrilled her as much as their joining of bodies—no. *More.* This happiness filled her heart until the foolish thing wanted to burst from her chest. She, alone, had the power to destroy the hard-won control he'd fought so hard for so long to manage, just as he was the only man capable of melting her heart. She held no regrets about giving herself to him. And never would.

"You don't have to be in control," she whispered into the shadows around them. "Not with me."

He nuzzled her shoulder. Neither of them was in a hurry to release the other and end the moment. Then she felt him tense, and she held her breath—

"Don't go to France. When all this is over, stay here." He placed a kiss to her shoulder so tenderly that she ached from it. "With me." He murmured breathlessly into her ear, "I'll tell my mother and sisters the truth about what our fathers did, once Horrender's caught and can't harm any of us ever again."

He was giving her what she wanted. But what he expected in return...could she do it? Could she stay in England and begin a new life in the place that had taken the old one?

A hot tear slid down her cheek, and she whispered the only consolation she could offer, "I love you, Devlin."

His arms tightened around her. "I love you, too."

A long breath eased from her. There were no secrets left between them now. She was drained, physically and emotionally, and what she knew, without any doubt as he held her safe within his arms, was more than that he'd finally agreed to tell the truth about his father, more than that she could trust in him and take comfort in his strength and solidity—

She knew she had to find a way to put the past behind them. Once and for all.

Chapter Twenty

PEYTON STOOD ON the footpath edging the wide Mayfair avenue and stared up at the old townhouse as the bells of St George's rang the midnight hour. Four bays wide, three stories tall, made of white stone and edged by wrought iron, the windows still shuttered against the night and against the past... The Chandler townhouse.

Her home.

Only it didn't feel at all like home. Instead, she felt as if she'd fallen into one of the nightmares she used to have when she'd first fled to France, when thoughts of home and all she'd lost hit her so hard, she often woke sobbing with tears. Proctor and Wilkins did their best to comfort her, but even their love and attention couldn't give her the consolation she needed. Nothing could. Her parents and the only home she'd ever known had been ripped away from her. How she'd managed to survive...

Perhaps Devlin was right. Perhaps she was stronger than she'd realized.

Now the shell of that former existence stood before her, silent and dark...lifeless. She'd avoided coming here since she'd arrived in London. She'd told herself she'd been too focused on gaining her revenge to visit here, too cautious about making mistakes that might have revealed her true identity. *Lies.* She'd simply been too frightened of the ghosts haunting the place.

As she gazed at the façade, she held her breath and strained her ears to listen for any sound.

Silence.

Her shoulders sagged. What else would have greeted her if not silence and stillness? She didn't really know what she'd expected to happen now that she was finally here. Even as she stared up at the house, not yet daring to venture a toe over the threshold, she half-expected specters to come drifting out of the darkness toward her.

But the only way forward was through that front door. So she stepped up the front stairs, took a deep breath to steel herself, and opened it. A slow creak welcomed her as the door swung wide and revealed the darkness beyond.

A chill ran down Peyton's spine. This was the very last place she wanted to be! But Chase and Devlin insisted she come here tonight. They could protect her here. Even now, in the darkness surrounding the house, she knew the two dukes and their hired men lingered somewhere unseen in the black shadows lining the street, watching over her but remaining hidden until necessary.

But their presence provided little comfort. Horrender would be coming for her, if not tonight then tomorrow, and she had to let herself be found.

"Come into my parlor said the spider to the fly," she murmured and with a shaking hand, lifted the small carriage lantern she carried with her to guide her way. Having no other choice, she stepped inside.

She paused in the entry hall. Goosebumps formed on her arms and legs that had nothing to do with Horrender. Apprehension knotted her belly, and she forced herself to breathe slow and steadily.

Oh, she was being silly! There was no good reason for the chill that swept over her, or the tingle at the back of her knees.

"It's only an empty house," she whispered to calm herself.

When she entered the dining room, she realized exactly how

empty. Gone—everything she remembered about the room had been removed, leaving only a gaping space. No large table that could seat fourteen, no Chippendale buffet tables, no china dresser—no *china*. Her mother's treasured collection was gone, along with all the crystal and silver that had made their dinner parties so grand. So were the large porcelain vases with their tall ostrich feathers that had once framed both sides of the bay window overlooking the square, the rug that had come all the way from Persia, the Murano glass chandelier her father had given her mother as an anniversary present... Even the marble fireplace mantel had been pried away, leaving a massive scar on the wall in its place.

It was the same in her father's study, where empty book shelves now lined the walls, and in the garden room where her mother had loved to take in the afternoon sun and gaze out at her tiny plot of flowers. All the rooms on the ground floor had been stripped bare, most likely by creditors who feared their debts wouldn't be paid any other way, given how the estate had no heir.

But enough decoration remained for a rush of emotion to hit her. The blue wallpaper with large flowers of raised velvet, the checkerboard floor in the entry and stair halls, the plastered ceilings in the main reception rooms with their designs of grape vines and myrtle trees, the rose ceiling medallion in the morning room—even the little plaster bird tucked into the carved leaves that decorated the outside edge of the marble stairs that circled toward the first floor, the same little bird that had fascinated her so much as a girl. All of it churned a flood of memories inside her of happier times, love, and peace.

But it was all a lie.

The money to buy all those beautiful pieces of furniture and decoration, all that crystal and silver, every single book in her father's study, every bit of plaster and marble—it all came from the illegal businesses her father financed for Dartmoor and Crewe. Charles Chandler had hidden it well, too. Oh, their house was lovely, but it wasn't conspicuous for a man of her father's status. He'd made certain of that by hiding most of the money in accounts and businesses on the Continent where his activities couldn't be traced. The same accounts and businesses Peyton had used to live on in France, to take care of Wilkins and Proctor, to buy fencing lessons from Armand Marchand…to pay for her return to London and her revenge.

With numbness and anguish flashing over her in turns, she held up the lantern to light her way and slowly climbed the stairs, passing the first-floor landing en route to the old nursery under the eaves. Her earliest memories of the house and her parents came from there. If anything survived—

She stopped in the doorway to the nursery and choked back a pained sob.

The room was the same as she remembered. Nothing here had been removed, nothing stripped away. It was *exactly* the same, right down to the pink ribbon she'd tied in her hobby horse's tail and the dolls arranged at the tiny table as if waiting for the tea party to begin.

She stepped stiffly into the room, set down the lantern, and picked up a little stuffed bunny. The furry creature with porcelain blue eyes had been one of her favorites, left behind in the nursery when she moved downstairs into her own bedroom. As she ran her fingertips over the soft fur, her throat constricted, and her eyes and nose stung.

Had even her toys been purchased with blood money? Peyton had been the same age as those children caught up in the dukes' illegal enterprises, chained up like slaves in factories or forced to do far worse in brothels. Her father hadn't wanted children to be involved, had balked at what they'd done when he'd discovered it—but how could he have not known that men like Horrender, Crewe, and Dartmoor would do anything to increase their wealth and power, even at the expense of children?

She swung her watery gaze around the room to take it all in. Her childhood had been absolutely ideal, so perfect…

Until the night it wasn't.

She set the bunny down, picked up the lantern, and left the nursery. She would have to do something with all these toys before she sold the house, ended her stay in London, and returned to France where she belonged. She had friends in Lyon and Marseilles and contacts she'd made through Armand and his acquaintances in the military. Here, she had only ghosts.

She halted as she turned onto the first-floor landing. A shadow moved at the bottom of the stairs below. "Devlin?"

When no answer came, the little hairs on her arms stood on end. No, not Devlin.

"Who's there?" she called out, lifting the small lantern, even though its light wasn't strong enough to reach past the bottom step and into the hall below.

She held her breath. Her blood pounded so hard in her ears that the roar of it was deafening, her arms and legs numb as fear flashed up her spine. Armand had taught her well when it came to fighting, as the knife strapped to her thigh attested.

But he hadn't prepared her for acting as bait.

That old familiar taste of helplessness rose sickeningly on her tongue, a horrible metallic taste that she *never* wanted to experience again. Helpless… Everything she'd done since the night of the attack had been to prevent that, only for it to return now with full force.

"Tell me who you are." Anger rose on the heels of her fear, and she demanded, "Now."

The man stepped into the dim circle of lantern light and looked up at her. "Welcome home, Peyton."

Her breath left her in a relieved rush. "Wilkins."

With a faint smile, her shoulders easing down, she descended to the ground floor. She'd never been so happy to see her friend in her life! But he wasn't supposed to be here. According to the plan, the only man who should have been in the house with her tonight was Horrender.

She set the lantern onto the stairs behind her. "You should be at the inn."

"After your announcement tonight at the party, telling everyone you were coming back here? You shouldn't have done that."

"You don't need to worry about me, not anymore." The old guilt tightened her chest at the thought of all he'd sacrificed for her over the years, only for her to exclude him now from their plans. But she had no choice. Chase, Crewe, and Devlin had insisted she tell no one, not even Wilkins. "That's what tonight was about—breaking clean with the past. That's why I had to reveal my identity."

"You didn't share any of your plans with me. Tonight's accusations, your new friendship with Dartmoor, your visit to Seven Dials—" Exasperation laced his voice. "Don't you trust me anymore?"

"Of course I do." She always would. But in stopping Horrender, she had to trust the three dukes more. "You and Proctor dedicated your lives to me." Her throat tightened—Proctor had most likely even given her life for Peyton. "I had you when I had no one else. I will always be grateful for that."

"Now you think you have Dartmoor on your side?"

Something about the way he said that twisted uneasily down her spine. "Yes."

"Then you're an even bigger fool than Betty and I thought."

His unexpected words struck her like a blow. *"Pardon?"*

He ground out in a low voice, "You're ruining everything, all our plans, all those years of waiting and plotting... I won't let you do that."

"That isn't your decision to make," she corrected quietly. She owed him her loyalty for the friendship and protection he'd given her over the past decade, but she wouldn't let him stop her. Her life depended on what happened now. "You should go. We'll talk again in the morning."

"I'm not going anywhere. I've waited too long to return and worked too hard to put everything into place to let you interfere."

A chill prickled across her skin. "What do you mean?"

"Seeking revenge against Dartmoor—you thought the idea was all yours. But you believed only what I wanted you to." A strange expression lit his face—*pride*? "All those investigators you had me hire to find information about that night...you had no idea I'd hired them to work for me instead. Servants always know what their employers are doing, and I knew how your father had been moving money overseas. At my behest, the detectives tracked down all of it. You were told about the land properties and businesses because I couldn't sell those without your signature on the deeds, but you never knew about all the bank accounts, or how I kept them for myself."

Her mind spun. "No—you showed me all the papers, gave me the investigators' evidence..." Then she'd oh-so carefully woven them together into the puzzle she worked inside her armoire like a spider's web, each piece of information building upon the next and illuminating what happened that night.

No, what she *thought* had happened that night.

"I gave you reports I created myself." His eyes gleamed. "All meant to make you believe Dartmoor was there that night, that he was the one who tried to rape you. You were more than happy to blame him." A dark laugh rose from him. "It was all so easy."

The world tilted beneath Peyton, and she reached out to place her hand on the stair banister to steady herself.

"Why?" she rasped out. "*Why* would you do something like that?"

"Because I needed Dartmoor out of the way. What better way to do that than to turn you loose against him?" He stepped toward her, and Peyton retreated around the banister toward the stairs. "You wouldn't have left France if I hadn't convinced you that Dartmoor was behind your parents' murders, that the time was right for you to finally exact your revenge."

He took another step, and Peyton glanced back at the stairs behind her. Every instinct inside her screamed that she had been cornered, yet she couldn't bring herself to strike out, to attack as Armand had taught her. Wilkins had meant nearly everything to her for the past decade. For God's sake, she'd trusted him with her life!

Now he was a complete stranger.

"Letting you destroy Dartmoor would have cleared the way for me to put the old business back together. *My brother's* business, with new peers to protect me and an accountant nearly as sly as your father to hide all the profits."

His confession reverberated through her like a shot. She couldn't believe—"Josiah Horrender...is your brother?"

"Step-brother. *Was*. He's dead now. Dartmoor and Crewe have been chasing a ghost." His ghoulish smile chilled her. "He fled to Ireland after the attack and got his throat slit. I was supposed to deliver you to him that first winter, then join him in restarting the enterprise." He shook his head as if disappointed. "Instead, I had to rebuild it all myself. It wasn't easy doing that from France, especially during the wars, but your money and my brother's connections made it easier. Even then, I was nearly discovered. But I put an end to him, and then you had no one to turn to for protection but me."

A horrible sickening rose into her throat. She knew who... Dear God, her grieving heart *knew*! "It was you," she whispered, barely a sound on her numb lips. "You killed Armand."

A jealous tone darkened his voice. "He'd gotten too close to you."

The way he said that alarmed her, and the shouting inside her head turned to screams. *Too close*... He meant as her lover. Peyton swallowed hard and pressed her hand to her belly. She was going to be sick!

"And Betty Proctor," she breathed out, unable to find her voice. "You murdered her, too."

"No, not my Betty. I couldn't have killed the woman who has been my right hand all these years, who convinced you that I was right whenever you began to doubt me. She's waiting for me right now in Southwark."

Peyton's head swam. The betrayal by the two people she'd trusted most in the world was simply agonizing. "No," she whispered. "That can't be…"

"Such a pretty little fool you were." He lowered a lascivious look over her, and she shuddered. "I couldn't have hoped for a better distraction for Dartmoor than you."

Unable to run past him for the door, knowing he would catch her before she reached it, she slowly shifted back toward the stairs. Her foot brushed against the bottom step, and her hand gripped the banister. She didn't dare turn her back on him. The trust she'd placed in him over the years shattered inside her like glass.

"Except that you distracted him *too* well." A cold fury pulsated from him. "Exactly when did you first lift your skirts for him, hmm? Was it the night you bested him at Barton's, or was it in the opera box?" He cast another glance over her, this time not bothering to try to hide his jealous anger. "Did you enjoy yourself, pet? Did you pant and beg and moan for it like a well-trained little whore?" The icy gleam in his eyes frightened her. "Or did he take you by force?"

When he reached up to trace his fingertip over her cheek, she turned her head away and swallowed hard to keep from casting up her accounts. "Do *not* touch me."

Ignoring her, he continued, "I've heard some women grow to like their attackers. Are you one of those?"

"No," she bit out fiercely. "I am *not* one of those."

"Pity."

An icy warning cut through her belly. She didn't want to fight with him. He had been her friend and protector, and she didn't want to believe what he was telling her because she didn't want to lose yet another person she'd cared about.

But the way he looked at her, the harshness of his words… Could she bring herself to hurt him if she needed to?

"The fire is rising in you, isn't it? The anger. The fight." He caressed his fingers down her neck to her shoulder, where he played with the thin strap of her gown. "Marchand knew that about you, too. That's why he always fought with you before he bedded you. But then, he always did know too much," he muttered, a furrow forming between his brows. "Like the truth about my role in your parents' murders."

Peyton froze. Every muscle in her body turned to stone.

"You haven't figured it out yet, have you?" An amused smile teased at the corners of his mouth. "All that information, all those clues you mapped out so carefully...yet you still can't connect the pieces."

He leaned toward her, so close she could feel the heat of his breath fanning across her cheeks, and she cringed. Even now, she couldn't bring herself to shove him away as he deserved. She had to know, *had* to learn the truth about everything that happened that night...

"I was the footman who walked ahead of the carriage that night in the fog, holding up the lamp to guide it through the city." His eyes gleamed like brimstone. "I led them right to the attackers."

She darted her gaze past him into the darkness, desperate for any sign of movement in the shadows that signaled Chase's men were ready to help her. But only stillness returned her stare. They weren't there!

Her heart plummeted. Of course they weren't. They were outside where they were supposed to have been, watching and waiting. Like her, they would never have thought the enemy would have come from within.

"You were supposed to have been my prize that night. If Dartmoor hadn't interfered, I would have had you." He took a half-step back, but the relief speeding through Peyton proved short-lived when he laughed. "Better late than never."

He lunged.

Peyton sidestepped to the left and threw up her right arm to fling away his hands as they reached for her throat. She tumbled off-balance against the banister and fell. Her back hit the stairs with a hard, teeth-jarring thud and ripped the air from her lungs. But fear kept the pain from registering in her mind, kept her fighting back with all her strength. Without a weapon to use against him, she clawed at him with her fingernails, pushed her thumbs into his eyes, scratched across his face—

With a furious growl, he shoved her hands away, but not before she grabbed at his cravat, yanked his collar away, and revealed his bare neck beneath.

A sickening horror rose up inside her as she stared at his neck where old scars cut jaggedly across his skin. The same scars *she* had put there ten years ago. *Good God...* Her blood froze.

"It was you that night." Her accusation emerged as nothing more than a rasping hiss, as if straight from her nightmares. No— straight from the fires of the hell she'd been cast into once more. "It was *you!*"

He laughed, happy that she'd realized his true identity. More than happy...God help her, he was *aroused*. The face leering in front of her sparked a horrible recognition inside her head, and with it came the flood of memories, terror, and helplessness she'd suppressed since the night of the attack.

That night crashed back over her as if she were once again there on the wet and cold cobblestones beside the carriage. She remembered the impenetrable whiteness of the fog, the acrid smell of the city's coal fires...the hardness of the cobblestones beneath her hands and knees as she scrambled to crawl away, choking down the rising vomit in her throat at the sounds and movements around her. No one heard her screams. No one was coming to help! Then a hand caught her ankle and yanked her to the ground, dragging her back as her fingertips dug into the cobblestones so hard that her nails tore away. She kicked and clawed as she fought with every last bit of strength to somehow stay alive. Sticky blood trickled from the scrapes on her hands and knees, and her throat burned, raw from the relentless screams that tore from her and echoed off the empty buildings around her.

It wasn't until all the air expelled from her lungs that she realized she was once again screaming for her life.

"That's it," Wilkins panted as he used his strength and size to pin her to the stairs beneath him. "Put up a grand fight. Make it worth my while." He grabbed her by the throat with one hand while he shoved the other between them to grasp at her skirt and yank it up past her knees, baring her legs.

With an enraged cry, she kneed him hard between his legs.

Air whooshed out of him like a burst balloon, and he sank onto his side with a plaintive cry.

She scrambled up the stairs, desperate to get away. There was no going down. She would never be able to safely crawl past him, even with him doubled over in pain. The only way to survive was up.

An animal-like growl rose from behind her as she scrambled up the stairs as quickly as she could, ignoring the loud rip of her skirts as the hem caught beneath her feet. But she didn't dare stop, didn't dare slow down even to glance back. She could hear him pounding up the stairs after her, charging right behind on her heels. He was so close that he was almost on top of her when she'd reached the third-floor landing, when her hand grabbed the banister and she propelled herself into the nursery.

She slammed the door after herself so hard that the wall shook. She reached to throw the lock—

There was no lock! No key, no bolt. With an anguished cry, she'd remembered that the nursery had never been locked. Her parents had forbidden it. For her own safety. They hadn't wanted to risk that she'd ever be accidentally locked inside.

Desperately, she grabbed one of the little chairs at her doll's tea table and jammed it under the handle.

She backed away from the door as Wilkins's footsteps reached the landing, then paused. He knew where she'd gone—for God's sake, there was only one door on this floor!—but the silence of that pause boomed over her like thunder, then slithered up her spin when it gave way to the metallic turn of the handle, the soft banging of it against the little chair that kept him from opening it so easily.

The handle fell still.

Peyton held her breath, afraid to move, even to breathe, as a thousand needles of helplessness pricked her skin. She stared at the door, and all her heightened senses strained to figure out what he was doing behind it, why he wasn't coming after her.

Then came the sound of running footsteps. Cold terror spiked in her chest as she suddenly realized—

Wilkins let out a fierce yell and rammed into the door like a bull, shoving his shoulder into it and bashing it open. The door flung back and slammed against the wall. For one moment, his lanky frame was silhouetted against the moonlight shining through the doorway as he paused.

A pause just long enough for Peyton to snatch up the doll's teapot and hurl it at his head.

It smashed against his skull and shattered with a dull thud. He staggered back from the force of the blow, only to be hit again by a barrage of cups and saucers. He threw up his arm to cover his face.

Now. Peyton ran toward him and shoved with all her might, sending him flailing backwards. She raced past him for the stairs. Only two stories, and she would be on the ground, out the door, safe—

A hand grabbed the back of her dress and yanked.

Her feet flew up from under her, and she tumbled down the stairs, each hard marble step bruising her arms and legs as she threw out her arms in a futile attempt to break her fall. She rolled to a stop on the landing. Every inch of her burned and throbbed with pain, but she barely felt it in her desperation to flee. She crawled forward on hands and knees toward the next flight of stairs.

Wilkins stepped in front of her, his black boots blocking her way. She froze, still on her hands and knees, each breath tearing from her lungs as her blood pounded in her ears.

"You think you can leave me?"

Slipping her hand down to the hidden pocket in her skirt, she squeezed her eyes shut as he bent down on his heel and leaned over her to caress his fingertips across her nape. Her hand closed around the slender piece of ivory, and slowly, she rolled onto her back beneath him.

"You think I'd ever let you go?" he taunted in a terrifyingly amused voice.

"Not without a fight!" She gritted her teeth and stabbed the knife upward. The resistance of his flesh gave way beneath the sharp blade.

Wilkins howled with pain. He shoved her away and clamped his hand over the gaping wound in his side. Blood seeped through his clothes and onto his fingers. His face twisted with hatred and fury. He pulled back his fist to punch her—

"Peyton!" The shout landed only a heartbeat before Devlin's large body charged down the hallway from the rear servants' stairs.

Devlin lowered his shoulder and ploughed into Wilkins, sending him tumbling backwards against the banister, then falling down the stairs. A faint trail of blood dripped down the marble steps in his wake and led to his crumpled body as he lay back against the wall halfway to the first-floor landing.

Devlin started downstairs after him.

"No!" Peyton grabbed Devlin's leg to stop him. He'd have to drag her down with him before she let go. She knew—he was reliving that night from so long ago, exactly as she was, but this time, he wouldn't fail to catch her attacker. And kill him.

She couldn't let that happen. The past would not win. *Not this time.*

"Stay with me, Devlin," she pleaded softly. "Save me, just as you did before." She slid her hand up into his as it dangled at his side and laced her fingers through his. "Don't leave me."

He paused in indecision, his gaze flicking between Wilkins

and her. Then his fingers tightened around hers, and he knelt down to sit beside her on the landing and gathered her against him. She wrapped her arms around his neck and held on tightly, safe and protected.

Wilkins let out a snarl of fury at seeing Peyton in Devlin's arms and clenched his fists. He foolishly started back upstairs, his eyes flashing with determination even as bright blood blossomed at his hip. His boot left a red smear on the white marble as he took a step in their direction.

"She's there!" Crewe called out from the stair hall below. Chase followed only a step behind.

"It's Wilkins!" Devlin shouted down to them. "Don't let him get away!"

Chase and Crewe charged up the stairs.

Wilkins took a long look at Peyton, and beneath his gaze, she felt her skin crawl from his betrayal and depravity. Then he raced up the stairs toward them. Peyton caught her breath and braced for a fresh attack.

At the last moment, Wilkins changed direction and hurled himself through the tall window. He launched himself out into the night in a shower of shattered glass and cracked wood.

Peyton bit down a scream at the dull thud of his body hitting the ground below and shuddered violently. Over Devlin's shoulder, she watched Crewe draw a pistol from beneath his greatcoat and charge outside into the dark night.

Chase held his own pistol with one hand and gestured orders with the other as half a dozen men flooded into the house and began to search through the rooms to secure them. The once silent house now thrummed with voices and movement; lanterns blazed to life.

It was all too much, and Peyton gasped for breath to fight back the hot tears that threatened to fall.

"Peyton." Devlin tenderly took her chin in his fingers and lifted her face to exam her. Worry filled his eyes. "Are you all right?" His voice shook. "Did that bastard hurt you?"

She knew what he meant—had he physically harmed her. But the wounds Wilkins cut into her were so much worse than simply physical. She shook her head and whispered, barely louder than a breath, "I trusted him and Proctor. They were family to me." She tightened her arms around his neck and pressed her cheek against his, both to hide her anguish and draw from his strength. "But it was all a lie…" She choked back a sob. "How do I trust anyone now?"

"By not letting them win," he murmured. "They stole your past from you." Devlin rested his lips against her hair to provide the only comfort he could. "Don't let them steal your future, too."

She gave a jerking nod and buried her face in his chest. The emotions finally overwhelmed her, and the tears fell, soaking into his jacket. "It was Wilkins, that night of the attack," she choked out between tears. "I remember it now." Then she lifted her head to look at him through stinging eyes. "I remember everything. Including you."

Silently, Devlin brushed a lock of her hair from her face that had come loose in the fight and tucked it behind her ear.

"I'm so sorry." She tightened her arms around him and clung to him, just as she had all those years before, the first time he'd saved her from Wilkins. But this time, it wasn't from fear. "I'm so sorry I ever doubted you."

"You had every right."

She didn't believe that, but she loved him for saying so. "You saved me." She didn't mean from Wilkins, not this night nor the night of the attack.

Devlin had quite simply saved her soul.

Crewe returned with an unhurried gait and a solemn expression. He slowly holstered his pistol as he climbed the stairs to them.

"Wilkins is dead." He avoided Peyton's gaze and told Devlin quietly, "He didn't survive the fall."

Peyton let the air seep out of her lungs with a ragged, cleansing sigh. Wilkins's death felt like the lifting of a sickness, one which had been a part of her for so long that she only recognized it now by its absence. The same with the house around her, whose dark shadows had finally been exorcised of their ghosts, once and for all.

When Devlin tenderly kissed her, to soothe away the last of her grief, absolution and acceptance warmed through her. She knew then that the past would never harm her again.

Chapter Twenty-One

D EVLIN STOOD AT the window of the drawing room at Dartmoor House and looked down into the street.

The cold, foggy night had given way to a beautiful morning. Children would be running through the parks with their nannies. Lords and ladies would be riding along Rotten Row on the back of finely bred horses or in barouches with the tops all down to take in the sunshine. Servants would be scurrying to markets or filling service yards across London with their gossip as they completed their work. Laborers would be going about their jobs at warehouses along the river, at storefronts or factories tucked into less savory parts of town. Not one of them would be aware of the bombshell that struck last night and that was already working to change so many lives.

Starting right here in his own drawing room. He turned away from the window and sent his mother and Margaret a reassuring smile he certainly didn't feel.

The time had come to pay the piper.

He cleared his throat. "Thank you for joining me."

As if sensing his nervousness, Margaret poured him a cup of tea and held it out to him.

His shoulders fell. Sweet Megs. Finding her a good and loving husband would be the next challenge he'd have to face, now uphill all the way after last night's events. But that would be a completely different conversation from the one he was about to have.

He'd made this promise to Peyton, and he planned on keeping his promises. *All* of them.

"You sounded so dire when you asked us to join you." His mother glanced at the door. "Should we also ask Teddy?"

"Not yet." He accepted the tea cup from his sister, even though he didn't want it. What he wanted was a bottle of whiskey. No, a barrel of it. "I need to speak with you two first. Alone."

"And Peyton—shouldn't she be here?" The duchess eyed him curiously. "I am assuming she's the reason for this conversation."

"She is." He leaned back against the arm of the sofa across the table from them, unable to find the patience to actually sit. "And no, she shouldn't be here." Which was why he had gathered them here while Peyton was still at Brechenhurst where she'd spent the night. He'd taken her there because it was the only place in London where she felt safe without him, while he Chase, and Crewe waited at the Chandler townhouse for the authorities. He would retrieve her later, once everything here had been brought into the light of day. "This concerns the Raines family. I'll leave it up to you two to decide how much to tell Teddy, if anything."

His mother's mouth pursed into a grim line. "You're leading me to believe this will be a very uncomfortable conversation."

"Yes." There was no point attempting to soften that. He'd never wanted to have this conversation. Yet he also knew Peyton was right. They couldn't move into the future until they'd put the past to rest. In every way. "It's about the old Duke of Dartmoor." Even now, he couldn't bring himself to call the bastard his father. Some things would never change. "You need to know the truth about what he did."

The two women visibly steeled themselves, their fingers tightening around their cups and their expressions turning grim.

Devlin set aside his unwanted tea. "Let me start at the beginning."

By the time he'd finished sharing what Dartmoor, Crewe, and Chandler had done all those years ago—although even now, he left out the more grisly details—the tea had grown cold, and the two women's faces had paled as white as the cups in their hands. Silence stretched over the room, interrupted only by the soft ticking of the mantel clock.

Devlin said nothing more and let the information settle over them.

Margaret turned her face away, but not before he saw the glistening in her pained eyes.

The duchess rested her tea cup on the saucer that had balanced on her knee this whole time, but her spine remained ramrod straight, her shoulders held just as imperiously as ever. "And Peyton knows all this?" she asked cautiously, unable to prevent a raw hitch from catching in her voice.

"Yes." Devlin pushed himself away from the sofa and drew himself up to his full height. "She's the one who insisted I tell you, once you were no longer in danger. She wants no more secrets."

"She's right," Margaret said quietly, then set down her cup and pushed herself to her feet to pace behind the sofa. "Secrets like those are never good. Who else knows?"

That was just like Megs, to already begin assessing the damage and potential destruction. Their father had taught her that lesson well: don't ever assume the best when the worst could always come. He answered, "Lucien Grenier."

She nodded, taking it in. "And Malvern and Greysmere, too, I suppose."

"Not Malvern."

"Pardon?" She turned her good ear toward him. The small movement nearly undid him. The Raines family would live with the scars of their father's deeds for the rest of their lives.

"Not Malvern," he repeated, slightly more loudly. "Shay has his own burdens. There was no reason to share ours with him, too."

With another nod, she began to pace again while his mother remained very still and kept her eyes focused on him, but he knew both women's minds were spinning. Even though they knew what evils Dartmoor had been capable of inflicting, to hear of his cruelty to strangers was still a terrible surprise. Devlin had felt the exact same way all those years ago when he'd first learned about them. Their shock had been delayed, but it was no less overwhelming.

"So what do we do about it?"

The small voice from the doorway stole their attentions, and three sets of eyes darted to Theodora as she stood in the half-open door. *Christ.* How long had she been standing there, listening in?

With her hands folded demurely in front of her skirts, she stepped into the room and moved her gaze between the three of them before settling on Devlin. She waited patiently for an answer.

Devlin raked his fingers through his hair. "How much did you hear?"

"Everything." No guilt showed on her face at that confession. "I'm more mature than you think, you know. I'm able to handle news like this, too, especially if it involves our family. And Peyton."

Double Christ. "Yes, I think you are, too."

Her tight nod confirmed it. Yet like a dog after a rabbit, she didn't let her question go. "So what are we going to do about it?"

The women seemed to collectively hold their breaths as they waited for him to answer. Instead, he deflected, knowing this decision had to be made by all of them. "What do you think we should do, Teddy?"

"We should try to make restitution." A serious line formed between her brows as she considered the options. "For those we know were harmed, and for their families. I think that would be a good start."

"So do I," Devlin agreed quietly. He'd never been more

proud of his sister in his life.

"But…" Teddy continued thoughtfully, her gaze falling to the carpet at his feet. "I think we should also keep it private among ourselves. That is, us and Peyton and Crewe. Papa is dead, and there's no reason anyone else needs to know what he did. It was years ago, after all, and what good could come from telling everyone now? Revealing it might even prevent us from helping those who were harmed."

Yes, she was definitely wise beyond her years. "I think that's a good plan."

"And Peyton should be put in charge of it."

His heart skipped. Perhaps that wasn't such a good plan after all. As far as he knew, Peyton still planned on leaving as soon as she could. "She's returning to France, Teddy. She won't be here to help."

"Have you asked her to stay?"

His mother raised a curious brow at Teddy's question, and Margaret waited expectantly for his answer.

"She was clear about her intentions." Even after they'd made love, even after that wonderful joining of bodies and souls—even after admitting to loving each other—she thought her future lay elsewhere. All that had changed was that the way to a new future had been opened for her, one without fear or revenge. One without him.

"Yes," Margaret pressed. Then she repeated Teddy's question, "But have you *asked* her?"

"She thinks there's nothing here for her."

"We're here for her! You have to tell her that." Before he could argue, Margaret threw up her hands as if begging for help from heaven to cure them of the plague that was her brother. "You can be so daft at times, Devlin, you know that?"

His eyes narrowed. "Hold on. I think I've done—"

"Not nearly enough to persuade her to remain in London," his mother interjected. "I agree with the girls. She needs to stay— *we* need her to stay." Her face softened on him. "*All* of us."

His sisters nodded, while his mother continued to watch him curiously. He'd never been more under scrutiny in his life.

"Margaret and Theodora," his mother called out over her shoulder to his sisters, her eyes never leaving him, "why don't you give me a moment with your brother, please? I'd like to speak to Devlin alone."

Normally, such a request would have brought grumblings and whines from both sisters at the thought of being excluded, but this morning's extraordinary revelations had them behaving. Margaret gave his hand a squeeze as she passed him on her way toward the door. Teddy, always wearing her heart on her sleeve, threw her arms around him and hugged him.

"See?" she said. "I told you I'm more mature than you give me credit for."

He placed a kiss to the top of her head. "Absolutely."

Her eyes gleamed. "Does this mean you'll finally let me learn to drive?"

"Absolutely not."

Teddy let out a loud sound of aggravation, clenched her fists at her side, and marched out the door after Margaret. "We haven't finished talking about this!"

"Oh, yes, we have."

She sent him an aggravated glare over her shoulder, then loudly shut the door. He could hear her angry footsteps stomping away down the hall.

"She's right, you know," his mother said quietly as he joined her on the sofa. She leaned forward to pour them both fresh cups of tea. "About Peyton."

"To help with whatever restitution we can provide?" He shook his head. "She most likely wants to put the past behind her and move on."

"I didn't mean that, although having her help would be a wonderful idea." She stirred in a dollop of honey and held out the cup and saucer toward him. "I meant asking her to stay."

"I have asked her." He took a sip of the tea and welcomed the earthy warmth down his throat. "She wants to return to France. She thinks her future lies there."

"Perhaps you didn't ask her the right question." She raised her own cup to her lips and peered at him over the rim. "Did you ask her to marry you?"

He choked on his tea. Sputtering, he scrambled to sit up. He turned toward his mother and gaped at her between coughs. "*Pardon?*"

"If she doesn't think she has any reason to stay in London, then perhaps we need to show her she does. A grand reason." His mother calmly reached for one of the tiny lemon biscuits resting on a plate on the tea tray and placed it onto his saucer. "*You* need to show her, Devlin."

He blinked. Had news of what her husband had done addled her brain? "You want me to marry her?"

"Yes." With that blunt answer, she settled back against the sofa as if they were discussing nothing more important than the weather. "You're a good pairing. There's certainly physical attraction between the two of you. I've seen the way you look at each other."

He set down his tea on the table and promptly came to his feet. "I am not having this conversation with my mother of all—"

"Heavens, Devlin! Where do you think you came from—a stall at the market?"

"Yes." He shot her a hard look over his shoulder as he strode toward the bookcase in the corner. It was time for something far stronger than tea. He pulled down the fake front of a row of books that turned the shelf into a liquor cabinet and retrieved the bottle of Glenturret hidden inside. "As did everyone in my family." No fresh glasses sat inside the hidden shelf, so he turned back toward the tea tray and unceremoniously poured his tea into Margaret's abandoned cup. "And all my friends."

"Even Lucien?"

He paused before splashing the golden liquid into his cup. "No. Lucien was the unintended consequence of Lucifer bedding a hellhound, then being left at the front door of Bladdenham Park like a changeling."

Devlin's caricature of his friend's creation was only half facetious. No one worked harder at crafting a blackguard's reputation than Lucien Grenier, Duke of Crewe. But then, no one had greater reason to.

That was one secret the Raines women would never learn about.

His mother thoughtfully rubbed the tip of her index finger around the rim of her cup. "Peyton Chandler is...well..."

Beautiful, intelligent, feisty yet feminine...the most wonderful woman he'd ever met in his life. None of which his mother needed to hear coming from his lips.

"Troubled," she finished with a small frown.

"Yes." He took a healthy swallow of whiskey. There was no warmth in his throat this time. There was only a long, welcomed burn.

"So are you."

The concern in his mother's eyes stabbed him in the gut. He slowly lowered the glass from his lips. He didn't bother denying it.

"For some of the same reasons."

He couldn't deny that either. So he stared into his cup and slowly swirled the whiskey just to watch it sheet off the china in dark legs.

"If life with your father taught me anything, it was to find allies who understand me. Peyton understands you, Devlin, and the pain you've suffered. She's one of us." She paused. "She deserves to become one of us in every way."

"You mean marriage." He shot her a quelling look. "I thought you wanted me to help her, not punish her."

Not rising to the bait of that failed attempt at humor, his mother leveled a hard look at him. "She loves you."

His heart skipped, and he covered any emotions that might have strayed across his face by shaking his head. "I don't know if what she feels is—"

"She *loves* you," his mother repeated firmly. There would be no brooking an argument with her over that. Yet she paused. "Do you love her?"

The simple question hung in the air between them like a roll of thunder announcing an oncoming storm. He could barely remember to breathe beneath the weight of it and had no idea how his lungs filled with air, how he managed to stay on his feet, or how he was able to answer, "Yes, I do," without his voice breaking.

"Enough to want to be with her, share a family, and create a real home together?"

"Yes." Then he put voice to his deepest fears. "But is that enough reason for her to change everything about her life?"

"Two people who need each other the way you do, who are equals in intelligence and capabilities, who can work together like true partners to create a happy life for themselves..." she murmured thoughtfully against the rim of her tea cup. "Seems to me to be the perfect reason."

"Amid all the scandal of her return, she's also supposed to withstand the gossip of becoming my wife and the trials that come with being Duchess of Dartmoor?"

A small smile played at her lips. "Duchess of Dartmoor isn't such a bad position, I daresay, for the right woman. One who has the spine and resolve to match her duke in every way."

That was the god's truth, even if he didn't want to admit it. But it was an even deeper worry that concerned him.

"And if she says no? If she would rather return to France and the life she knows there versus the struggle that awaits her here?" *If she would rather keep me in her past with the ghosts who used to haunt her than walk into the future together?* It was a fear he didn't have the courage to raise with Peyton before, not even when he'd held her trembling and satiated in his arms. "What do I do then?"

His mother gave him a reassuring smile as she stood and approached him. "She won't." With that certainty, she removed a ring from her finger and placed it onto his palm, then closed his hand around it. "Take this when you propose. It was your grandmother's engagement ring. You deserve to have the same happy, loving marriage that your grandparents had." She leaned up to kiss his cheek. "If not more."

When she moved away, she took the bottle of whiskey with her.

He looked down at the ring and shook his head. "Is it really that simple?"

"God no!" She poured the whiskey into her tea, then set the bottle aside and lifted the cup to her lips to take a tentative sip. "Marriage is the most complex situation in the world, at some times happy, at others thoroughly miserable, and always a challenge, even when both people care for each other. But when you have love, support, and acceptance, it's also the most miraculous."

He felt the tiny ring dig into his palm as he tightened his hold around it. "I have your blessing, then?"

"You have a wonderful future ahead of you." Her eyes softened on him. "I cannot think of anyone more perfect for you to spend it with than Peyton Chandler."

Neither could he.

Chapter Twenty-Two

"ALL RIGHT, THEN." Peyton clapped her hands, and the children lined up in the street, some so excited about their game that they bounced up and down in place, unable to stand still. "First—David." She pointed at the towheaded boy of ten who stood first in line. "Count to five."

The boy's face lit up at such an easy pitch. "One, two, three, four, five!"

She pointed at the downspout halfway down the street. "Good! Take your base."

The boy ran forward, and a little girl in a dress that was barely more than a collection of rags stepped up next.

"Spell your name."

The girl scrunched up her nose. "M-A-R-Y."

"Go!"

The children advanced a base, working their way around their improvised game of rounders. They had no ball, no bat, and only stations along the street to serve as bases, yet they were making a go of it. Instead of pitching to them, each child was asked a question that they should have learned in Sunday school. When they answered correctly, everyone advanced a base. If they answered wrong, the child in the lead could help. If the answer still wasn't correct, then they all went back a base, and the lead child went to the back of the line. An out. But Peyton made certain the questions were just hard enough to tax their brains without being so difficult as to frustrate them.

She'd felt the need to do something fun with the children this afternoon after her night at Brechenhurst. She owed it to them and to Mrs. Martin, who made her feel welcome here.

After the fight at the townhouse, she certainly didn't want to stay there. Nor could she stay in a townhouse that was empty except for old toys and ghosts, although the fight with Wilkins had seemed to exorcise them, and Devlin's strength and comfort had pushed them completely into the past. Yet she also couldn't bring herself to stay at Dartmoor House with his mother and sisters. Oh, they would have welcomed her, surely...until they learned the truth about her father's role in helping the old duke destroy so many lives. She doubted they could ever forgive her.

So she asked Devlin to take her to the one place she knew she would find comfort—Brechenhurst. After all, if it gave shelter to forsaken children who had no place else to go, then she would be right at home.

Mrs. Martin took her in without a single question, not even when she helped Peyton with a warm bath with salts meant to soothe the black and blue bruises forming across her body and brought her warm comfort food on a tray down into the basement bedroom. This morning, the kind manageress miraculously found a dress for her to wear because her own gown—no, *Margaret's* gown, she couldn't forget that she no longer had anything in this world to call her own—wasn't fit to wear. The woman was a saint. A silent, non-judgmental saint.

Now, this afternoon, Peyton was doing her best to put the darkness of the past few weeks—and especially last night—behind her by playing and laughing with the children. It was more than just a game. It was her chance to say goodbye. She'd promised them that the child who answered the most questions correctly would receive a shiny coin and new coat, although she'd already sent one of the shelter's helpers to the market to buy new coats and shoes for all the children. Their new clothes would be waiting for them when they arrived back at the shelter this evening. So would a bag of shiny pennies for each of them.

But she would be gone by then, like a wraith in the night, leaving London as secretly as she'd arrived. It was for the best. The Raines family needed to heal, and they couldn't do that if she were a constant reminder of past sins.

"My turn, miss!" A little boy who couldn't have been more than five or six stepped up to bat.

"All right then." Despite the sudden sadness that swept over her, she ordered, "Sing me a song."

The boy thought a moment and then belted out the first verse of a sailor's drinking shanty that left Peyton staring at him, wide-eyed. *Goodness*. Did the little bit of a boy even know what was meant by calling a woman Miss Laycock?

He grinned, knowing he was stirring up trouble.

"A miss," she called out. "Back to the end of the line with you. And next time, try a nice hymn or nursery song, all right?"

The boy only grinned wider and moved to the back, where one of the other boys stole his hat, then rubbed his head in slight punishment for slowing up the game. The warning was clear. If he attempted to disrupt the game again or embarrass Peyton, he'd find himself pummeled in the alley by the other boys.

She turned to the next child. "Sing me a song—a *proper* one."

The boy nodded and sang a few bits from a song he'd learned in Sunday school. Peyton applauded and sent him on. All the children advanced around the bases, with one coming back to the start.

"Score! A point!" All the children shouted and jumped up and down excitedly as the oldest boy made a mark in a patch of dirt at the side of the street. They'd been promised treats if they managed to score more than ten points. Peyton would make certain they did.

"Who won the Battle of Waterloo?" she called out to the next child.

"England!"

"Wellington!" the lead boy on base corrected.

"Excellent!" she called out. "A team answer. Go!"

Another child returned back to home and scored another point.

"Here's a hard one." Peyton leveled a challenging look at the girl who stood in line next. She was the oldest of all the girls and just on the cusp of being too old to stay at Brechenhurst any longer. Peyton made a mental note to give Mrs. Martin funds to find the girl a position as a maid so she might have a chance at a good life. "Recite a poem to me."

The girl thought a moment. Peyton could almost see the nursery rhymes spinning through the girl's head as she tried to choose one to share. She opened her mouth—

"She walks in beauty like the night."

The deep, masculine voice came from behind Peyton, its velvet richness twining around her like a ribbon. She froze, not daring to turn around... *Devlin*.

"Of cloudless climes and starry skies, and all that's best of dark and bright," he recited softly as he stopped directly behind her, so close she could feel the heat of him down her back and smell that now familiar scent of leather, port, and man, "meet in her aspect and her eyes."

He took her shoulders and gently turned her to face him, and the crooked smile that greeted her melted her insides. He'd always had that effect on her, even years ago when he'd been nothing but a careless young man who hadn't paid her any attention whatsoever. But now that she knew the man he'd become... How could she ever love anyone else as much as she loved him?

"Do I get to take a base?" he asked cheekily. The girls were all giggling, and the boys were irritated that he'd interrupted their game with love poetry. Then his chocolate brown eyes landed on hers. "Or perhaps I scored a point."

Oh, he'd definitely scored a point, all right. And not in any way that made leaving London easier. Just when she thought she might be able to put her feelings behind her and move on, he had to go and do something as romantic as recite a love poem to her. Did the blasted man have any idea how much her heart was breaking?

"You cut the queue," she informed him instead, somehow gathering enough strength not to break down. Or throw herself into his arms. "You're disqualified."

The children let out a flurry of laughter at Devlin's expense.

He eyed them knowingly. "That's not the support I'd expect from my team. And after I asked Mrs. Martin to open Brechenhurst early today, too, so that you could all have warm sticky buns and cups of chocolate."

The little faces lit up with excitement. They didn't move, not wanting to break the spell and have what he was saying be nothing but a terrible joke.

"She's waiting for you now." He nodded in the direction of the shelter halfway down the street. "Go on."

The children let up a cheer and raced toward the front door of Brechenhurst, their game quickly forgotten. All but one ran away. A little girl named Charlotte lingered behind.

"But you promised the winner a coin and new coat," Charlotte reminded her in a quiet voice that broke Peyton's heart. The girl had already learned in her brief life how few people kept their promises.

"So I did." Peyton reached into the pocket of her pelisse and withdrew a shiny new penny. She bent down on her heels to the little girl's level and held it out. "I don't have the coat with me, though. That will be coming later today. But you've won this fair and square."

Charlotte bit her bottom lip in hesitant distrust as she slowly approached, as if she expected Peyton to pull the penny away and laugh at her. Peyton didn't move, except to place the coin in the girl's outstretched palm.

The girl closed her hand around it as if it were as valuable as a gold sovereign, then pressed it against her chest. "Oh, thank you, miss!"

"Ah-ah!" Peyton held up her finger as the girl turned to walk away. "Spell your name."

The girl hesitated, sliding an uncertain look at Devlin for help. When he didn't interfere, letting her do this on her own, she pulled in a deep breath and spelled, "C-H-A-R-L-O-T."

Peyton smiled sadly, knowing she wouldn't be here to help the little girl learn to spell. "Close enough."

With a quick hug, she sent Charlotte racing back to the shelter and the treats waiting there.

"You're wonderful with them." Devlin held out his hand to help her up. "They trust you a great deal."

She shook her head. "They don't trust anyone, not really." She rose, bringing herself face-to-face with him. "But I understand that."

"I'm certain you did. Once." He didn't release her hand. "But I hope that's changed, that you've come to trust in my family. And in me."

She dodged answering that by tossing him a saucy smile. "How could I distrust a man who flatters me by reciting Byron?"

He curled her arm around his and slowly began to walk with her toward the shelter. "Did it work? I hear most women like sweet nothings and charming flattery."

"I am *not* most women."

He leaned down to caress his lips against her temple and murmured, "How well I know that."

Ignoring the butterflies in her belly that launched into full flutter, she quickly changed the subject, and her amusement from only moments before vanished, along with her smile. "You've done it, then? You've told them everything about our fathers?"

"Everything they need to know."

That was a duck if ever she'd heard one. But she understood. Only so much shock could be absorbed at one time. The rest of what their fathers had done would come little by little, when the moment was right.

She turned her face away. "They must hate me."

"Not at all."

She bit back a grim laugh. "How can they not? My father made their evil possible. Your father and Crewe's wouldn't have been able to fund their enterprise if he hadn't handled the money for them." Then the butterflies in her stomach turned into sickening knots. "The money I found after the attack, all squirreled away in investments and properties—all of it is tainted."

"Not all of it. Your mother had a large dowry that your father invested into legitimate businesses and bonds when they married, and his salary with the Bank of England was more than enough to buy property." An amused grin pulled at his lips. "Including the small estate in Sussex that you used for collateral the night we became reacquainted at Barton's."

Her shoulders sagged. "I can't keep any of it."

"You should. You deserve that part of it. Use it for whatever you want. My mother and sisters raised some very good suggestions for it." He paused, barely a heartbeat, but she felt it, so attuned had she become to this man during the past few weeks. "Such as your dowry."

Laughter spilled from her at the ludicrousness of that. "You saw the looks of shock and horror on the faces of everyone in Malvern House when I announced I'd returned. Who would want to marry me?"

He kept his gaze straight ahead on the street. "The Raines women have some determined ideas on the subject."

"Of course they do." She blinked rapidly. If they found her a husband, they could send her away with him and thoroughly wash their hands of her and any association society might think connected them. "But they don't need to worry about me. I'm a survivor, you know. I'll be just fine on my own, wherever I am."

"I know."

They stopped in front of the shelter's door, and Peyton stared at it, unable to bring herself to look at Devlin for fear he would see the anguish glistening in her eyes. She rasped softly, "This is goodbye, then."

"No." With a gentle tug, he led her onward down the street. "This is just the beginning."

She glanced up at him, surprised. "What do you mean?"

"Don't you want to know what other ideas my family had for your inheritance and for the rest of the money still left to be uncovered?"

"Yes?"

"Restitution."

She blinked. "Pardon?"

"They think you should use it for restitution for the people our fathers harmed." He shrugged. "Or reparations, as the case may be. And I agree with them."

He led her toward the small pocket park at the end of the street, where a lone chestnut tree protected the only patch of green grass in the neighborhood. Someone—perhaps Mrs. Martin—had planted a small bed of flowers beneath the spreading boughs to make it as inviting as possible. Peyton couldn't help but compare it to Brechenhurst. A small refuge of beauty and peace in the midst of an otherwise colorless, impersonal city.

"It means hiring detectives to hunt those people down, enduring disappointment and grief, and it won't be easy, either in finding the people involved or in figuring out the best way to provide help." He reassuringly squeezed her arm, then posited carefully, "You would need to remain in London to oversee it all."

"No," she whispered, barely a sound on her lips. "I *can't*... Your family, Lucien...you—you would all hate knowing I'm in the same city with you, that I'm digging through your pasts to discover more sins..." She shook her head, but not before her eyes began to sting and the world around her blurred beneath her gathering tears. "I have to leave. You all need time to heal. How could you ever come to terms with what our fathers did if the sight of me constantly dredges up painful memories and grief?"

She turned her back to him and swiped desolately at her eyes.

"Good Lord," he murmured, stunned. "That's why you want to return to France, why you've been so determined to leave? Not because you want to live there." He took her upper arms and gently turned her around to face him, and his eyes searched her face for answers. "You want to leave because you think you'll cause us more pain by staying."

She closed her eyes to keep from seeing the expression on his face at the stark truth of what she'd planned. She couldn't bear it. "Yes."

"You're wrong." He cupped her face between his hands and rested his forehead against hers. His breath fanned warmly across her cheeks. "We need you here with us, Peyton. We need to heal together—all of us." Another pause, and in that hesitation, she felt the world shift beneath her. "I need you, Peyton. *I* need you here with me."

Her eyes flew open and stared at him, his face tear-blurred. He couldn't possibly mean… Her shoulders sagged in defeat. "I would only cause you pain if I stayed."

"You would cause me infinitely more pain if you left."

She stepped back, needing space and air to breathe. She simply couldn't trust in what he was saying. "And your family?" she argued. "How are they supposed to move on if I'm haunting them?"

She'd learned a hard lesson during the past few weeks. There were more ghosts than just those in graveyards.

He leveled a solemn gaze on her. "My family wanted to make certain that I delivered a very precise message to you."

She steeled herself for the worst. "Which is?"

He reached into his jacket's inner breast pocket as he took her hand and lowered himself onto one knee in front of her. "Marry me."

Peyton couldn't move, couldn't speak—she could barely find the strength to keep standing as she watched him slide a small ring onto her finger.

Devlin looked up at her, not with expectation but determination. She'd always known he was a force to be reckoned with, but she never knew exactly how much until that moment. His expression held no uncertainty whatsoever as he waited for her decision, only strength and resolve.

"You said you loved me," he reminded her as he folded both hands around hers and slowly rose to his feet. "You meant it. So did I."

A knot filled her throat, and she began to tremble.

"So we should spend the rest of our lives proving it, don't you think?" He raised her hand to his lips and placed a tender kiss to the back of her fingers. "I can't think of any better way to put the past to rest than to focus on a new future. Together." He paused, then took a deep breath and asked again, "Will you marry me, Peyton Chandler?"

The burden of loneliness and fear she'd carried for too long lifted from her shoulders, and the hollow in her chest vanished. With every beat of her heart, they soared away into the distance. In their place came hope, purpose…love.

She nodded as a tear slipped down her cheek. "Yes," she whispered, her voice shaking with the enormity of the new life rising up before her. With this man she loved. "I will marry you."

He murmured her name as he took her into his arms and held her, loved and protected, against him. So much affection and trust blossomed between them that she warmed from it, all the way down to her toes. His embrace tightened around her, and as she nestled against him, she knew this was exactly where she was meant to be.

In his arms.

Epilogue

October 1817

DEVLIN PAUSED IN the open French doors leading out onto the rear garden terrace of Dartmoor House and smiled to himself.

The autumn harvest party to benefit Brechenhurst was in full swing. The festivities had taken over the rear gardens, the terrace, and the ground floor reception rooms, with the guests enjoying themselves with this bit of country fun transported to the city. For once, the English weather had cooperated and given them an unseasonably warm afternoon, and now the light from the setting sun fell in golden hues across the property and gave the gathering even more of an autumnal flavor.

A small fair filled the garden, with wooden stalls set up across the narrow patch of lawn and down the garden path. Manned by the children of Brechenhurst, the booths held various games and foods, including roasted chestnuts and hand pies. On one end of the stone terrace, a large half barrel had been filled with water and bobbing apples for anyone brave enough to try to capture one, while on the other sat a puppet theatre where wooden marionettes bounced back and forth on strings to the delight of both laughing children and adults. There was even a small dog performing tricks, a fortune teller in a tent, a trio of musicians, and a special booth where guests and patrons could purchase toys for the children—along with pillows, bedrolls, soap, and more, all donated immediately back to the shelter.

Inside the house, the reception rooms were only a bit less chaotic, with more sophisticated refreshments and none of the autumn decorations that filled the garden. The inside rooms had become the refuge of elderly dowagers and statesmen needing escape from the rambunctious children. But even there, the importance of the shelter could not be ignored. Every bit of the day's event was carefully planned to benefit Brechenhurst as much as possible, to help even more children find better lives away from the streets.

"This is all your own fault, you know," Lucien Grenier, Duke of Crewe, warned in a low voice as he came up beside Devlin and followed his gaze across the garden. He nodded at the trick dog.

Devlin frowned as the dog rose onto its hind feet and turned a perfect pirouette. With a tiara on his head and wearing a pink dress, the mutt looked uncannily like Queen Charlotte at a palace ball. "How is this my fault?"

"Everything was going along just fine when you were pretending to be Mr. Hunter and keeping your involvement with Brechenhurst secret. But then you had to let everyone know that you'd been helping the shelter, and that led to this."

Both men paused to stare, speechless, as the dog curtsied.

"This just goes to prove what I've said all along," Lucien drawled.

Devlin arched a brow. "That men face consequences when they keep secrets?"

"God no!" Crewe looked aghast at the suggestion. "That men shouldn't ever let their secrets be known. Oh, it starts off with the best of intentions only to end up with…" He waved a mug of hot cider at the garden and muttered, "Dancing dogs."

Devlin grinned and shook his head. "Secrets aren't for me. Not anymore."

Revealing his connection to Brechenhurst was simply one more step in that direction. He hadn't made any grand announcements about his role; he'd simply stopped referring to himself as Mr. Hunter and allowed his true identity to become known to the staff and children. Mrs. Martin hadn't been surprised in the least. She had simply shrugged at the news and hurried off to clean the kitchen before the children arrived for the night. His family hadn't been any more surprised, and they'd supported him in his desire to turn the shelter into a full-fledged charity. Their work with the children proved more healing for them than he ever would have imagined.

So was the help they were trying to give to the victims. Together, they were working to find the people who were harmed by their father's criminal enterprise. It was slow going, with many of the leads given to the detectives coming to nothing.

Yet they'd sworn not to give up until every last person who could be found was contacted and reparations made, however they could.

Speaking of missing people... Devlin turned back to Crewe. "Any information from Chase about Betty Proctor?"

The woman never resurfaced in London. She had simply disappeared, fleeing the night of the explosion and undoubtedly running for her life when she learned that her partner, Wilkins, had been killed. Any more news Chase discovered, no matter how slight, wouldn't bring Peyton any comfort. Ultimately, she had lost another person she loved, someone she should have been able to trust.

But perhaps news of Proctor's whereabouts would finally allow her to stop blaming herself for Wilkins's betrayal. They had been chameleons, leading double-lives even when working for the Chandlers, and no one could have known Wilkins was related to Horrender or the deceit he and Proctor were capable of committing. Peyton had no reason to think they were anything other than dedicated servants. Until they weren't.

Crewe frowned down into his cider with distaste, as if just realizing that it wasn't spiked with rum. "I don't think Betty Proctor will be a concern."

Devlin's eyes narrowed at that unexpected answer. "You

think she's dead, then?"

"I think too many people have come back from the dead lately to say for certain one way or the other."

That was the God's truth. It had been six weeks since Peyton's grave was removed from the churchyard, and all of them—including Crewe—were still growing used to its absence. After all, its specter had hung over them for years.

"Chase traced her to Portsmouth," Crewe added. "The last anyone in England saw of her, she was setting sail for America." He took a reluctant sip of cider. "Tell Peyton whatever story you think will bring her the most solace. That's all that matters now. The past is gone."

Devlin's gaze landed on his mother and sisters as they stood in the center of the lawn and supervised festivities; they were in their full glory running it all. The warmth of relief filled his chest that they were finally safe. His father couldn't hurt them any longer.

"At least we're out of danger now," Devlin acknowledged.

"Speak for yourself." Crewe's eyes narrowed at a woman who was wandering among the booths and entertainments, carefully swinging her gaze around the garden, searching for someone. "If you'll excuse me," Crewe muttered as he slapped Devlin on the back. "I have to be somewhere."

"Where?"

Crewe jerked a nod toward the woman. "Anywhere she isn't."

Devlin bit back a knowing smile as Crewe hurried to disappear into the crowd of guests at the far end of the terrace and avoid the woman who was searching for him.

Some things never changed.

But others… He smiled at his mother and sisters. The party was their idea—a fun event that both guests and children could enjoy together, as well as letting any possible patrons interact with the children they would be helping with their donations. Although how the Raines women were able to put it all together so flawlessly, he would never know.

His mother was in her element as dowager duchess, greeting old friends with deep pockets and encouraging them to see the benefits in a place like Brechenhurst. A more regal woman Devlin had never seen, even as she expertly ordered the footmen to bring more apples for bobbing and a bowl of water for the dancing dog.

Teddy was busy playing with the children. For all her protests that she was a grown woman, ready to debut and learn to drive, she still possessed a youthful exuberance and sense of fun he hoped time never diminished.

As for Margaret…sweet Megs never strayed far from the side of Robert Davidson, her new suitor for whom she'd developed a genuine affection.

Devlin liked the man…well enough. As well as he could like any man with designs on marrying his sister. Davidson was the third son of an earl, which no one in the Raines family held against him, because he was hard-working, intelligent, and as down to earth as anyone in society could be. A self-made man, he'd accumulated a small fortune for himself by cornering the market for new warehouses along canals and turnpikes needed for all the American and French goods flooding into Great Britain now that the wars had ended. Davidson might have been only a businessman, but he'd become one of the most successful ones in the empire. His fortune would keep him, Margaret, and their family in the comfortable life they deserved. More importantly, the man doted on Margaret, unable to hide his affection for her even when he tried.

Devlin expected Davidson to request a meeting with him soon to ask his permission to marry Margaret. He anticipated a wedding by Christmastide.

And as for weddings… Peyton stood in the middle of the party madness, as regal as a princess, perfectly at home, and completely happy.

His lips curled into a smile. Dear God, she was lovely. Even now, even after all they'd been through in the past few months—

the engagement, the wedding, their wedding trip to the estate followed by settling into Dartmoor House and resettling his mother and sisters into a dowager house across the square...with long, languid nights wrapped in each other's arms that stretched into lazy, sun-filled mornings—the sight of her still took his breath away.

He prayed time never dulled that feeling.

He strolled down the terrace steps and into the garden to take his place at her side. He had to satisfy himself with an affectionate squeeze to her elbow to let her know he was there when what he wanted to do was pull her into his arms and thoroughly kiss her.

When a devilish smile played at her lips, he knew she'd read his mind, and a knot of hot desire formed low in his gut. He nearly said to hell with the party and scooped her into his arms to carry her up to their bedroom.

"Both His Grace and I are fully committed to Brechenhurst," she said to a small circle of guests who had gathered around her. Of course, they had. She was simply magnetic. "As we hope all of you will be, as well."

The guests smiled and nodded, easily won over by her charms.

Thankfully, though, the attention she received was no longer due to the gossip that her sudden reappearance and wedding had stirred across London. Oh, neither of them really cared what anyone else in the *ton* thought about them. They had each other—that was all that mattered. But being Duchess of Dartmoor wasn't easy, and whispers and stares had only made it more trying. Yet she'd paid little mind to the vicious tongues, preferring instead to focus on her work with the shelter and reparations for her father's misdeeds...and in preparing Teddy for her official debut in January, at a grand ball with hours and hours of dancing.

Devlin couldn't imagine any other woman enduring it as graciously as Peyton, and he would gladly spend the rest of his life as a true partner in whatever she wanted to accomplish.

"What do you think, Dartmoor?" A member from the House

of Commons raised his mug of cider to punctuate his question. "Will the new parliamentary reforms have you committed to Whitehall day and night in the coming session?"

Devlin smiled and placed his hand at the small of Peyton's back. "Fortunately, I'm already committed to my wife for all the days to come." He smiled in apology to the group as he led her away, then leaned down to murmur wantonly in her ear, "And all the nights."

When a faint blush pinked her cheeks, he knew she longed to be alone together as much as he did. "Well then." She paused as they walked through the garden to take a small sack of roasted chestnuts from a booth as they passed. "Parliament's loss is my gain." A wicked smile tugged at her sensuous lips. "And a-gain and a-gain...."

He laughed. He'd never been happier in his life.

"I think," he began as he stole one of her chestnuts and popped it into his mouth, "that you and I should let my mother and sisters—"

A loud crack of flesh on flesh punctuated the noise of the festival. Everyone's attention bolted to the terrace, where Crewe stood in front of the woman he'd wanted to avoid...the same woman who had just slapped him.

"*That* can't be good," Peyton muttered.

Devlin watched as Crewe said not a word to the woman but gave her a formal bow and sauntered away as if being slapped at a party was the most expected event in the world for him. "That's Lucien for you."

"Perhaps we should inquire about the matter," Peyton suggested.

When she started forward, Devlin stopped her. "Lucien has it under control." Well, as much control as Crewe could ever have over his life. "Let's just enjoy the party. How about we visit the fortune teller?"

"I don't need to." She rested her hand lovingly on his bicep, and he couldn't help the longing flex of muscle beneath her fingertips. "I already have the future I've always wanted—a wonderful life with a man straight out of the past."

He leaned down to scandalously kiss her, the watchful guests around them be damned.

She stopped him just as his lips were about to touch hers and leaned away. She dropped her gaze to her fingers as she fussed with his cravat, and her smile vanished, her face growing serious. "But there is one thing I'm lacking."

His chest tightened with concern. Was she not as completely happy as he was? "Which is?"

"I'd like to have a baby." She looked up at him coyly beneath lowered lashes. "Do you think you might be willing to help me with that?"

A mix of wolfish desire and unbridled love blazed inside him. He'd been wrong earlier. *Now* he'd never been happier in his life. "Gladly."

He wrapped his arm around hers and led her into the house to their bedroom.

About the Author

Anna fell in love with historical romances—and all those dashing Regency heroes—while living in London, where she studied literature and theatre and found herself lost nearly every day. A USA Today best-selling author, she loves to travel, fly airplanes, and ballroom dance, and when she isn't busy writing her next novel, she can usually be found in her garden, fussing over her roses. She loves all things chocolate and tea, is a terrible cook, and hopes one day to use her oven for something other than shoe storage. She loves to hear from her readers.

Website – www.annaharringtonbooks.com
Facebook – facebook.com/annaharrington.regencywriter
Amazon – amazon.com/stores/Anna-
Harrington/author/B00ZNNG3XW

Milton Keynes UK
Ingram Content Group UK Ltd.
UKHW020813200824
447135UK00004B/168

9 781963 585018